DOUBLE-CROSSING THE BRIDGE

Cole,
Best of luck on your
writing adventures!
Sad J Sa

DOUBLE-CROSSING THE BRIDGE

A TROLL CAPER

SARAH J. SOVER

FALSTAFF
BOOKS
WWW.FALSTAFFBOOKS.COM

To Ashlynn and Lily. I told you magic was real.

THE HOLE IN THE WALL

Granu snatched up the quivering rat, the latest victim of Critterhole freed by a bad toss, and snorted at its futile efforts to wriggle free. The mahogany table in the low-lit cavern tavern wouldn't offer salvation tonight, not with two trolls tossing back flagons of grog in the corner booth. Any hopes the creature harbored of escaping its gruesome fate, inevitable impalement on the spike within the game's painted wooden platform, came to an abrupt end.

Not one to ruin frivolous entertainment, Granu tossed the rat back to the waiting swog. The porcine underling with an upturned nose and beady, wide-set eyes grunted in thanks, a string of snot leaking from his nostril as his tiny wings fluttered in appreciation of her attention. His black-speckled tongue darted out to clear the mucous as he arched an expectant brow at her. She smiled but turned away. The would-be suitor picked up on her lack of interest and returned to his friends, a knot of trolls, swogs, and other sun-avoiders jostling one another for a turn at the tavern game.

Voices echoed off the stark stone walls, and a persistent drip from the cavern ceiling added to the water collecting on the table. Granu used the back of her stubby hand to clear the puddle. A green neon sign bearing the name *Goron's* flickered over the bar, illuminating the vinyl upholstery throughout the tavern and giving the place a mossy feel common to the outermost caverns of New Metta.

A shrill shriek followed by rowdy cheering marked the death of the rat and a point for the swog's team.

"He said that to her? What was he thinking?" said Fillig, picking up the interrupted conversation. He sat in the cracked forest-green booth across from Granu, gobbling fried fairy wings by the fistful.

"Kradduk only thinks of one thing, you know that."

Granu gazed after the swog, who was no longer visible through the crowd. Snot aside, he wasn't a bad-looking potential mate. Granu had no idea why such a tasty hunk of meat was interested in her.

"Ah, my favorite topic! Me."

A well-groomed, large troll with three chins and a killer smile appeared at the end of the booth. He used his tree-trunk thigh to shove Granu farther in, taking his usual seat beside her at the corner table past the Critterhole platform. Granu knew Kradduk only chose the spot next to her because it offered the best vantage point for scouting the tavern for mates and launching to his feet in pursuit if the opportunity arose.

Kradduk Chert wore the latest in corporate fashion, a solid black jumpsuit fitted against his bulging chest, adorned with a red burlap necktie. His booming voice and huge, rectangular head caught the eye of more than one species of female scattered throughout the cavern. Granu rolled her eyes at the flirty glances.

"And I think of more than one thing, thank you very much. I think of finely ground fetus bones, perfectly aged grog from the hills of Friddum, the feeling of Maise granite beneath my head at night, and only the sweetest, plump rumps of the most beautiful females in New Metta City resting on my slab after a full day of strenuous exercise. "He waggled his heavy eyebrows in a way that made Granu laugh.

She could never take Kradduk seriously with his goofy expressions and endless catalog of pick-up lines, no matter how obscene his words. Fillig, on the other hand, sneered in disgust as he took a long slurp of grog.

"Kradduk, you sicken me," he muttered, setting the flagon back on the table with a sloppy thud.

Granu shook her head. She'd first met Fillig Schist in stone-blasting class. He'd been her study partner back at Vinkle U, and they'd spent countless late mornings cramming for exams. She wasn't sure how she would have gotten by without him, but he always seemed to miss the humor in life.

"You know it's just his way. He's a dirty cud-chewer when it comes down to it." She smacked Kradduk's arm with the back of her hand, emphasizing the insult. He curled into himself as if the blow hurt, and a flirtatious smile played at the corners of his mouth and touched his eyes.

Fillig snorted. "He should show some respect, if not for the females of the world, at least for you."

"Trolls!" said Kradduk, "I'm sitting right here and my hearing is great. But, as long as we're on the topic, I could do more for you than that, Granu." Kradduk stuck out his tongue playfully, eliciting another groan from Fillig and a chuckle from Granu.

The tavern was bustling at this hour, when those with day jobs celebrated surviving the sun and those with night gigs pre-gamed in anticipation for the long hours to come. The clientele of Goron's was comprised primarily of trolls and swogs, but a few brightly-feathered grawbacks and small-boned, pink-skinned molents sat scattered throughout the tavern. There was even a sniggle, small for her species but still hulking over the other patrons, her gray flesh stuffed into an alcove on the opposite side of the room like the contents of an over-filled suitcase.

Goron's didn't discriminate based on species, unlike some of the other establishments in New Metta, which allowed only higher-level creatures such as trolls, swogs, and other intelligent underlings. Some still excluded trolls due to the Billy Goat Blight, though they'd never admit it. Treating high-level creatures that way would be downright rude, not to mention illegal. Not Goron's. Any upstanding sun-avoider with cash was welcome. It was one of the things that drew Granu to the tavern.

Goron's was far from the classiest establishment in the sector, but it was relatively clean. The green paint on the cavern walls chipped away to reveal gray stone in many places. The furniture was rotten and wobbly, and the smell was always a pleasing mixture of compost and cooked meat, never of rot or flowers, scents trolls found intolerable despite their prevalence throughout the city.

A grawback with bright blue tail feathers, iridescent green and blue down framing her face, and a razor sharp beak and tongue, made her way to their table. Dreatte was their regular server.

"Is Kradduk at it again?" she laughed as she set another round of drinks down, expertly keeping her trailing arm feathers out of the condensation accumulated on the table. Her claws rattled against the glasses. "I'm surprised he hasn't died of the yellow fingle yet."

Grog shot out Granu's nose at the lewd reference. Fillig doubled over in laughter, nearly slamming his forehead into the thick wooden table.

Kradduk's face fell, his shoulders slumped, and he cocked his head to the side, reminding Granu of a mongrel caught eating scraps from a table. Then his mouth tightened as his wide nostrils flared in mock anger. "No tip for you."

"I'm not concerned. You never tip well anyways," quipped Dreatte, her round yellow eyes sparkling. Kradduk was known for throwing money around nearly as much as for throwing himself at every female, eligible or otherwise. He'd even taken a pass at a sniggle or two, though it was largely unheard of since the creatures were repulsive on so many levels. Granu couldn't fault him, though. She'd once seen a sniggle smash an entire table with his thumb simply because he wasn't happy about the way Dreatte spoke to him. Skin lesions or not, it was hot. Granu blushed at the memory.

"Pouting doesn't become you," said Dreatte as she sashayed away, her tail swishing back and forth with each step. Kradduk craned his neck to watch her, and Granu smacked his arm again.

"What was that for?"

"Grawbacks now? Really?"

Kradduk shrugged. "Nothing wrong with diversifying your portfolio."

It wasn't that Granu thought less of grawbacks. Some of her closest grade school friends had been grawbacks. But mating was a different story. Their anatomy didn't mesh with trolls'. Where trolls were wide, they were narrow. Where trolls were large, they were petite. Brittle bones didn't hold up to the dense mass of a troll in the throes of passion, so the two rarely intermingled. Besides, angular features were far from alluring to trolls, as small-boned Granu was acutely aware.

"A fine, sexy lady deserves to be appreciated. I don't discriminate," Kradduk said.

Granu laughed, shaking her head. "Next it'll be molents or worse, humans."

"What is your problem with molents, Gran?" asked Fillig. "You're forever putting them down. I didn't peg you for a back-cavern bigot."

"Besides, Kell is a damn fine-looking dude," added Kradduk. The bartender looked up at mention of his name then went back to his duties with the shake of his head.

"Kell is different. He brings the grog! And I don't have anything against them, I just don't find them attractive. I'm allowed to have my preferences. Besides, Kradduk would probably kill a molent if he tried to get it on with one. I mean, he's a thousand times the size of one."

"So, you've noticed my size, then, Granu?" asked Kradduk, nudging her with his arm. Amongst trolls, the bigger, the better. A large troll could have the personality of a wet mop and the brains of a unicorn and still bring home the ladies.

"Everything is suggestive with you!" Granu said, her face flushing. "You're the largest troll I've ever met, but that doesn't mean anything. You're like my brother."

When Kradduk and Fillig got together, they had a way of keeping her off balance. Fillig took everything so seriously and lured her into a real discussion while Kradduk snuck in for the kill when her defenses were down. She was fairly certain that Fillig's part was unintentional at least.

A large female troll walked past on her way to the restroom, giving Granu a reprieve as both males paused to watch, Kradduk with his flagon poised in mid-air and Fillig with his mouth agape.

"Seriously, guys, do you think staring a girl down will get you into her pants? You're like juvies watching the kiddie tank at Flopps."

"Hush Granu, she's looking this way," mumbled Fillig.

"You don't have a chance in heaven," said Granu.

"Speaking of Flopps, you want to grab dinner there sometime this week?" asked Kradduk, bringing his attention back to Granu. No longer staring at the passing troll, he watched her with his head propped on his hand, the picture of nonchalance.

"Um, it's a little out of my budget right now," said Granu. She stared off into the distance as if there were something really interesting near the far wall of the tavern.

"I'll cover you."

"Honestly, I don't care for that place. I think it's kind of cruel to keep the humans alive until you pick one to eat. I mean, I know it's no different in the long run, I guess, but it kind of makes me a little sick."

"Like they're smart enough to know what's happening?" Kradduk grinned.

"Wow, our Granu is a humanitarian and a speciesist. What a combination. Did that old roommate of yours get to you? What was that human-lover's name? Gill? Garve?" asked Fillig, laughing.

"Bood, you idiot. And no, I'm not about to become a vegetarian and join the human rights movement. I hunt more than you do, I bet. When's the last time you even left the city anyway?"

When Fillig didn't reply, Granu tacked on, "Yeah, that's what I thought. I just prefer my killing done quickly and with finesse. I don't like seeing their ugly little faces crying for mommies that were skewered days before. It kills my appetite."

"If it makes you feel better, they do it too," said Kradduk."Unlike our shut-in here, I frequently leave the confines of New Metta. Ever been to a seafood restaurant topside? They keep their prey in tanks right by the front door, so it's the first thing you see when you walk in."

"Of course I haven't been to a restaurant topside. I don't make a habit of dining with my food. You know, you can get a lobster skewer and a plate of oysters at Fred's without having to mingle with the herd." Her lip curled in disgust. "Besides, I thought humans didn't accept our existence? Most think we're stories to frighten their young ones. Do you mean to tell me they tolerated you at a table with them and didn't run screaming?"

"Not exactly. TCB had a high-end seafood joint rented out so we could experience dining the way humans do."

"Why on earth would you want to eat like an uncivilized beast? Better off chewing hay at the unicorn ranch. At least then you might get a rainbow laser show if you spook one."

Fillig interrupted. "Hold up for just a second. We're glossing right by something huge here. Kradduk, did you just ask Granu out?"

"No, of course not. I'd never do that." Kradduk caught Granu's expression of faux offense and began to stutter in a very uncharacteristic way.

She decided to let him off the hook. "I don't think I'm his type any more than he's mine," she laughed.

"What is your type, anyhow? Based on your dating history, I'd say you have a thing for the uggos," said Kradduk.

"Hey! My dating life is none of your concern."

Fillig tossed a few bucks on the table to cover his share of the bill and returned his wallet to his back pocket as Granu protested and Kradduk laughed.

"Well, gang," he said, "as much as I love ragging on Kradduk and watching Granu squirm, I've got to get some sleep, so I can get up with the sun for work."

"You have some truly terrible hours, dude. You need to get a sweet gig like mine," said Kradduk, momentarily distracted from Granu's love life.

"Yeah, well, not all of us are lucky enough to snag a job at The Covered Bridge. Some of us have to resort to hauling boulders."

"Luck had nothing to do with it." Kradduk waggled his eyebrows at Granu again. She tried to puzzle out the implication but was afraid to ask. Fillig, however, couldn't let it pass.

"Come on, we all know you got that job through your family connections. You're nothing but a trust fund troll turned manager to appease mommy. If it weren't for her, you'd never have landed that gig!"

The air seemed to leave the room, the lights seemed to dim. Kradduk's shoulders tightened, a red tinge creeping over the whites of his eyes. His voice lowered. "You know nothing about my mother," he growled, the softness of his voice conveying the threat better than any amount of screaming.

Fillig blanched. "I've met your mother, and she's a wonderful troll. Really. She's great."

In all the years they'd been friends, Granu only saw Kradduk fight once, the cause similar to the current situation. It was an experience she had no desire to repeat and the offender had no ability to. She had to intervene and quickly.

"Krad, he didn't mean anything by that," she said, hoping she could pull Kradduk back. He didn't anger easily, but he had his soft spots just like any troll, and his mother was one big squishy weakness.

"Yeah, man, I'm not insulting your mom. Just you." Fillig tacked on the joke like a life preserver, likely realizing how close he was to becoming chopped meat for the unicorn farm. As quickly as the moment emerged, it passed.

Kradduk's body relaxed, his eyes cleared, and he grinned. "In that case, I guess I won't have to eat you."

Fillig let out a long breath. He made a show of rolling his eyes as if he weren't terrified just moments before, but Granu knew better. He couldn't get out of there fast enough. Shooting a departing wink at her as he muttered hasty goodbyes, he walked away, stopping at the door to carefully don his coverings, a sunsuit with the quarry's logo plastered on the back.

Staying out of the sun was integral to a troll's continued existence, hence the lack of windows on the external wall of Goron's and all other underling establishments. While only trolls turned to stone, the sun affected all underlings to varying degrees, which was why New Metta was located entirely underground with the notable exception of the The Covered Bridge. Most sun-avoiders tried to secure jobs during the night hours if they worked outside the city, but only the upper echelon succeeded. Fillig had to sleep in short shifts in sub-prime hours like most of the working class, covering his body from head to toe for his morning commute.

Granu would love to work, even day hours. She was unemployed, having lost her previous job when the young trolls she taught both entered wontog—raging troll puberty—at once. Their eyes turned red, their mouths foamed, and their bodies convulsed. They charged the smaller troll with vicious abandon and nearly turned her into a troll fillet. When she awoke in the hospital, she discovered that her high performance in academia was worthless to employers who couldn't trust her to stay alive long enough to care for, let alone teach, their little monsters. Granu, thinking about her brush with death, scratched at the scars on her arms.

"Thinking about getting a job?" asked Kradduk, his eyes lingering on her hands. For such a self-involved troll, he had moments of astute insight, which were more off-putting than his casually offensive comments.

"Don't change the subject. You almost made Fillig mess himself."

Kradduk shrugged. "That troll's too twitchy."

"He likely needs a change of undergarments after that." When she got no response, Granu took the hint that he didn't want to discuss it further, so she pulled out her phone and began scrolling her Friend-Zone feed.

After a few minutes, Kradduk continued where he'd left off. "Any leads?"

"On what?"

"Work. You know, that thing most underlings do to earn money?"

"Oh, right. No. All the entry positions outside my field say I'm overqualified, and the ones in my field require hands-on work with wontog-aged teens. I'm just not willing to go through that again."

"Well, my offer still stands. I have some pull at the tar fields. Work is work."

Granu crinkled her wide, upturned nose. She wasn't quite ready to resort to shoveling tar, however much it paid. She didn't attend Vinkle University on a full scholarship to go home sticky and stinking of the pits every morning. Then again, her degree in Early Trollhood Education hadn't prepared her for the onset of wontog, so she lacked means to pay her bills. She sighed.

"I appreciate the offer, but I'm not that desperate. Yet."

"Suit yourself, but I don't think it's very healthy to be sitting around in your own filth waiting for something to fall in your lap," replied Kradduk.

"Well I never! My filth is fragrant, thank you very much, and while you've been seducing your way through New Metta, I've been scouring the city looking for any job remotely connected to my degree. If I didn't know better, I'd think the goats were at it again."

"Nah, that's not their style. They go for trolls getting promotions and moving up in the world, not ones on unemployment. Besides, if the billys are involved, you know it."

"Yeah, they'd at least leave the hoof print on the classifieds or something." When the billy goats successfully foiled a troll's plans, they always left their signature mark, a cleft hoof print, somewhere. "Didn't you have a run-in with them once?"

Kradduk sneered and slouched. "Yeah. When I was a junior manager. I was about to be promoted to executive level despite the Blight, but they showed up to the most important meeting of my life. Dropped out of the ceiling like cud-chewing ninjas, dressed all in black, and armed with paintball guns. They shot up my charts and my chance at a promotion too. They even got a shot off at Marla, the only troll to reach VP level in the last ten years. She walked around with one green eye for a week, and I was stuck pushing paper for another year before advancing."

Granu shook her head. "You'd think somebody would do something about them."

"Well, at least most companies have Blight discrimination policies.

TCB does too, so they'll never admit that was the reason I didn't get promoted. It would open them up for a lawsuit. They did come up with some fantastic goat-repellent technologies after that incident, however, and I take full credit."

Nobody knew how the feud with the goats began, but whenever a troll was about to accomplish something important in life, the billys showed to sabotage the poor sap. They never killed or did permanent damage, but they plagued the trolls like bedbugs, a constant itch that could never be scratched.

Years ago, New Metta tried to create goat-proof seals on many entrances, but the billys were sneaky, and they had ways into every cavern in the city. The exclusion project was an enormous flop, wasting thousands of tax dollars with no success. The project ended with the resignation of Mayor Grugg, the troll who had spearheaded the campaign and the last troll mayor in present times.

Billy goat pranks were so reliable, many businesses shied away from hiring trolls, hence the moniker Billy Goat Blight. But recent litigation made many businesses fearful of lawsuits. Still, trolls rarely held the most powerful or highest paid positions for long.

"Damn billy goats," they said in unison.

"Anyhow, I didn't mean any harm. I'm just worried about you. In all the years I've known you, you've never been one to idle," said Kradduk.

"Where did this sudden concern come from? I'm beginning to think you have actual feelings, my friend."

Kradduk quivered in a way that made the material of his jumpsuit stretch across his chest and arms, causing a swog crossing the room to trip and land on her face. Her tiny wings fluttered in a too late attempt to catch her balance. Granu snickered as her friend attempted to hoist her up, resulting in both swogs flopping onto the hard floor. Kradduk didn't notice.

"Perish the thought. So, how's your friend Tanna? I had a dream about her last night. The things she did to me would give you palpitations." He licked his lips and widened his black eyes.

Granu had known Kradduk since grade school. Back then he was awkward and sweet, far from the wealthy womanizer he was today. It wasn't until his mother ate the Secretary of Underling Defense and took over the position that he became wealthy, and with money came toys, wild nights, and females aplenty. As if his looks weren't enough to accomplish the latter.

Granu threw a napkin at him, enjoying the envious way the swog looked her up and down as she finally climbed to her feet. Granu decided to play it up, leaning toward Kradduk and biting her bottom lip, keeping the female in her sight just beyond Kradduk's wide head. Kradduk shifted uncomfortably and leaned in slightly. Granu grinned, and Kradduk laughed in his utterly contagious way. She couldn't help but laugh with him, though she wasn't sure they were entertained by the same thing.

"When are you going to find a nice girl and settle down?" she asked as the swog trotted away to her own table, friend in tow. Granu nearly felt bad for her.

Kradduk's laugh ended abruptly and he leaned ever so slightly away. "You concerned about my future? That's rich. I have a plan, for your information. Once I've made my way through all of the female trolls, swogs, and other sexy ladies of New Metta in the 21-30 range, I'll find an eligible life partner, not romantic, of course, but someone I could travel with to scour the rest of the world for lovely, willing females. Maybe we'll adopt, eventually."

Every time Kradduk was asked about his romantic future, he gave a different story, plan, or excuse.

"That one was lame."

"Yeah, I know, I'm off my game today." Kradduk poked at the bowl of fried fairy wings, withdrawing his attention from Granu.

Granu spent the next few hours taking in flagon after flagon of grog and even attempting to help Kradduk pick up a female troll with skin like toad hide and the largest backside either of them had seen. She was way out of his league. He failed splendidly, and the troll nipped his hand, drawing blood, before rejoining her friends at the bar. Watching Kradduk on the hunt made Granu self-conscious, even if he wasn't successful this time. It was true that she occasionally caught the eye of a troll or swog who appreciated a different sense of aesthetics, but she was keenly aware of her smooth skin and off-putting eyes. By the time Kradduk turned in for the day, Granu was ready for some time alone. She would catch no such break.

"Granu Scoria!" The voice sounded like tires on wet asphalt, and unfortunately it was familiar. A pink molent in a Hawaiian shirt tucked into high-waisted khakis approached, and by his pointed movements, he meant business.

"Mr. Picketts, how strange to run into you in *here*."

"It's no coincidence! I know your type, and this is the closest sin hole to *my* cavern."

Of course. Her molent landlord had hunted her down at the closest watering hole.

She sighed. "What can I do for you?"

"Where's my money?" The high-pitched squeak sounded more like plastic on Styrofoam than a speaking voice, and Granu did her best to suppress a shudder.

"I didn't expect to see you today," said Granu as the molent hoisted himself into the booth next to her. She stifled a gag at the feel of his oiled, bristly skin against her leg. Granu tried to be progressive, to accept everyone as they were, but Fillig was right. Molents creeped her out. She'd never admit it aloud, though.

"Out with it, troll! I need my rent money, and I need it now," he demanded, beady eyes unreadable as usual. Molents didn't have eyelids, so they constantly looked shocked by some horror known only to themselves.

"I don't have it yet. I'll get it for you soon. Please, just give me until next month," pleaded Granu.

Picketts' long front teeth dug into his chin, and his whiskered nose twitched as he considered her. "Fine. You are on notice. One month. You will pay me what you owe plus 20% interest, or you will be out on your rump," he said, emphasizing his words with a jab of the forefinger. "You haven't been having gentlemen callers in my apartment, have you?"

Granu's mouth dropped open. "My personal life is none of your business, old man," she gasped.

"Get my money!"

Granu felt the blood rush to her eyes. She counted to ten, breathing deeply. It would do no good to eat the little creature, especially in front of witnesses. One of his brothers would inherit his holdings, and she'd be in the same position—or worse— if she could manage to avoid legal recourse.

"Yes, Mr. Picketts. I'll get your money. Thank you," she replied, clenching her teeth. If she lost this place, she'd be forced to seek government housing in the fifth sector, which was not a place for a troll to live alone.

The exorbitant cost of living in New Metta, the most expansive city of its kind, was supported by waiting lists a mile long, and Granu had scored big to find an affordable apartment in a great location. Picketts was more patient than most landlords in allowing her any leeway on rent. All the same, his smug little face made her feel violent.

Granu was thankful when Picketts climbed out of the booth and left with a disgusted look around the tavern, but the feeling didn't last.

"Harlot!" he mumbled when he was just out of her reach. Granu's vision blurred as she lunged from the booth, intent on ripping out the molent's throat, but Dreatte stepped in her path.

"Have a drink," chimed the grawback, slamming a flagon into Granu's hand as she grasped the troll's shoulder with the talons of her left hand and ushered her back into the booth. Granu's sight cleared enough to see the cavern door slam shut behind her very lucky landlord.

2

THE CRUNCH

The grog did the trick. After draining the flagon, Granu left a more generous tip for Dreatte than planned and made her own way to the internal door of Goron's, located on the opposite side of the tavern from where Fillig had exited in his sun gear. It led to the cavernous maze that was New Metta City.

New Metta, the shining jewel of underground life in Fairbax, was a cultural hub like no other in underling society. A labyrinth of passageways large enough to accommodate the most hulking creatures linked and crossed with smaller thoroughfares, providing access to different sectors of the city. Public transportation in the form of motorized flatbeds moved underlings through the city, but most simply walked or used Segways. Horizontal breaks in the rock lining each passage sometimes provided a view to nearby passages, sometimes collected the tainted water that seemed to endlessly drip everywhere in the city, and always glowed with recessed lighting in shades of blue, red, green, or purple. The thick smell of sulfur permeated the cavern air. It was the smell of home.

The miles of passages and crevices in the rock radiated from a great canyon which split the land above in two with a huge covered bridge as the only topside connection. A river ran at the bottom of the canyon, providing underlings with potable water unlike the magnesium-laden drippings in the caves, which were only good for teenagers impressing would-be mates with displays of flatulence.

Granu sloshed along the passageway away from Goron's. All residents of New Metta developed mechanisms to cope with being constantly waterlogged. Molents groomed frequently, grawbacks produced an oil coating for their feathers, and swogs were protected by layers of fat. Thick troll hide, impervious to pruning, sheltered Granu from the less comfortable aspects of cavern life.

The recessed lighting along this cavern glowed green; the passage would take her to Vermin Square if she followed it into the heart of the city. The lights of New Metta indicated which major sectors the paths intersected—green for government, purple for commerce, or was it blue?—only the original swog engineer knew for sure. She walked the other way, toward the canyon.

The cave opened into the large, bustling gorge known as Barter Sector. Expanses of space gave the impression of being open to the night sky, but it was an illusion as the cavern peaked leagues overhead. She turned left. Red lanterns hung from stalactites over the sides of the street. Voices bounced off rock as vendors called wares to passers-by who sometimes stopped to trade at one of the countless shops lining the passage. Money was as valuable here as anywhere, but exchange of goods was the expected currency in Barter Sector.

Granu passed shops with roasted cats stretched on hooks, tables with shiny gems and bits of metal arranged to catch the covetous eye of a passing troll or molent, and open caverns with vendors screaming into the gorge to anyone who would listen. On the street, grawbacks sang about paper products in front of a tiny shop specializing in securing rare and illegal items. How that place wasn't closed down by now was beyond her.

Water swished through Granu's Crocs as she sloshed her way through the throngs. Eventually she reached Gore Pass, the passageway containing a narrow staircase which led to the door of her studio cavern. Hers for now, at least. She knew it was only a matter of time before the pink rat threw her out.

Granu made a sound of disgust in the back of her throat just thinking about molents hoarding piles of coins in tiny caves along the eastern outskirts. Molents loved nothing more than money; at least, that's how it seemed to Granu.

Her neighbor, a nosy troll named Len, peeked out of his observation hole to watch as Granu approached her door. The blue glow of a large computer monitor backlit his ill-proportioned silhouette. She nodded to him, suppressing an eye roll at his persistent staring and let herself in. Snagging the most recent copy of the New Metta Chronicle from her kitchen table, she sank into her Laz-E-Bones to spend another day combing over the wanted ads.

A picture of The Covered Bridge sprawled across the front page. There had been another attempted robbery. With the tolls they collected, TCB Corp provided the largest source of income for New Metta, and it was guarded with technologies she couldn't wrap her head around. Yet every idiot crook seemed to take a turn trying to rob the corporation. When would everyone learn that the place was untouchable? They'd have better luck robbing the human fortress, the Bellagio, on the topside. Morons.

The wanted ads were flimsy, as usual, with a few listings for cooks, electricians, tar workers, boulder haulers, and so on. Nothing for a well-educated troll looking to shift industries.

Bold letters caught her eye.

"Attractive executive seeks female troll with wide set eyes, boulder breasts, and thunder thighs. I'm a sad troll who just had my heart broken, and I need a little TLC. No uggos or over 30s please."

Granu nearly choked.

"Oh, Kradduk, do you really think any female is stupid enough to answer that piece of refuse?" she muttered with a shake of the head before ditching the paper and busting out her laptop. It seemed like only the elderly and Kradduk still posted in the newspaper these days. No viable job prospects showed in any of her search engines either.

This is my life, she thought as she gave up the hunt and opted for a cup of scotch instead.

An unexpected knock made her close her laptop and pray to the

Underlord it wasn't Picketts again. There was no barmaid to save his ass here. She cracked the door to find Fillig waiting with slumped shoulders.

"Fillig, what are you doing here? Done at the quarry already?"

"In a way. They fired me. Apparently after six years on the job, I am now officially overqualified. If you ask me, I think that punk Pikey was worried I was after the job he had his eye on. It was supposed to be mine! A ridiculous notion since the quarry isn't too keen on promoting trolls, if you know what I mean."

Granu gasped. "But you just told me last week that you were about to nail that promotion! You can't think the Billy Goat Blight is to blame! That's discrimination!"

"Yeah, it is. And yeah, I do."

"You could sue."

"And they'll just claim it was performance-related. I should have known better. I thought Onee liked me enough to overlook the Blight, but he wouldn't even answer my calls after I got word from HR. I heard Pikey was promoted before I even made it home. Oh well. I guess I'm joining the ranks of the unemployed. Got any Giddle?"

Granu moved aside so Fillig could squeeze through the doorway into the tiny living room. While large enough for Granu alone, her apartment wasn't constructed to entertain guests, at least not large ones. It would have been expansive for the smaller creatures of New Metta, but it was downright tiny for a troll. She was so short and slight, though, she hardly noticed.

She rarely had visitors, except Francie, her friend from college. Francie wasn't much larger than she was, so the spatial limitations didn't bother her. She went to the kitchen and emerged with a rocks cup and the bottle of the Giddle Scotch Kradduk had bought her in celebration of her graduation. She refilled her own wide, wooden cup made specifically for powerful troll hands to hold delicate liquors, and poured one for Fillig. She'd been nursing the bottle for the last few years since she'd never be able to afford the liquor on her own.

"Ah, the 20 year. Thanks, Gran." Fillig took the glass. "No job, no girl, no future. That's me. No future Fillig," he muttered as he downed the contents of the cup.

"Fillig. Stop with the pity party. This is just a little hurdle. New Metta is enormous. You'll find something in no time," she said, mustering up all the enthusiasm she could.

"Oh really?" replied Fillig, "So I guess you're just lazy then?"

Granu snarled and slumped into her overstuffed recliner. "That's not fair."

"I'm sorry, Granu. It's just been a really bad day," Fillig said. "I know you're trying to lift my spirits, and that was uncalled for."

"Honestly, Fillig, you have a Masters of Destruction in Rockworking. You'll find something. My degree is job specific, and the real world is nothing like university. I wish they'd told us that when we chose our majors."

"Yeah, because wontog came as a complete surprise," Fillig said with a smirk.

"Hey, now, I'm an only child. I didn't have to fend off my siblings like the rest of you, and most of my class was quarantined with Flea Pox when they went through it. I mean, I saw a few turn, but I never had to manage it myself."

"I know, Gran. I didn't mean anything by that." Fillig took a long swig of his Giddle. "Not to beat a dead unicorn, but you've never really talked about that night. I mean, I know the Rockborn juvies tried to make a snack of you, landing you in the bite ward, but what really went down?"

"There's not much to tell. Two juvies out for blood, one me. You've seen the scars."

"What about your training at Vinkle U? Didn't you oversee wontog during your three months of clinicals?"

Granu nodded and sighed. "Yeah, but it was supervised, and only one juvie turned the whole time I was there."

"There's really no predicting when it's coming?" asked Fillig. "Mine happened two days after I turned fourteen, not that I remember much about it, but our school was prepared with quarantine cells."

It was a fair question. With all the recent advancements in underling technology, Granu thought there should be some way to better pinpoint wontog, at least within a year or two, but she'd learned the hard way that wasn't the case. And with a five-year window of possibility, all anyone could do was learn how to handle it when it did happen. But even that training had proven ineffective.

"That's private education for ya. I was supposed to be on the lookout, and I did see it coming in Tigg. I could have handled him alone, but siblings turning together? There was a three year age-gap for Underlord's sake!" Granu shuddered. "But that smell. I'll never forget that smell, like acid in my lungs. It was the smell of death."

Fillig cleared his throat, bringing her attention back to present times. "What happened to the one who turned during clinicals?" he asked.

"My professor was right there, and she stepped in to restrain while I called in the authorities. She acted like dealing with wontog would come naturally."

Fillig snorted at that. Handling trolls during wontog couldn't possibly be natural for anyone.

"I know. I was naïve. My parents are both educators, but they work with older underlings."

"Yeah, I know. I was your date to your dad's lifetime recognition ceremony, remember?"

How could Granu forget? If it weren't for Fillig slipping her a flask under the table, she didn't think she would have made it through the night, not with her aunts clustered around pestering her about her career trajectory. This was just after the incident and before the short-term gig she took as a tutor. Nobody in her family would let her forget the shame of nearly becoming troll fillet for wontog-raging teens.

"Have you thought about that? Using your father's connections to get a job on the faculty of Vinkle?" asked Fillig.

"Come on, Fil. Everyone my dad works with knows about my epic failure as a teacher. You know they won't hire me, and dad won't give a recommendation for fear of tanking his own career. I was so stupid, thinking I could restrain the little demons."

"Granu, you are the smartest troll in New Metta. Nobody has your brilliance, drive, or dedication! Like I told you when you were in the bite ward, you can do anything you set your mind to."

Granu laughed. "Apparently not. I graduated with honors and a degree in Early Trollhood Education, and I'm contemplating work at the tar pits. I'll be the most overqualified rake-pusher there."

"Don't be ridiculous. You didn't get that degree to be a rake-pusher."

Granu's shoulders slumped. "You don't need to sound like my dad. I was obviously underprepared. I didn't exactly plan to become a meal for juvies."

"Underprepared. You're telling me," replied Fillig. "Life after college isn't what I thought it would be either. I was supposed to start at management level with my degree, but I've been in the trenches for six years and for what?"

"Some of those years were before graduation. You were lucky to be able to work there part-time while going to school, and now you have experience."

"Yeah, unfortunately experience doesn't pay bills," Fillig countered.

"Sure doesn't," Granu replied.

"Here's to society failing to prepare us for the real world even as we sign those tuition checks," he said, tossing an arm over her shoulders. There was the Fillig she knew, comforting her even as he was struggling with his own problems. Fillig may be more sensitive than most, but he truly was a good friend.

"Hear hear," chimed Granu, raising her second glass of Giddle. "Hey, did you see Kradduk's personals ad?"

"Underlord, yes! Can you believe that troll? I do have to hand it to him, though, he snags more ass than I could ever dream to!" Fillig's voice held a note of awe, perhaps even envy.

Granu gave a half-hearted laugh. "It's frightening that he gets laid so frequently. There must really be some truly stupid creatures out there."

"And here I am, alone. What does that say about me?" asked Fillig.

"You're not alone. You're with me."

"You know what I mean. It's not like you're lining up to marry poor, jobless Fillig."

Granu scoffed. She knew she was no catch and Fillig had no real interest in her. Petite with a narrow face, high cheek bones, and a full head of thick, black hair, she stood nearly as short as a human. Her ears pointed upright rather than sagging and flopping over like proper troll ears, and her skin was smooth.

The real kicker, however, was her eye color—bright green instead of the favored black, and if that weren't bad enough, they were close-set. If it weren't genetically impossible, one might accuse her mother of mating with a disgusting feeder human, spawning a troll-prey hybrid. Alas, no such cause could be blamed. Granu just was, and despite her high-level achievements in academia, she was aimless. Fillig, while unremarkable as far as trolls go with perfectly troll-appropriate proportions, could do better.

"Alright, that's enough. You're bringing me down," said Granu. "Go get some rest. I'll catch up with you at Goron's tomorrow, and we can commiserate to your heart's content."

His habit of alternating between condescending intellectual and self-pitying bump-on-a-log wore on Granu. Even if he was a good friend, she had enough to worry about without a sad-sack Fillig cluttering up her apartment.

3

THE REAL WORLD

Kradduk kissed his black-haired, tough-skinned troll companion for the early morning goodbye. He forgot her name, so he decided to call her Miss Blue in honor of the baby-blue yak hair sweater stretched over breasts the size of twin swog heads. Miss Blue was pure perfection.

He celebrated another victory when the elevator door closed behind her. Any time his conquests didn't stay for the daylight hours was a win in his book. He locked the deadbolt after her before heading to the kitchen for a cup of day-tea to take with him to the bedroom. The herbal additives helped him fall asleep, and he needed to grab some if he was going to tolerate his coworkers in the evening.

After a solid day's sleep, Kradduk dressed in a fine Flusterberry suit of deep green with gold pinstripes and headed into the office for the night. He was making rapid progress climbing the corporate ladder at TCB, despite his early career run-in with the billy goats.

Kradduk started at the company in middle management a few years back and won a series of promotions more by hustling and networking than by performing well. He was even featured in Zud's 100 under 35 feature, a comprehensive list of influential underlings with promising career trajectories. Still, he didn't really need the gig.

Fillig wasn't lying. Kradduk's family had money and connections, which was how he got hired on in the first place.

His mother had grown tired of his playboy lifestyle and set an ultimatum: get a job or get cut off. So he took the job at first as a way to appease her, but he kept it for more personal reasons. He quickly discovered just how underhanded TCB was, how they paid off police and politicians alike to cover up their shoddy practices. While the company had more political weight than any other entity in New Metta, they were surprisingly careless with their bookkeeping, so Kradduk made himself invaluable by covering their asses time and time again. He'd pulled TCB out of the flames so frequently, you'd think he had a law degree. He wasn't sure how the company would function without him, and that was the first part of his plan. It was the only part of his plan so far, if he were honest.

Before Kradduk, they'd spent thousands on bribe money, but now he kept their dealings from prying eyes, saving them cash and, on a few occasions, jail time. He sat behind his desk, staring at the computer and wondering if he should continue to work for these vile animals. TCB was known for eliminating all competition by whatever means necessary, and their fees were outrageous, even for sun-avoiders. They violated every business law in Fairbax, yet they pulled in profits and paraded around like puffed up grawbacks during mating season. He shrugged his shoulders as if answering himself. He may not need the money, but some things were more important. He was on a mission here, and it was personal. He'd take them down one way or another.

He popped open a file on his desk and shook his head. Given to the wrong person, the information on the first page alone could tank the company. Kradduk ran his fingers over the damning words, imagining the headlines should these documents conveniently fall into the hands of Inspector Quinn or Bernside Forrage, the investigative reporter for UGH. No, this wasn't how it was going to happen. It lacked finesse. He stuffed the file into the shredder beneath his desk. The bin was full. Again.

Just then, the CEO of TCB walked by the large glass window that served as Kradduk's wall. TCB creed didn't allow for privacy for any managers under VP level, and Kradduk was the only one permitted to turn his computer away from the glass wall. The precaution was due more to the privileged information it contained than to any fondness for him.

Kradduk made eye contact with the swog. Bartock Figg made a motion as if his two fat hands were guns, pulled the triggers, and winked at Kradduk. Bartock's head was perfectly round with flabs of fatty flesh jiggling beneath his wide mouth. His round snout dominated his face, making his beady, dark eyes appear even smaller, and he had the snaggle-tusk common to the Figg family. Now there was an inbred lot. In a gaudy display of wealth, Figg had his tusk gold-tipped to match the four gold rings signifying his family rank piercing his right ear. His torso was barrel-shaped, and tiny wings stuck straight out from the back of his jumpsuit. He wore a bright green power tie with little golden swogs in flight littered over it like tacky porcine confetti.

The Figg family of swogs all but owned New Metta due to their control over TCB, the single largest cash influx into the city. On paper, there was a council, a mayor, and a justice department, and all decisions were made based on polite discourse and voting. It was all very civilized in the eyes of the public. In reality, no law, ordinance, or directive was passed without crossing the desk of the Figg secretary. The Figgs controlled the entire legal process, from introduction of bills to enforcement on the streets once they became law.

There wasn't a single government official not on the payroll. With more money than the Underlord, they got away with the worst crimes in the underworld—fraternizing with humans, extorting from churches, 3rd degree deviousness. In a world where impulse ruled, planning wrongdoing far outranked crimes of passion, and TCB redefined what it meant to enact a plan.

No, Kradduk had to stay close to Bartock if he wanted to exact his revenge. When the time was right, he'd ruin that prick and all of TCB with him.

Kradduk decided that he'd worked hard enough for one day, so he packed up his things and headed to Goron's. Setting his own hours was a luxury he'd earned with the nature of his service to the company. As long as the reporters, police, and feds stayed well away from TCB, Kradduk was free to do as he pleased.

Granu and Fillig were already parked in their usual corner booth when he arrived. The tavern was empty aside from the handful of nightly regulars giving Kell a hard time at the bar, but their alcohol-amplified voices bouncing off the stone walls made it seem as if the place were packed. Kradduk generally avoided conversing with the regulars, who were currently occupied parroting inflammatory phrases from the popular podcast Bigot Begot. He dealt with enough buffoonery at work. As the current argument echoed off the stone walls, Kradduk wondered why Goron's didn't invest in some tapestries to absorb the sound. Most respectable establishments in New Metta were lined with them. Granu seemed to have a soft spot for the place despite its shortcomings, so he didn't complain.

"My trolls, how's it hanging?"

Granu's bright green eyes cut to him, and she shot him one of her equal parts amused and irritated looks with which he'd become intimately familiar over the past fifteen years. If she'd give him the slightest hint of interest, he'd take her out and show her the world. Her emerald eyes were fascinating, her skin enchanting, and her ears adorable. And that mind—sharp as a filed bone shank. She was so different from the trolls he took home most nights, from anyone he'd ever met, really.

"Baby, you know you like it," he said, using his thigh to push Granu further into the booth once again so he could sit on the outside. She never seemed to notice the single opportunity he took to make physical contact, other than the occasional exclamation of pain as the skin of her thighs stuck to the vinyl seat when he shoved her. Oh well. He did prefer to sit on the outside, ready to pounce if a sexy female sauntered by. Fillig tossed Kradduk a bowl of infant spines, a step up from their usual fried fairy wing snack.

"Mm. What's the occasion?" He asked as he stuffed a fistful into his mouth.

"Unemployment," answered Fillig.

"Ooh, ouch. Joining the ranks of Granu? That's low. Sorry to hear it cuz," Kradduk replied through crunching. "What happened?"

"I'm overqualified apparently."

"After this long? You know what? I bet they realized you were overdue for a promotion but didn't want to risk a billy appearance. The goats could do some real damage at the quarry."

"There's no telling, but if that were the case, they'd never fess up. It doesn't change the situation. It's alright, though. Now I have more time to hang with my girl here," said Fillig flashing his canines at Granu.

Kradduk grunted at Fillig's obvious flirtation. "We should find you a new gig pronto. Want me to sweet talk the head of the Demo department at TCB? I bet I can get you hooked up. He owes me a favor."

Fillig narrowed his eyes at Kradduk for a moment before a smile spread over his face. A position at The Covered Bridge was the most coveted opportunity in all Fairbax.

As the only canyon crossing within a hundred miles, TCB was the shining jewel of New Metta and the only government-sanctioned contact point between underlings and humanity. Humans happily paid tolls to trolls on the bridge, then convinced themselves that what they saw wasn't real, attributing their impressions to flights of imagination. Later, they wrote stories for their offspring about trolls, goats, flying pigs, and wishes, convinced they had created entire worlds from nothing but their own minds. The human ego was nearly a match for human stupidity. As a result of this mass delusion, New Metta went undiscovered by humanity. Of course, if any issue did arise, the human feds would step in to keep the peace.

Much of the city's security stemmed from the strictly enforced law that kept trolls and other humanivores from hunting within 50 miles of the city limits. With no missing persons, there was no threat, so if any humans did begin to question their false reality, the others just ridiculed them.

Of course, if the tolls went unpaid, all deals were null and void, and human life would be forfeit to TCB. That's when cleaners were employed.

For underlings, working at TCB was a dream job as it meant money, life in the relative open, and prestige enough to impress any mate.

"See, Fil," Granu reached over the table to smack him in the arm. "I told you it wouldn't be hard with your background. I don't suppose TCB has any need for juvie sitters?" Granu asked.

Kradduk laughed, and the resulting frown on Granu's face made him laugh more. "TCB offering childcare? What next? Maternity leave? Paid disability? Unthinkable."

Besides, Granu should be doing something more with her life than watching a bunch of ne'er-do-wells. She was brilliant. He didn't say that last bit out loud, of course, so she continued to scowl in his direction.

Fillig ignored them both. "It's a good thing Kradduk cares so much about how I occupy my time," he growled.

Granu cocked her head to the side. "What?"

"Nothing."

Kradduk rolled his eyes. Fillig was so transparent. He didn't know how Granu could be so oblivious to the troll's intentions. But then, she never seemed to notice any potential mates.

"What do you think? Do you want the job or not? One condition, though, you really have to like tacos," he said.

"Tacos?" Fillig looked dubious. "I mean, who doesn't love tacos?"

"Anyone who works at TCB. It's all they serve. It's great at first. Kid tacos, turkey tacos, crunchy fairy tacos, but eventually, you get a little tacoed out."

"Really?" gasped Granu. "We live in a hub for imported delicacies thanks to the hunting ban, and all the company that enforces the ban, serves is tacos?"

Kradduk scowled. "They're swanky tacos, if that helps. Unicorn fillets, pixie parts, pickled toes."

"There's nothing swanky about unicorn flesh. The farm is just outside the city," said Granu.

Fillig looked pensive. "I could just bring my own meals."

"You would turn down free tacos? What's wrong with you?" asked Kradduk, flabbergasted.

"Didn't you just say I'd get tacoed out?" asked Fillig with his face contorted into a quizzical expression.

"Free tacos, dude." Kradduk stared at Fillig like he'd just descended in a space ship.

Granu burst out laughing. "Males," she muttered.

"Do you want the job or what?" asked Kradduk with a sheepish smile. Granu's laugh was infectious.

"TCB. Hmm. I know they're an evil corporation bent on the destruction of the world, but how could I turn it down? They consistently rank #1 in Transparent Business Monthly."

"Oh, because that's not rigged," Granu said, puffing in a way that lifted a lock of her hair before it settled back on her forehead.

"Keep your jealous comments to yourself." Fillig turned back to Kradduk. "What's the job?"

"Hey now, Granu does have a point. TCB owns the Transparent Business Corporation along with the rest of the city. I don't want you coming into this thinking it's all moonlight and weeds. There's an ugly side to TCB. But it is *the* place to work, and the Demo department is integral to the success of the company. Its sole purpose is to remove all competition. That's where you come in."

"Competition? For TCB?" Fillig looked skeptical.

"I know, right? There is none. And why do you think that is? Every other company in New Metta has rivals, but not the biggest money-making enterprise in all of Fairbax? There's a reason for that. Every so often, someone gets the bright idea to build a bridge. Sometimes it's underlings looking for a revenue source, sometimes it's the humans upstairs getting cranky about paying the toll. They get to thinking, and humans thinking is never good for anybody."

Granu and Fillig both chuckled. The only animal less intelligent than a human was a unicorn, good only for their meat, horns, and testes. Humans, though gamey as adults, made for the choicest of entrees before the age of ten, so underlings tolerated their continued existence.

"The Demo department makes sure these new bridges don't ever reach completion. Simple as that. A new one pops up, *boom*. No more competition."

Fillig was nodding along, probably unconsciously. Blowing things up was the epitome of fun for a troll with a Masters of Destruction in Demolition. "Sounds like a sweet gig. What's it pay?"

"Enough to get by on. More than the quarry, I'd wager, plus the occasional under the table corpse."

Granu gasped. "Isn't that in violation of the hunting ban? You're telling me this is sanctioned by TCB?"

"Come on, Gran. It's TCB. They can do what they want. Besides, that's why it's under the table. Who wants to pay taxes on a little snack anyway? And, technically it's not hunting. It's protecting the income of the city. Everyone knows what happens if you don't pay the toll."

"Everything about The Covered Bridge seems shady to me," said Granu.

"Maybe, but the benefits rock, the pay is good, and the prestige will land you all kinds of ass." Kradduk gave her a quick punch in the arm. "Don't worry Gran, you'll find something sooner or later."

"I don't really have a later to figure it out," she replied. "The damned molent is demanding his rent now, *or else.*"

Kradduk could see worry lines forming at the corners of her eyes. He kicked himself for not realizing how stressed she must be. "I didn't know you were so backed up. I'll take care of it until you get back on your feet," he said pulling out his wallet.

"Absolutely not! I will not be your charity case," snapped Granu. Kradduk put his wallet away with a shrug.

Kradduk really didn't know what the big deal was. Money was nothing but a necessary evil, and he had plenty to cover anything Granu needed and more. If her pride wouldn't let her take his money, he'd have to find another way to help. An idea began to form, one that would help him take down TCB and help Granu all at once. But he'd have to play his cards perfectly or she'd never agree to it. For now, it was best to focus on Fillig.

"Ok then," he said, motioning to Kell for another round. This time of night, business was too slow to have a server on staff. "What do you say, Fil? Do you want me to pull some strings?"

"That would be amazing," Fillig answered, looking almost apologetic as Granu sulked. "Lighten up, Gran. Things will turn around for you."

"Yeah, sure."

They fell into a silence broken only by the crunching of teeth on infant spines. Kradduk slurped his grog as he considered his genius solution to Granu's predicament, though he kept his head swiveling to appear focused on female-watching.

Shouting shattered the moment. At the bar, chaos broke out. Forin, a sniggle who dwarfed his companions and was known for spouting off, stood abruptly, knocking over a stone stool. He hollered something unintelligible at Girr, a female troll who remained seated as if his size were no threat. He lifted his fat fist to pummel her, and Kell vaulted the bar, landing on the enormous creature's shoulder. The tattooed molent seemed to be everywhere at once, zipping down the sniggle's side, around his legs and back up his torso to land on the bar with a satisfying thud. The giant gray mountain hit the ground, his legs bound by the wire cord Kell used to take his feet out from under him. The impact shook the cavern, sending bottles from the shelf behind the bar to the floor, where they shattered on contact.

"Don't even think about getting up," snarled the quiet, if sometimes sarcastic, bartender. Kell's chest heaved, but he stood atop the bar like a tiny ruler of a broken kingdom. Forin looked as stunned as the rest of the tavern patrons. Nobody said a word in the loaded moment.

"Maybe I'll go home with Kell tonight," laughed Girr, finally breaking the spell with her slurred words.

Kell inclined his head to her before addressing the sniggle. "Go home and sober up, Forin. I don't want to see you back here until you've learned to treat a lady with respect."

"Aw, Kell. You know we don't have the same rules in our species," drawled the sniggle as he writhed around on the floor, freeing himself from the wire.

"I don't give a fuck. You're in my bar, you'll act right. Now, get out."

Remarkably, the sniggle got to his feet, holding his head low. He paid his tab and left without a word to the troll or anyone else.

"Holy shit," said Granu when it was all over. "Kell is a badass."

"I once saw him take down three trolls single-handedly," said Kradduk. "I'll never underestimate a molent again. Yo, Kell, come do a shot with us!"

The molent shook his head. "Nah, I don't drink on the job. Besides, I gotta keep these punks in line."

The stunned silence in the place made it clear there'd be no more trouble for the rest of the night. Kradduk was pleased that his policy of never crossing a bartender was validated, though perhaps not in the way he'd imagined.

4

THE ONE-NIGHT STAND

Kradduk spent what felt like eternity giving Fillig a rundown of the ins and outs of TCB while Granu sat in the corner, blocked in by his troll-spreading limbs. She stared idly into her flagon as she swished the contents around. Some kind of insect had made its way into the foam, and she watched it struggle to get to the edge of the container, sloshing it free every time it managed to grasp on. Every time the conversation hit a lull she tried to change the subject, but Kradduk would think of one more thing to add, some juicy tidbit about a hidden room for grabbing a nap or a custodian with a Giddle hook-up.

Finally, Fillig told Kradduk he was ready, and they left together, Fillig to study some materials Kradduk emailed him and Kradduk to schmooze the head of the demolition department on Fillig's behalf. Granu sucked down the contents of her flagon, floundering insect and all.

She spent the rest of the night drinking through the remainder of her cash. She had nowhere else to go. As the night wore on, the tavern filled. When Dreatte arrived for her shift, the place was packed with sun-avoiders playing Critterhole, drinking, and dancing by the digital jukebox to the beats of Warted Woebegone. Flagon after flagon of grog surged down her throat until she began to see double and sway to the music. She knew it was time to head home when she found herself flirting with a molent with gray, bristly hair and one red, wandering eye. As she settled up with Kell, she felt a hand on her shoulder. She turned to swing defensively and was met with an uncomfortable giggle.

A troll shorter than Granu with round, flushed cheeks and tiny eyes set on either side of a wide nose stood, flashing a shaky smile even as he cringed in anticipation of Granu's fist smashing into his skull.

"You're Granu," he blurted.

"I'm aware."

"Oh! Sorry. I live next door. I'm Len." Len's eyes twitched as he spoke, causing Granu to feel the need to look at his forehead in an effort not to stare.

"I know who you are. You're forever sticking your head out your window when I come up the path." Granu was aiming for haughty but only achieved a tone just above sloppy drunk. She cast her eyes toward the door.

The troll snickered. Granu couldn't look away from his grotesque face. He was like the decomposing road-kill that was always smashed into the street at the eastern end of the Bridge. The color had left his cheeks, so they returned to the brown hue natural to the troll, but they were smooth, high, and tight. His neck was long and protruded from his body at a strange angle, reminding her of an incorrectly-assembled grawback. His limbs were short, too short for a proper troll, and entirely disproportionate to his torso. If Granu was unattractive, Len was downright repulsive.

"It's just that you're so beautiful. I can't resist a chance to look at you," he said with his hand nearly completely covering his mouth. He snickered into it.

"That's not funny, and you're one to talk," replied Granu, taking his awkwardness for sarcasm. How dare this little cud-chewer make fun of her!

"No, I mean it. I'm sorry. I shouldn't have spoken to you. I'll go back to my table now. I'm sorry to bother you." Len looked as if he'd been punched in the nose, his cheeks flushed once again, and his eyes downcast.

Granu realized her mistake and felt like she'd kicked her child-hood pet, a bunny she'd plucked from the jaws of the young troll next-door. She'd always had a soft spot for bunnies, and Len's eyes glis-tened just like Mr. Fluffernutter's. She sighed as she debated going after him. He had taken a chance, and she'd shot him down. Badly. He was already halfway across the room when she called out to him. He stopped abruptly before slowly turning around.

"Yes?" he asked, his dark eyes widening, this time in hope rather than fear.

"Are you here alone?" she asked, eying the empty table he was approaching.

"No. Well, I guess, yes. I have my laptop. I was engaging in a heated debate about who is superior, Giddeon Gamut or Zelna Zoombig when I thought I could use a drink to cool off. Which do you think is superior?" His words seemed to trip over one another in an effort to leave his mouth as quickly as possible.

"I'm not much into television to be honest."

Len scoffed before he caught himself. "The television versions are shit anyways, I was talking about the graphic novels. In the graphic novels, Gamut is much larger, and his accent is Vovnian, not Ichian like in the TV series, and Zoombig, what can I say about the incompa-rable Zoombig? She's the epitome of everything a hero should be, with inherent flaws crippling her and holding her back, all the while pressing her forward to overcome the loss of..." He trailed off, taking notice of Granu's disinterested face. "Oh, well then. Do you like music? I happen to know the lengths of every song ever written down to the second."

"Every song? Like, ever?"

"Well, every song in that jukebox over there, I'm sure. Want to test me?" He pulled his wallet out of his back pocket and offered it to her.

Granu stared at his outstretched hand. This was the strangest pick-up tactic she'd ever seen, not that she had much experience on that front. "Why would you memorize song lengths?"

"Uh, well, I don't know why exactly. It's just something I picked up over the years." The troll adjusted his stiff, white button up shirt while slipping his wallet back in his pocket.

Granu took pity on him. "Um, well, that's interesting. What about this one?" The Shrieking Shambles' popular hit 'Pass the Bone' was playing.

"Five minutes, twenty-three seconds."

Granu didn't know exactly how to respond, but the eager look on Len's face made her decide to cut him a break. She laughed. "Well, I can't dispute you, so call me impressed," she said. The little troll's face lit up with the brightest smile she'd seen. With that expression, he was almost cute.

"Do you want some company?" she asked. It's not like she had anything better to do.

Len's mouth dropped open then snapped closed. He nodded excitedly without saying a word and scampered the rest of the way to the empty table. Granu followed, taking the seat opposite him. They sat, staring at each other for a long moment in silence before Len gasped.

"Oh, you'll be wanting a drink!" He motioned for Dreatte and ordered a bowl of unicorn testes, expensive but delicious and believed to be an aphrodisiac for most underlings. Granu swallowed the vomit that crept up her throat at his overt attempt at seduction. But Len had another flagon of grog brought for her, and before long, she forgot how repugnant he was. She even forgot about wallowing in her depressing life. Len chattered on about things she cared nothing for, but it felt nice to escape herself for an evening. Hours passed quickly, and Granu found herself laughing, dancing, and feeling free for the first time in months.

"Kell," she half-whispered, half-yelled when the bartender passed the dance floor during a particularly erotic song, "Am I dancing with him? Oh, Underlord, tell me I'm not dancing with him!" Her voice was far louder than she intended, and Len's ears were mere inches from her face.

Kell shook his head and kept walking. Len continued to grind against her leg in time with the music, either drunk or oblivious. Granu leaned into the thumping rhythms and overwhelming urge to just let go.

The next evening, Granu awoke in someone else's cave. She looked around frantically, but nothing was familiar. The granite bed was comfortable and warm. Len lay next to her beneath the burlap covers, a stubby arm draped over her chest. A snore loud enough to wake the dead echoed throughout the chamber, and his sickeningly sweet breath made her wince.

"Oh. Oh no," she gasped as realization washed over her. "No, no."

"Good night my putrid petal," he murmured as his eyes fluttered open. Granu shifted away, blood rushing to her face. Len removed his arm from her chest and used his hand to gently push the stray lock of hair back from her eyes. Gone was the unsure, sweet troll from the day before, and in his place was a troll convinced of his own prowess.

"Shy, are we? You weren't so shy last night."

"I, um, I have to go right now," she stammered, bolting up from the bed and taking the blanket with her, leaving Len naked. He posed seductively, propping his head on his hand and bending one leg to frame his stumpy trollhood. Granu did her best to look away as she searched the room for her clothes. There, on the chair in the corner. All she had to do was get them on without dropping the blanket, and she'd be home free.

"No need for modesty. I saw everything last night." Len snickered in that insufferable way of his, causing a shudder to run down Granu's spine. She gave up and dropped the blanket to the floor so that she could hastily pull on her pants and top. Anything to get her out of there faster.

Len's tone changed from playful to uneasy as he took in Granu's humiliation. "I can make us breakfast. I have goat." He puffed out his chest as if buying the meat of his enemies at the grocery store somehow proved his trollhood. When Granu didn't respond, he continued, sounding more deflated with each offering. "Dragon eggs, and a touch of human blood in the fridge. A freshly killed rabbit—want me to cook it up?"

She swallowed a mouthful of bile at the thought of consuming bunny meat, but Len wouldn't know about Mr. Fluffernutter. Most trolls ate rabbits by the hutchful.

"No, but thanks. Really. I, um, had a great night, but I need to get home now," she said, all but fleeing the poor troll's home. He watched from his observation hole window as she scrambled down his steps, up the passage, and up her own. She slammed the door behind her, stomping her feet and shaking her arms in a chaotic dance of disgust as soon as she was free of his gaze. That's when she realized she'd lost her phone.

"Oh, bloody heaven. Please don't let it be next door."

Granu took a scalding shower, stalling to ensure Len wouldn't be at the window any longer, before sneaking out as quietly as possible. Her plan must have worked since he didn't pop his head out as she passed at a near jog. She slowed her pace when his cave was out of sight, making her way past the shops and apartments lining the way back to Goron's. The entire time, she prayed to the Underlord that her phone was there and not at Len's. Her prayers were answered.

"You left this sitting on the bar when you joined that, um, handsome young man last night," teased Kell. He winked at her, and Granu thought she might burn a hole in the floor right there.

"Don't you ever go home?" snarled Granu.

"I'm just ending my shift now. Here." Kell set a bloody fixture, an alcoholic beverage known to cure the worst of hangovers, on the bar next to her phone. "It's on me," he said, laughing.

"Thanks," muttered Granu, pocketing the rogue phone as she pulled herself up into a barstool. "Got any pixie powder? My head feels like it may explode."

5

THE ESTABLISHMENT

F illig entered TCB the way all underling visitors did, through an expansive gift shop filled with brightly colored Bridge paraphernalia offered at outrageous prices. Each of the four cornerstone towers perched on a natural ledge halfway up the canyon, created by hundreds of years of erosion, and they were topped with guard towers. The river ran leagues below the outcropping, too far down to hear from the top of the bridge, much less from the ridge that served as the base for the towers. Each cornerstone was a gateway from New Metta City into the company, with entrances through the caverns located at each floor and stairwells on the first emerging from deep within the ground. It was through one of the ground hatches that Fillig emerged after climbing the stairs carved into the cavern's rock floor and walking through a metal detector.

The gift shop, bright and loud, spanned the entire distance between the western towers, and there was an identical one located between the towers on the other side of the bridge. TCB radio blared a Grimey Virus pop song, and bridge figurines, post cards, key chains, plushies, and t-shirts lined the shelves and display cases. A zimble with eager eyes and a wide grin greeted Fillig, his gaze following the troll all the way to the marble staircase positioned equidistant from both elevators. As he climbed the stairs toward the reception desk, Fillig couldn't help but look back to see the goofy smile still plastered across the zimble's striped face. He grimaced in return.

"Can I help you?" the grawback at the front desk asked, her expression thankfully less chipper than the gift shop greeter's. The brightness of her green and purple feathers was offset by her bored demeanor, and she seemed to be chewing something, though Fillig had no idea what it could be. Grawbacks couldn't chew gum without damaging their beaks. He stared at her for a moment before clearing his throat.

"Yes, Kradduk Chert told me to check in here for my interview."

"Ah, you must be Mr. Schist. Go through the double doors to the elevator and take it to the admin offices on level two. Take a seat in the waiting room. I'll notify Mr. Squeath's secretary of your arrival." She used her wrist feathers to wave him through, her beak working on whatever she was eating all the while. Things like that drove Fillig mad. He nearly yelled at her to stop, opting to shake his head to clear the thought instead.

"Thanks."

What struck Fillig most about TCB was how clean and white everything was. Fluorescent lighting gleamed off the floor and walls, making him squint. It was a strange contrast to the rickety bridge above and the dank, dark caverns below. The humans expected a warped wooden bridge, so that's what they got: a rickety, worn, bumpy façade to hide the corporate monster lurking beneath.

Inside, it felt as if the architect tried to wash away every piece of gravel and dirt, as if TCB were something better than the earth that provided them all with sanctuary. Masking true underling nature with something so squeaky clean and foreign rubbed Fillig the wrong way.

The waiting room on the third floor was no different. Hard metal chairs squealed against bright white tile, and an assortment of creatures sat shifting and fidgeting, reading magazines or staring at the screened devices in their palms. The *bleeps* and *bops* of someone playing Fairy Pop bounced around the room.

After longer than Fillig cared to wait, a male zimble's hooves beating against the tile preceded an announcement that Mr. Squeath was ready to see him. A female sniggle who'd been waiting for who knows how long shot Fillig a dirty look as he followed the multi-colored creature through another set of double-doors. They passed down a long hallway lined with glass-walled workspaces to a corner office where a medium-sized swog sat behind a large, wooden desk. Finally, something that wasn't clinical and white.

Two others, a troll and a second swog, joined them in the office, taking seats on a cream-colored unicorn hide couch after bumping fists as a form of greeting. Fillig awkwardly held out his fist and watched in horror as they exploded it out one after the other. He wondered how he would ever fit in here.

"Fillig!" The troll.

"Fiiillliggg!" The swog.

The swog behind the desk grinned and poured four glasses of scotch from a crystal decanter. By the smell of it, it was the good stuff. Not Giddle, but Friddum at least. Well, maybe he could make it work.

"Filly, Fil, Fillman, I hear great things about you. I hope you can live up to them, if you know what I mean." Both occupants on the couch nodded, clutching their drinks in front of them.

Fillig had no idea what he meant. Before he'd agreed to interview, Kradduk had warned him that TCB was very much a bro club, but he hadn't really believed it could be this bad. Mr. Squeath, the manager of the demo department, was the epitome of everything Fillig hated in school, right down to the goatee and innuendos.

"Not too great, I hope. I wouldn't want to disappoint," replied Fillig with a thin smile. Just then, a loud thud made Fillig bolt from his seat. Behind Squeath, the open blinds revealed the form of a goat, dressed in black spandex from head to toe, with the exception of a hole for the tail, ears, and eyes, sliding down the window. Fillig's eyes widened in horror.

Squeath turned his head at the disruption and erupted in laughter straight from the gut, and a beat later, the two others did as well. Fillig chuckled awkwardly as he lowered himself back into his seat.

"Invisiglass. Bastard thought he was going to ruin your interview, but don't you worry. We're accustomed to the billy inconvenience, and the vile little creatures are no match for TCB. Don't you worry about the Blight or the windows, either. There are none in the common areas. They are only in offices if people request them, and we've got UV blinds for daylight hours."

Fillig tried to appear mollified, but he couldn't help casting a nervous glance at the glass wall of the office. Squeath's face was smug as he explained. "As an extra precaution, the glass walls filter UV rays too. No need for alarm."

At Fillig's nod, he continued, "But let's get to the point here. Kradduk is very respected in our organization, and if he says we should give you a shot, I'm inclined to agree. Can you tell me about your work history?"

Fillig didn't take his eyes from the figure in the window, backlit by the rising moon, still sliding slowly with the squealing of spandex on glass. This was his first encounter with a billy. Thankful that TCB was equipped to deal with them, he answered the question. "Well, most recently, I worked middle management at the—"

"Fil, I'm just bustin' your balls. So, you tag a lot of tail?"

"Excuse me?"

"Oh, you know what I'm talkin' about. This guy here, he knows what I'm talkin' about." The swog and troll made grunting, appreciative sounds before chuckling again, low in their throats.

The rest of the interview went on much the same, with the swog making inappropriate jokes, Fillig nodding along while swallowing bile, and the two others nudging, grinning, and snorting on cue. If he had to hear the phrase "You know what I'm talkin' about" one more time, Fillig thought he might march right out of the interview, job be damned, but he really needed the gig. He wasn't willing to tell his dad that he was unemployed, not when the old troll gave him such a hard time about his career path.

Somehow, he made it through, and Mr. Squeath's pink face split into a smarmy grin as he told Fillig that he'd "nailed it" and that he'd "soon get a crack at a hot zimble secretary."

Shuddering at the complete disrespect, Fillig rose to leave. "I greatly appreciate your time, and I look forward to working for you," he said.

The goat plastered to the window blinked big yellow eyes and slid another three inches.

"You should, just wait until you get a look at Mona." Squeath's fat tongue ran along his wide mouth.

"I'm sure," said Fillig, performing obligatory fist bumps all around.

On his way out, he took notice of things he'd breezed by in his eagerness to get to the interview. The most notable observation after the off-putting window placement was the species diversity of the workers. All manner of underlings bustled about their job-duties, but that was expected. It's what those job duties were that was concerning.

Kradduk had explained the undeniable speciesism at TCB but seeing it first-hand was something else. Swogs were all in positions of power. Their high sun tolerance, combined with their ability to fly, gave them the distinct advantage of being able to survey the entire bridge easily with little damage beyond sunburn if they didn't oil up first.

It didn't hurt that the company was owned by a family of swogs who tended to promote their friends and family over more qualified applicants. Trolls and grawbacks worked in every facet of operations including management, custodial duties, and security while molents and zimbles tended toward secretarial duties and front office staff. The custodial staff was entirely molent, a fact that hadn't gone unnoticed by the New Metta Chronicle during a recent piece on speciesist policies.

After the piece ran, there were protests outside of TCB, but the hoopla died down after the Figg family made a sizable donation to the SunDown foundation, the equal rights group that had pressured the newspaper into running the story in the first place. The New Metta Chronicle had cried carry-over speciesism from the days of segregation, but they printed a retraction two days later.

Hostilities between species, overt and otherwise, had certainly survived anti-discrimination legislation, especially from the more established families in society who went from ruling over creatures they deemed below them to working alongside them after the Species Act passed 30 years ago. Fillig's family was progressive, believing in equality and shunning the old school mentality that trolls were better than grawbacks, zimbles, or molents, but TCB seemed stuck in the dark ages.

Fillig couldn't stand being in the building for a moment longer. How he was going to work here was beyond him. He rubbed his hands over his arms as if attempting to wash the filth of corruption from his skin as he made a beeline to Goron's. Granu was already perched at the bar, her hair in tangles and dark circles underscoring her bright eyes. Fillig looked her up and down with his mouth twisted into a half-grin as he took a seat on the barstool next to her.

6

THE BRIGHT IDEA

ey, Kell, fill me up," Fillig said before turning his attention back to Granu. "What happened to you?"

"Not a damn thing. Did Kradduk get you an interview?" asked Granu, offering up a weak smile in an effort to get Fillig to focus on himself instead of playing another round of Fix Granu. It worked.

"Yep. I just came from it, and I nailed it, as my new employer said."

"Granu nailed it too," said Kell, placing a flagon down on the bar in front of Fillig. Damn. So much for her diversion.

"Kell! You promised you wouldn't tell anyone!" Granu's lip pulled up to reveal her sharp canine teeth.

"Simmer down, green eyes." Kell winked at Granu again.

"What's this about? You do look rough this evening. What did you get up to yesterday?" Fillig grinned. "Did you go home with somebody?"

"None of your damn business. And you sure know how to compliment a girl, by the way. Idiot." She raised her flagon. "Here's to your new job." Granu shot a warning look at Kell, who shrugged and walked away to see to his side work.

"Cheers!" Kradduk's booming voice filled the room, causing more than a few patrons to turn and give him a once over. He was wearing a suit with shiny, silver accents designed to catch the eye of creatures with covetous natures. Granu quickly averted her gaze.

"Squeath loved you. You start tomorrow night," he said, tossing an arm over Fillig's shoulders and ruffling his light brown hair.

"A night shift? You've got to be kidding me!" exclaimed Granu. It was enough that Fillig got a job at TCB, but to score a night shift was unheard of for a newbie.

"You'd think Granu would be in a better mood. She got lucky last night," said Fillig, his head cocked to the side.

"I don't know if I'd put it that way," said Kell as he returned with a green drink for Kradduk.

"Would you shut your lentian mouth?" snapped Granu.

"Whoa! No need for slurs. I'm not the one who went home with a two." Kell was as good-looking as molents came. He was larger than most and tattooed all over, his pink skin almost entirely hidden beneath the intricate ink. His right ear was pierced with a gold ring.

"Watch it, Gran, you've seen Kell in action," said Kradduk.

"Oh, Granu, you didn't!" said Fillig.

"This is nobody's business. So, Fillig, did they go over the benefits package with you?" she asked, desperate to shift the conversation away from yesterday's exploits. This time, she wasn't so lucky.

"A two? Really? I'm disappointed in you, cuz," said Kradduk as if she never spoke.

"Like neither of you have done it," replied Granu testily. "Need I remind you of Igra or Franni?" Both trolls shrugged and Kell snickered.

"Igra was a lovely troll," said Fillig, fluttering his lashes innocently.

"Franni was skilled," said Kradduk, nodding and holding his hand up for a high five from Kell, who promptly slapped it.

"Ugh! Males! You're all disgusting. Looks aren't everything. I'll have you know that I had a great time with Len last night. He made me forget how awful my life is."

Fillig's mouth fell open. "Len? As in your creepy next door

neighbor who spends all day picking fights on the internet Len? As in, nearly the size of a human Len? As in—"

Granu cut him off. "Shut it cud-chewer."

"Yeah, give her a break, Fil. I'm sure Len is a perfectly pleasant troll," said Kradduk, his facial expression giving away his heavy use of sarcasm.

"And you!" Granu rounded on the bartender, "What about Seagum? You were with her for two months, and that girl was as trashy as Kradduk here. If I had to hear about her bathing habits or catch a glimpse of her thong one more time, I thought I'd vomit."

Kell shrugged. "Fair enough. Another round before I take off?"

Garva was clocking in as Kell packed up for the day. She was a homely zimble with a long neck, faded pink stripes, and eyes that looked in different directions. Granu suppressed a gag at the overwhelming smell of lilac that poisoned the air whenever she was in the cavern, and the way her mane was braided was unnatural. The trio moved to their regular booth to continue celebrating Fillig's new gig and ragging on Granu. It was well past noon when they began talking about what she should do with her life.

"You could sell those bracelets you used to make," said Kradduk.

"When I was twelve? Um, no."

"I thought they were pretty, with all those shiny minerals and bits of broken teeth."

"Kradduk, every juvie female made them. Nobody's going to buy silly friendship bracelets. Be real."

"You could teach little trolls, you know, before they reach wontog age," said Fillig, sloshing grog over the table.

"Nobody's going to hire an education major who quit after her first wontog. Besides, that requires referrals, which I don't have, childcare certifications, which I also don't have, and a lot of time that doesn't pay."

"You quit?" said Kradduk. "That's the story now?" He ignored Granu's glower.

"Oh, I know! Why don't you rob the bridge like all those other geniuses?" slurred Fillig. "A good hit, and you're set for life. Kradduk said it himself just the other day. Ouch! What was that for?"

Granu laughed as Fillig rubbed his leg and glared at Kradduk. New Metta's gem, The Covered Bridge was the most policed part of the city and the now employer to two-thirds of the table.

"Yeah, I'll run a covert operation. We'll dress in black like the billys and synchronize our watches," snickered Granu.

"It really wouldn't be that hard if you were smart about it." Kradduk's mouth was tight, his face unreadable. "These stupid kids come at it aggressively. They attack. They don't think. If you took down the computer systems first, it would cause chaos. Then you could practically stroll right in and load all that cash up before anyone knew what happened. It's a wonder nobody's pulled it off already."

"That's what I'm talking about," spat Fillig, propping up his head. "And we could hire a computer guy, like a hacker or whatever. And we could hire someone to talk to the hacker so nobody knows it's us! Like, a go-between."

Ignoring Fillig's drunk babble, Granu turned to Kradduk. "You've given this some thought, haven't you?" She struggled to believe that Kradduk could really believe this was a good idea. He may be arrogant, but he wasn't stupid.

"I've worked there for years, and every month there's a new failed attempt. Of course I've considered what might actually work."

"That's what I'm talking about," said Fillig again, smacking his hand on the wet table. Splatters hit Granu's face, and she rubbed a sleeve across her brow absently. "You gotta do it smart." He dragged out the last word and jabbed a stubby finger into his temple, cringed, then glared at his own hand.

"You guys sound way too serious about this," said Granu, still smiling at the joke, though her lips wavered a bit. "Fillig's out of his mind, but you're not! You can't be considering this?" She waited for Kradduk's answer, which took a moment longer than it should have.

"Yeah, of course. We're just shooting off. Nobody wants to be caught by Bridge Protection. They live for these attempts. A botched job can feed their families for days," said Kradduk, but he was still chewing his bottom lip, and his black eyes were intense.

"You mean to tell me they get paid under the table too?"

"Here's to feeding families!" proclaimed Fillig, raising his flagon.

"With other people's carcasses." Granu lifted her drink and clinked it against his. She cringed as grog sloshed all over the table. Fillig pulled a straw from his water glass, splashing water in the process, and began to suck up the liquid on the table with a slurping noise. A nearby grawback turned and stared at Fillig, his beak agape.

Fillig met his eyes. "What? You never see a troll drink before?"

Granu groaned as Fillig made to stand and fell back into the booth. She smiled apologetically at the grawback, who turned back but kept watch with a wary side-eye. To another grawback, it would be an invitation to fight, but to a troll looking after her drunk friend, it was a merciful dismissal.

"He's going to regret that cave water in the evening," said Granu, watching a drip from the ceiling hit the table and mix with the spilled grog. "I'd better get him home."

Kradduk laughed. "And I'd better get her home," he replied, nodding toward a buxom redhead at the bar before getting up, straightening his suit, and strutting in her direction.

Granu slid out of the booth and hoisted Fillig to his feet. She struggled beneath his weight, grunting and stumbling her way through the twisting cavern paths. To make matters worse, he was going on about the merits of life underground and the injustices associated with sun intolerance, as if she hadn't heard this spiel every time he'd had one too many. It was only a matter of time before he waxed philosophical on the meaning of life and the place of trolls in the grand design. It was going to be a long walk.

Why does Fillig have to live on the other side of New Metta? she thought as she half-dragged him along. It was unfortunate the caverns weren't wide enough for streets like they were on the north end. If the sun weren't shining outside, she would have taken an elevator to the surface and called a cab to pick him up, but Red Cab didn't guarantee their window tinting, and sun exposure wasn't something a troll chanced. It would serve this fool right to end up a statue in the back of a taxi.

Once Granu finally got Fillig safely home and tucked into his own bed, she headed back to her place. Her muscles throbbed but seemed relieved to be rid of the weight of an inebriated troll. As she approached her door, Len stuck his head out his window. "Hello there, my putrid petal," he said with a grin.

"Hey Len," replied Granu without making eye contact. She strode by him, up the stairs, and into her apartment. Len was still hanging out his window as she shut her door. Granu had the feeling she'd be regretting yesterday for a long time to come.

7

THE FUNDS

Granu trudged the three miles to Kradduk's place with her head low, staring at the craggy ground before her as she kept to the underground passages. Cutting out into the canyon for a portion of the walk would be faster, but she had no desire to hasten this meeting. Even on the long route, most trolls could cover the distance in under an hour, but Granu's legs were shorter, so she took three steps for an average troll's one, a shortcoming she didn't mind so much on this particular trip.

She meandered until she reached the Knot, a huge cavern traversed by hanging bridges connecting various passages at different elevations with each other. Stairwells were carved into the rock walls, allowing for pedestrians to reach different bridges. Granu slowly climbed the one that led to the highest bridge, the one that would take her to the upper west side where the wealthiest of New Metta dwelled. She pressed on through the bustling passage, following the winding cavern toward the silver sector.

Eventually, she couldn't prolong the trip any longer. She was winded by the time she arrived at Kradduk's lobby. She stopped outside the gleaming glass doors to catch her breath and stall for a moment. *Maybe if I didn't walk everywhere, I could put on some weight,* she thought as she stretched her legs. But there was no way was she going to be seen zipping through the tunnels on a segway like some elderly tourist from Baxerton or Corvine. Gaining weight wouldn't make her any taller anyway.

She watched underlings passing through the purple light of the silver sector as they went about their business. A sniggle in a unicorn-hide miniskirt made her cringe but not nearly as much as the molent couple making out on the bench tucked into the rock alcove across the way. *They should get a room,* she thought before realizing that she was putting off the inevitable. She'd thought of anything she could to get her mind off her current mission, and here she was loitering outside Kradduk's door, creeping on molents. She couldn't believe she was stooping to this new low, but without borrowing from Kradduk, she couldn't pay Mr. Picketts, and without a place to live, she'd end up at the bottom of the canyon as sure as a toddler tastes gamey.

Len would let her move in with him even though their encounter had been short. She'd put money on it. The way he was waiting for her every night just so he could stick his head out of his observation hole window and stare was beyond unnerving. It used to be off-putting, but now that she'd slept with him, it was a little terrifying. She shuddered at the thought of coming home to him every day. The sun-soaked canyon was a preferable option.

Ever since her slip in judgment, he'd watched her comings and goings more obsessively than ever, frequently leaving her traditional courting gifts of maimed kittens and pickled human toes. While she did love the taste of freshly-killed kitten, keeping the gifts would send the wrong message. So, daily, she toted the treats over to his place and left them on the landing at the top of his steps. Once, she heard the unmistakable sound of blinds rattling as he moved away from the window. The whole mess was unpleasant, but it was either this or eat him. No matter how much he creeped her out, she couldn't get her mind around ending his pathetic life.

Eventually, Len got the message and stopped with the gifts, but he still thrust his head out of his window to stare at her every time she left her apartment. She thought of looking for a new place to avoid that judging stare, but nowhere in New Metta was as cheap as her current arrangement with Picketts. And it's not like she had a hefty deposit sitting in a bank somewhere. Granu had been avoiding her landlord for weeks, but the letter taped to her door yesterday was notarized by the first bank of Gimrod and said, in no uncertain terms, that if she didn't pay her back-rent by the end of the night tonight, she'd be out on her ass. So, she made the walk of shame to Kradduk's and was now stalling on the street.

The glass door swung open of its own accord, putting a quick end to her window of retreat. Kradduk lived in the prestigious Trollstop Lofts. Each unit had a private sheltered opening to the canyon which allowed fresh night air in during waking hours but kept the sun out during sleep, a commodity not offered by any other complex. The openings were along a sheer portion of the canyon, so there was no external pedestrian access to the apartments. Visitors had to enter through the black marbled lobby with its golden chandelier and sparkling diamond decor. It must be nice to be a trust fund troll.

A grawback with rust-colored plumage and a navy tuxedo held the door open. Finkin, the doorman, held his beak a bit too high but always greeted her with feigned respect. He peeked his head out of the now open door.

"Ms. Granu. Will you be coming in this evening or merely standing watch out there?"

"Oh, uh, yes, I was just um. Yes. Hello."

"I'll inform Mr. Chert of your arrival," he said, making his way behind a desk constructed of the same marble as the floor and walls. The room was rectangular, an oddity in a city of caves and caverns and a luxury that likely cost the builders a pretty penny. He turned his back to her as he pressed a button on the keypad on the wall and spoke into the nearly invisible headset fitted to his cranium.

"Ms. Granu Scoria has come to call, sir," squawked Finkin. "Right away."

"You are permitted to go up," he said to Granu once the call ended.

Finkin entered another code into the keypad, and the elevator across the room opened. Once Granu was in, it took her directly to floor 23. Each floor contained only one apartment, but there was a narrow hall with a door for added security—like anyone was going to get past Finkin. That door was open, and Kradduk was leaning against the frame waiting when the Granu stepped off the elevator.

"What a pleasant surprise," he said, embracing Granu. "I didn't expect to see you until the tavern later. Let me get rid of my guest, and I'll be right with you."

Granu was taken aback by Kradduk entertaining a guest at this time in the evening. She shouldn't have been. It was Kradduk after all.

A female troll with black hair, black eyes, and a wide face emerged from the back room. She wore a red faux-leather dress and heels that couldn't possibly be designed for a troll's fat ankles. Flesh rolls spilled over the tops, and she wobbled as she walked.

"Who is this?" she barked upon spotting Granu by the door, her eyes wide and her teeth bared in a snarl typical of troll aggression.

"Baby, calm down. You knew what this was, now out with you," said Kradduk, taking the female troll's perfectly manicured hand in his and bringing it to his lips before walking her to the door and smacking her on the rear. Granu rolled her eyes.

"Well I never!" the troll exclaimed.

"Oh, hush love, we had a great time, didn't we? Let's not ruin it now. I'll call you later," cooed Kradduk.

To Granu's horror, the troll's indignation faded and she giggled before standing on her tip toes to kiss Kradduk's cheek, peering at Granu all the while. Kradduk gave her ass a squeeze, and she giggled again.

"You'd better call me," she said with a purse of the lips, a look Granu was sure was intended to be flirty, not at all duck-like. She leaned against the elevator wall and pressed one foot up behind her, giving Kradduk a good look halfway to areas he'd already explored as the doors closed. Granu may never look like that, but she'd never act like that either.

"Now that's self-respect," she said. Kradduk shrugged and smirked.

"If they had self-respect, they wouldn't be here in the first place. Speaking of which, why are you here? Did you finally change your mind and come around for a piece of the Kradduk love machine?" He waggled his eyebrows and thrust his pelvis forward in a gesture too obscene to be taken seriously. Granu grunted. Used to getting a full laugh out of her, Kradduk's face fell.

"Like I'd follow that." Granu nodded her head toward the door. "Besides, I'm sure you've been at it all day. Aren't you tired? Wait. Don't answer that."

Kradduk chortled into his closed hand but thankfully didn't respond.

Granu took a deep breath then blurted her purpose. "Anyway, I'm here because I need to take you up on your offer to front me rent money. You're my last resort." Having said her piece, she slumped onto his unicorn-hide couch.

"Last resort? That's one I don't get every day."

"Come on Kradduk, you know this is hard for me."

"I could be hard for you."

"Kradduk!"

"Sorry, Granu. You know I'm here for whatever you need."

"It's just a loan. I'll pay you back as soon as I land a job, I swear."

Kradduk walked to his bookshelf, moved a few large tomes aside, and exposed a vault in the wall. He typed in a number combination, and it popped open. "Calm down, Gran. We've been friends since elementary school. I'd do anything for you, you know that. It's no big deal." He rifled around in the wall safe for a moment before extracting a checkbook.

"It's a big deal to me. I've been taking care of myself for longer than I can remember. I hate this," she said.

"I know." He handed her a blank check made out to her. "So, what do you want to do about it? The jobs aren't pouring in, and I've been thinking about our drunken talk the other day. You know, about TCB."

"Oh Underlord. You're serious?" asked Granu. "Kradduk, you've worked there for years, and you've seen everyone fail at getting to the treasury. Besides, it's not like you need the cash." She looked around his ritzy apartment appraisingly.

"No, but you do. Are you ready to consider the tar pits, then? I can make the call."

Kradduk was calling her bluff. He only mentioned the tar pits when he was pushing her in another direction, toward whatever agenda he'd devised. She knew he was manipulating her, but it was still effective. He was right. She wasn't made for the pits.

"You know I'm not, but robbing TCB? That's not exactly the logical alternative."

"Maybe not to you, but it makes perfect sense to me."

"Kradduk, even the professionals fail. And failure means death. Are you really prepared for that?"

"We won't fail."

"Ok, what's really in this for you?" Granu knew Kradduk loved her, they'd been friends forever, but that didn't warrant risking his life to make sure she had rent money. Besides, he could buy her apartment outright without noticing the missing funds if he wanted to—not that she'd let him. There had to be something more in it for him if he was seriously considering this.

"Granu, have you been to TCB recently? It's a hotbed of filth. Everyone there is dirty in some way, and they live in riches while the rest of New Metta scrounges for scraps."

"Yeah, scraps," said Granu, nodding her head toward the 95" screen on the wall. "When did you become so righteous?"

Kradduk shrugged. "I can't right a wrong when I see it? What must you think of me, Granu? You've known me longer than anyone save my own mother, and you think I'm some shallow cud-chewer. I'm not sure what that says about me."

"Right a wrong? How is cleaning out the company going to help the poor of New Metta? Are you going to redistribute the wealth?"

"Well, it may not solve all the world's problems, but taking down a giant evil sure is a start. I do care, Granu, whether you believe it or not."

"Ok, who is this oversensitive babe and what has he done with my Kradduk?"

Kradduk shook his head as if baffled by her. "Anyway, I wasn't claiming that I live in squalor, but many do. It's not right. Besides, Bartock Figg can kiss my bumpy ass."

Realization washed over Granu. This wasn't about the money. It wasn't about taking down an evil organization either. This was about Figg, and it was personal.

"Ah-ha! There it is. What slight did Figg commit against you?"

Kradduk sighed. "He nailed my mother, but that's not what pisses me off. He humiliated her, denied their relationship in front of a room full of the richest swogs and trolls in New Metta, and left her for his money-grubbing whore of a wife. She was so mortified, she had to drop out of the New Metta Society for Ladies of Means. She couldn't show her face in polite company for years without someone making a comment. She ate three of New Metta's most influential females in that time, just to survive the embarrassment. That pig needs to be brought down a notch, and a successful hit on his family's livelihood would do the trick."

"Is that what happened to Rebatt Stonewall and Furna Terra?" The deaths of the actress and senator had been in all the papers, but as was the case with most bouts of troll rage, the killer hadn't been named.

Kradduk nodded. "And Moldi Barkbottom."

"Whoa. So, revenge? That's what this whole thing is about? It's been years," said Granu. "Your mother is a respected politician and isn't hurting for anything at this point."

"She only began socializing again to get me the job. Everything she's done has been for me. I've been biding my time, waiting for the opportunity to take the fucker down."

"Underlord, Kradduk. I didn't know you were so vengeful."

"It's my mother we're talking about."

Granu sighed. "Yeah, I know. But what about your job?"

"Like you said, I don't need the money, especially if we succeed in emptying the TCB treasury."

"Oh Kradduk, isn't there some other way to exact your revenge? You said you do their dirty work. Can't you just leak some information to the authorities or the press? Hurt TCB in a way that doesn't get you barbecued?"

"I could, but where's the flair? The humiliation? Even if my information made a bit of difference, which is doubtful considering how much of the city is on TCB's payroll, there's no humiliation. Everyone knows TCB is crooked. They'd find a way to push it back under the carpet. Maybe they'd pay some fines. Maybe I'd get lucky and it would bankrupt the bastard, but that's not likely. No, robbing TCB beneath Figg's nose, on his watch, that's the way to do it. He'll be ostracized by his family, by the elite of New Metta. He'll be mortified. And he won't be able to show his face a year later, that's for sure. And I doubt he'll be able to make the come-back my mother did!"

"You're really serious? You're going to risk your life to get back at someone for embarrassing your mom?"

"Um, yeah Gran, I think I am. I'm a real troll. We risk our lives for all kinds of things, and if Mom doesn't rank up there, I don't know who does."

"Yeah, your mom is pretty great. I remember that time she made us pot brownies because she got marjoram and marijuana confused."

Kradduk grinned, and Granu was relieved to see his intensity melt away. This revenge-crazed version of her friend gave her the chills.

"But do you truly think we can pull off what nobody else has been able to in the history of TCB?"

"Nobody else had me, Gran. An inside job is the only way to make this work. The trick is doing it smart, doing it right. We'll need Fillig to break through the wall of the vault. I know where it is, of course. And it's not where everyone thinks. That's a security measure TCB employs, the spreading of misinformation."

"Have you considered that maybe they spread misinformation internally too? How can you be sure you know what you think you know?"

"Of course they do it internally! But you underestimate my importance. I keep their asses out of the fire. Lying to me is a risk they can't afford. I know where the cash is, Fillig knows how to get to it, and you, well we need you to make sure we don't get caught. You can get in by bringing a group of kids for a field trip or something. They come through all the time. That will get all three of us inside without arousing suspicion. The only thing we're missing is a computer guy."

"You're off your rocker, you know that?"

The simple truth of the matter was that TCB was not an entity to mess with. Even if a heist were possible, escape would not be, not with the company owning all the areas surrounding the city.

Despite all of this, Kradduk grinned at Granu. "Yeah."

"And you expect me to go along with this?" She shook her head. He couldn't be serious.

"Yeah."

"Why should I?"

"Because the system is broken, and the system in New Metta is driven by TCB. They're the enemy. You've always done everything right. You went to school, busted your ass for top honors, got a job, paid rent on time, did everything they told you to do to be successful in life. Yet, here you are, taking money from me, the one who did it all wrong. I flunked out, slept and stomped my way to the top, and I've got it all. It's not right. And TCB is the living embodiment of all that is wrong with the world. Plus, you love me, and without you, I'm likely to screw it up and end up a statue in the sun or on someone's dinner plate."

Ugh. He was appealing to her inflated sense of justice. Kradduk knew Granu better than anyone in the world. He saw her step in when weaker underlings were bullied, saw her write scathing letters exposing the injustices in marketing to the New Metta Chronicle, and he even knew about Mr. Fluffernutter. Now, he was using it all against her to get her on board with his suicidal mission. It was nearly impossible to argue with Kradduk when he wanted something. If one approach failed, he had another two or three arguments up his sleeve at any given moment. She didn't feel like facing his other arguments just yet.

"And how am I supposed to do that? Why me?"

"I need your brains. I have some general ideas on how to pull this off, but without someone clever and analytical to plan it all, I will slip up. I'm smart enough to know I'm not smart enough."

Granu grunted. He was probably right.

"Does that mean you're in?"

"No. Thanks for the money. I'll pay you back."

Granu left. The whole idea was crazy and would get them all stuffed on someone's dinner table before they could even begin to plan. They weren't thieves, they were good, hard-working trolls, even Kradduk. Besides, there was no way Fillig would be up for this, even if it was his idea. He was just spouting off thanks to the copious amounts of grog in his system. Now that he was sober, he'd see the idiocy of the idea. All he really wanted in life was to find a nice girl and settle down in the suburbs. Granu realized with sudden clarity that she needed to get to Fillig before Kradduk did.

8

THE RINGER

Kradduk sat in the dining hall of TCB sucking on a buttered goat taco. Across the table, Fillig worked through a pile that could rival the plate of any sniggle. The dining hall was abuzz with underlings devouring their midnight snacks, talking shop, and coming and going from their offices upstairs. When someone left, the swinging doors hardly shut before someone else shoved them open again. Midnight snack was the most popular meal of the night.

The Captain of Bridge Protection, Big Pig, stood by the doors to ensure no brawls broke out, his fat arms crossed over his bare, branded chest. Unlike most swogs, he embraced the connection to the porcine cousins as a sign of power. His counterpart, Little Pig, was likely down in the offices watching the camera feed. Discussing the heist here was dangerous. Kradduk swallowed hard, determined to pressure Fillig while they were away from Granu. He just had to wait for the opportunity.

"I don't know how you could get sick of these," said Fillig, mumbling through a mouthful of food. "They're absolutely divine!" He splattered the table with chunks of food as he spoke.

"Yeah, they're not bad. Chef Gonzo created the recipe. You know him, from that cooking show?"

Fillig nodded and shoved a whole taco in his mouth. His cheeks were round with chewed-up tacos.

"I guess it's no surprise that the most famous chef in New Metta would have designed the menu," he mumbled.

"Yeah. Too bad they didn't bother to have him come up with anything else."

"Hey, don't knock the tacos. You're the one that pitched them as a selling point." Fillig licked the juices off his stubby fingers with a slurp. His plate was so clean, it gleamed in contrast to the filthy mess on the table.

Kradduk decided it was now or never.

"Hey, Fil. That thing you said yesterday," he started. Sitting in the dining area of the intended target, under the nose of Big Pig, he couldn't say anything that would arouse the suspicions of the workers surrounding them. But if he was going to sway Fillig, he needed to lay the groundwork quickly, before the absurdity of the idea fully set in and Granu won him to her side. Pitting Fillig against her was the only way he could sway her. So far, he'd done his part well by introducing the idea, a manipulation Kradduk had devised weeks in advance and set in motion the night he scored Fillig the interview.

"I don't remember much about yesterday, to be honest. Not after that round of oozing bombs. How many did we have? Four? Five?"

Kradduk laughed. "You had four. You kept going on about celebrating life and your place in the cosmos."

"Oh, right."

"But, Fil, I'm serious here. I want to talk about the idea you had. You know, the one about raising funds for Granu."

Fillig's eyes went wide, and the smile faded from his worm salsa-covered face. A chunk of wriggling muck fell from his saggy cheek. "Oh, you mean—? Oh, that was just drunk talk. I didn't mean anything by it. Just crazy drunk talk after you mentioned—"

Of course he didn't mean anything by it. TCB was impenetrable, and the company's influence wasn't contained to New Metta. Clarksdale, the thriving human village above, was all but owned by TCB. The Bridge provided the only canyon crossing for hundreds of miles, so Clarksdale saw a fair amount of traffic; humans were forever trying to go toward something or get away from something, rarely content to settle down in one place. The humans of Clarksdale drew paychecks from TCB's coffers, so they carried out their duties without question.

Robbing TCB was nearly impossible, and even if they pulled it off, all of Clarksdale would be on alert, making escape tricky. It certainly wasn't an idea a troll like Fillig would concoct without his strings being pulled.

Kradduk, the master puppeteer, nodded as if deep in thought. "Yeah, I know. But I was thinking, is it really that crazy? I mean, if we pull it off, we'd be set for life."

"Um, yes, it's that crazy. It's certain death," said Fillig, his voice an octave higher than normal. "Even talking about it is certain death. What is wrong with you?" Fillig's eyes kept darting to Big Pig, who was now preoccupied with his own plate of tacos. Luckily, everyone around them was too busy devouring tacos to pay the slightest attention to two trolls chatting over midnight snack.

"Fillig, don't you get tired of being the responsible troll? The reliable one everyone knows will do the right thing? Ever wonder what it might be like to live risky? Dangerous? I mean, half the females you date find you reprehensibly dull. Do you think that maybe, for once, it would be nice to change things up?"

"Well, yeah, but by running a red light or having a second helping of toddler stew. Not by putting my life in danger for what? Money? Thrills?"

"Really, cuz? You consider a second helping dangerous? That's ridiculous. You'll never impress a proper mate living the way you do."

Fillig sighed. "You might be right, but at least I'll stay alive," he said.

"For what?"

"What do you mean? For breathing, for life. As Honki Fosma writes in his paper, "Trolldom and the Caves We Inhabit," existence itself is worth all the sufferings of the world."

"Fillig, don't quote your philosophy books at me. Your university education has nothing on life experience. Without some excitement, a troll is nothing but a worthless pile of unicorn dung. And staying alive means nothing if you don't enjoy life."

"Yeah, because your endless line of females is so fulfilling."

"Maybe not, but it sure is fun. My life may seem empty to you, but it means a great deal to me. Yours is nothing but waking, going to work, and going home. Same old thing every day." Kradduk had him on the rails.

"Whatever, dude. This conversation is stupid and dangerous for no reason. We are never going to—" Fillig looked around and dropped his voice to a loud whisper. "Go through with it."

"Oh, Fillig. Just think on it, ok? I'm in, one-hundred percent. I'm willing to do this because bad creatures deserve to pay, Granu needs the help, and because I'm a troll. A reckless, rugged eater of babies who isn't afraid to put myself out there. You should take a long hard look at your life. Who have you become? Is this the troll your mama raised? Is this the troll she would choose as a mate were you not her son? Is this the troll someone like Granu would ever choose to be with?"

Kradduk paused to let that sink in. Fillig's face turned red, telling Kradduk that the remark struck true.

"Kradduk, you're crazy. I've got to get to work."

"Maybe I am, but I'm also right. Think on it, Fillig. Think hard."

Fillig clambered from the table, strode across the room to empty his tray in the wash bin, and headed out the swinging doors without so much as a look back at Kradduk. When he was gone, Kradduk smiled. His plan set in motion, all he had to do now was wait until Fillig came to him. Then, he'd use the fool to pressure Granu. This was going to be the perfect revenge on Bartock Figg and all of TCB. When it was over, the place would be in chaos.

9

ALL IN

I t's a good plan, Granu."

Fillig looked serious, but there was no way he was really going for this. Kradduk, the infernal rake, may be off his rocker, but Fillig was a pillar of moral decency. Granu was devouring her half of a toad and gorgonzola pizza as she recited her experience with Kradduk the night before, fully expecting Fillig to side with her. Her efforts to ridicule Kradduk's plan seemed to be in vain, however, as Fillig now sat across from her wearing a contemplative expression and barely touching his food.

"I thought you were just drunk talking," she said.

"Well, I was. But if Kradduk's on board, well then...so am I."

"What? Oh, now I see. He got to you, didn't he? What did he do? Appeal to your desperation for a mate? I can smell his manipulation a mile away!"

"He did no such thing," insisted Fillig. "And I take offense."

"Come on, Fillig! You're supposed to be the one with sense! You're a traditional, good old reliable, law-abiding troll. There's nothing wrong with just wanting to find a nice female and settle down to raise a family. I don't believe what you're saying right now."

"Maybe I'm sick of being good old responsible Fillig. Maybe I'm embracing my dangerous side."

"Dangerous side? Really? I once saw you run from an itty bitty bunny rabbit when you thought it was a sprite."

"Hey, I ate that rabbit if you recall," said Fillig, giving Granu a pointed look. She frowned in response.

"Ok, I may not be that dangerous, but I do work at that hell-hole, and as much as it pains me to say, Kradduk's right. I need to live a little, and it might as well be at their expense. It's a giant corporation of swindlers and crooks. Do you know what Squeath said to me today? He told me that if I want to advance, I'll need to nail at least three co-workers and dismember one or two more! And I have to report to that swog! How can any company operate that way in this day and age and still control all of New Metta? It's archaic. I've only been there a few weeks, and I'm literally sick every morning when I get home. Ask my cat. I say we go for it."

"We go for it? Like it's just some off-the-cuff decision to hold up the most guarded structure in New Metta? Even the Carnage Gang couldn't pull off a hit on TCB. Don't you remember the headlines? The enormous plunge in crime after they were devoured by Bridge Protection?"

"Yeah, of course I remember. It was only a few years ago. I saw Lew's statue before they tossed him into the canyon. We're not going to hold them up like robbers, Bugsy."

"Well, do you want to end up like Lew? I mean, those guys were real pros. Tommy Tick-Tock, Billy the Boar, Frida the freaking hit-swog. All dead. How in all Fairbax do you think we can do what they couldn't?"

"I don't know, Gran, but TCB deserves worse than this. And it would set us up for the rest of our lives. I can buy that cozy cave in the Hormel school district, find a female, and take care of my family for life."

"Fillig, you don't have a family yet. You're not even seeing anyone. Failure means death. Not jail, not a parade. You'll never get any of the things you want when you're a stone statue at the bottom of the canyon—or worse, an entrée!" Granu took another bite of her pizza, the tendons and cheese stretching the distance between her hand and mouth. Fillig shrugged and offered her the bowl of fairy wings sitting in front of him. She grabbed a handful and mindlessly stuffed it in her mouth, the crunchy texture mingling with the gooey cheese on her tongue.

"You can't even decide what you want for dinner half the time, but you're ready to leap into this?" She choked on the ball of cheese and wings and succumbed to a coughing fit.

"See, Granu? You could die right now, killed by a bite of pizza. Live a little."

When she regained her composure, she took a hard look at Fillig. The one with the plan. The one who had his entire future mapped out. Here he was, convincing her to rob TCB. This was unreal.

"Live a little? By courting certain death? You've both lost your minds. That, or you're suicidal. As bad as things are for me, I'd prefer to keep my head attached to my neck, thank you very much."

"Granu, it's been months. There isn't a job out there for a troll with your degree that isn't in childcare or education. It's either this, live off Kradduk forever, or learn how to deal with juveniles going through wontog."

"You're really going there? I'll have you know—Underlord! That's it," she whispered.

"What?"

"Wontog. It's the distraction we need to bring Bridge Protection from their posts, to give us cover. Most of the guards are male. They haven't the first clue how to deal with a troll going through wontog. Kradduk had this harebrained idea about a field trip. It would be pandemonium if every juvie I brought suddenly turned, all of them at once."

"And how are we supposed to know when a teen is about to turn?" asked Fillig.

"Most can't!" Granu beamed. "But I think I can. I'll never forget that smell. I'd recognize it anywhere."

"I knew it! I knew you were on board!" Fillig said, clapping his fat hands with childish abandon.

As if on cue, Kradduk walked into the bar, and Fillig yelled to him, waving his arms wildly, earning dirty looks from a group of underlings playing Critterhole. Kradduk waited for the teen tossing a hedgehog to miss before navigating around him. Fillig was nearly bouncing with excitement by the time Kradduk shoved Granu further into the booth.

"She's in," he blurted with no greeting.

Kradduk looked downright smug, sitting there with crossed arms and a smirk.

"No, I'm not. I just had an idea for how someone could pull it off, that's all. If you two fools are going through with this, you can't go in with a half-cocked plan. You need to do it right, and you need a good distraction."

"It sounds like you're planning, Gran. It's just like when Burton got married. You hated the bastard but you basically served as his wedding coordinator, and it was a lovely affair. You just can't help yourself, so I don't know why you're fighting this. Besides, you won't let me die. You love me." He puckered up and leaned over her, kissing the air as she pushed him off.

"I take it you're on board too then, Fillig? I wasn't sure you'd remember thinking up the idea." Kradduk gave Fillig a pointed look.

Fillig nodded, his face flushed and eyes bright.

"Yes. It's utterly insane, but I'm in. It was my idea after all."

Granu narrowed her eyes at him, but Kradduk grinned. "So what's this great idea you have for a distraction?"

"Wontog!" Kradduk was looking at Granu, but Fillig answered. "There's nobody in New Metta who can tell when a troll is about to go into wontog. But Granu can! Even if she can't handle it, she can smell it coming!"

"I appreciate the vote of confidence." Granu scowled.

"How does wontog figure into the heist?" asked Kradduk, wrinkling his forehead.

"A bunch of juvies in wontog would be too much for Bridge Protection. They'd be overwhelmed. And that's when we strike!" Fillig was blabbering like a juvie on the Feast of Demons. Granu hadn't seen him this excited since that brunette smiled at him across the room at the film premiere of Love and Guts. She prayed to the Underlord this didn't land them in a similar debacle.

"TCB does have a program set up with the schools, you know, like community outreach. It's a pretty elite thing, though. Invite only," said Kradduk.

"But if we did get approval, we could just fudge some transcripts. Hand-pick some teens nearing the change to take the place of the better students," mused Granu.

"Yeah, we could probably swing that if we had someone who was good with computers. But, Granu, you're not exactly a teacher anymore. How would you get parents to sign off on something like this?" asked Kradduk. Fillig was swiveling his head back and forth between Kradduk and Granu as if watching a bout of frog-ball.

"Parents are desperate to get their little ones noticed by TCB. It would be great on a resume. I'm sure if I played both ends, I could— You know what? This is ridiculous. I don't even know why I'm talking about this."

"We're doing this with or without you, Granu. If we fail, that'll be on your conscience. Then you'll have no drinking buddies to complain to about your sorry lot in life." Kradduk smiled, waving down Dreatte.

Granu rolled her eyes, picked up her flagon, and drained it in one sip in preparation for the next round.

"Fine. I'm not letting you two knuckleheads get killed. As you so politely point out, I have no job, very few friends, and an empty bank account. As much as it pains me to say, life would be downright miserable without you."

Kradduk and Fillig hollered in triumph and shared a fist-bump. The whole room stared.

"Way to avoid attention. Don't ever do that again. Please."

"Sorry. Habit," said Fillig. "See why TCB needs to go down? See what they do to us?"

"What's wrong with a perfectly good fist-bump?" asked Kradduk.

69

"Listen you fools," continued Granu. "If we do this, we do it my way. The first thing is to not breathe a word about it to anyone, got it? The last thing we need is Bridge Protection or the meddling billys to get wind of this."

They nodded as Dreatte delivered their beverages.

"I'm serious. Not even to impress a female, Kradduk," she said as she sipped from the new flagon. The pair of them didn't look like they could last five minutes without blurting the plan out to the first underling to ask how their day was going. *What am I doing?* she thought.

"Hey!" said Kradduk, "Fil here's more likely to try and impress a female. I don't need bravado to get laid."

"Oh, really?" Granu shook her head as Fillig laughed. "We've all heard your lines. If that's not bravado, I don't know what it is."

"Charm."

Fillig rolled his eyes.

"Whatever. Listen, I want to screw over TCB and take their money, but I don't plan to die in the process. My goal is to keep us all alive. You will not jeopardize this. Understood?" Granu glared at the pair of idiots.

Both trolls nodded. The trio sat, drinking and munching as the sounds of underlings going about their normal lives surrounded them. From this moment on, their lives would change drastically, and they all knew it. No one spoke for a good five minutes before Fillig cleared his throat to get everyone's attention.

"So, the question remains, where do we find a computer genius we trust enough to bring in? We can't forge transcripts ourselves. Access to the TCB network is a must too, or Bridge Protection will apprehend us before we get within ten feet of the place."

Suddenly, Granu realized that they were both staring at her and grinning like idiots.

"No. No! Don't even think it! Absolutely not." she said.

"Len," said Fillig.

"Len," said Kradduk.

"Fuck," said Granu.

10

THE IT GUY

Granu navigated her crooked little passage slower than usual. She thought asking Kradduk for cash had been rock-bottom, yet here she was, groveling for help from her one-night-stand. Talk about being punished for her one indiscretion. Admitting to sleeping with the troll was bad enough; she certainly didn't want to bring him into her social circle. Len's head poked out of the observation hole as soon as her feet hit the limestone in front of his apartment. His little black eyes bored into her from the depths of his cavern.

"Hey, Len," said Granu, attempting to sound friendly.

Len's expression didn't change aside from a barely perceptible flare of the nostrils and lowering of the brow. After she spoke, he didn't respond or give any indication that he heard her other than a slight parting of the lips before he snapped his mouth closed. Granu didn't blame him for his surprise. Weeks had passed without her acknowledging him save to return a gift before shuffling back up her own stone steps.

"Do you have a minute?" she asked. "Can we go somewhere private?"

"What do you think I am? Some toy you can break out when

you've had a few too many?" His face reddened, giving him an odd glow that contrasted with the sharpness of his stare. When flushed, he resembled a giant pink, if somewhat angular, piglet being led to slaughter.

Granu's stomach lurched when she realized he thought she wanted sex. She took a deep breath to steady herself before speaking, ignoring the metallic taste on her tongue.

"No, it's not that. It's something else entirely. I want to talk to you about something, um, else." Her mind raced as she tried to puzzle out how to begin. She couldn't exactly open with "Hey, we're going to rob the most heavily-guarded corporation in the city. Wanna help?"

Luckily, he used her pause to duck his head back inside, the sound of metal blinds clinking against each other as they fell back into place.

Granu hesitated before climbing the steps to his front door. He left her on the stoop for so long she began to wonder if he was going to come to the door at all. Perhaps this was his petty revenge, leaving her alone outside the door until she went mad or beat it down. She thought about leaving, but Fillig was right; access to TCB's computers could prove integral to the success of their mission. It's not like she knew any other computer geniuses. Finally, she heard the rattling of Len messing with the lock. He pushed open the door and stood, wearing a completely different, yet no more flattering, outfit and reeking of Anal Gland Cologne. He must have bathed in the stuff. His body blocked the door as he stared at her for an uncomfortably long moment before turning and walking inside without a word. She assumed he meant her to follow, so she did.

A huge TV, larger than Kradduk's even, took up the entirety of the wall to her left. Cords connected it to a laptop and to a third monitor, both of which perched atop a SlugsMart wall unit. A burgundy couch sat not two feet from the nearest screen, and Granu wondered how he could see anything while sitting so close. He must really get immersed in whatever it was he was watching. The overall effect resembled some kind of command station for a high tech enterprise. A role-playing game was on the screen. She could tell based on the text prompt and the hulking, heaving, horned creature waiting to be directed. The creature turned to look her up and down before licking his bovine lips with a thick, pink tongue. She shuddered and looked away. Technology could be so creepy sometimes. Len sat on the couch and continued to stare wordlessly.

Granu moved to stand slightly behind the couch in the gaping void that was the rest of the room. Behind her was a floor-to-ceiling shelf holding manuals, comics, and action figures. The other walls were blank.

"Can you keep a secret?" said Granu, going for broke.

"I didn't tell all of New Metta how you had sex with me then ignored me for weeks, did I?"

"Um, well, I really don't know. Did you?"

"No."

Granu shifted and fixed her gaze on a half-eaten bowl of Eyeball Pops floating in milk perched on the end of the console. Len didn't offer her a seat or drink, so she stood with her hands clasped in front of her. "Ok, well, this is a big secret, and I'm only telling you because I feel like we've shared something special, and I really think I can trust you."

"You think it was special?" Len's tone changed from cold to something slightly warmer, buttery even. "Well, that changes everything." His eyes were alight.

Fuck, thought Granu. But she pressed on.

"Um, yes. Of course. I don't go home with just any troll off the street. But this secret, it's a big deal. I need you to promise you won't breathe a word of this to anyone, even if you decide not to join us. Do you understand?"

Skepticism returned to Len's features. "Join you? Who is us? Granu, what are you talking about? What game are you playing?"

"No games, alright? Just promise."

"Ok, ok, I promise," Len said, his tone earnest. Good. She'd broken through.

"It's highly illegal. Does that sit ok with you?"

"I'm a member of Nameless," said Len, puffing out his chest slightly.

73

"Oh, um, ok," replied Granu, not sure what to do with that information.

"I figured if I shared an illicit secret of mine, it would put you at ease. We're heroes, you know, no matter what the Chronicle says. We took down Kumbai Smite. You're welcome." Len gave a tight-lipped smile to accompany a seated bow, and Granu didn't know how to respond.

"Thank you for that. It helped a lot of creatures, I'm sure. This is a bit different than hacktivism, though. But I totally support your outing of the thieves of Bull Street. It's not right what they did to the economy," she said.

Len's face fell. "Yeah, that was Jerry."

"Oh, um, ok. Good job Jerry? Anyway, this kind of involves theft too, but not from little guys. From people who really deserve it," she answered.

"What I do with Nameless is important, Granu. We don't just take down the little guys. Just wait until you see what we're working on next."

"Oh, I didn't mean any offense. I know it's important. You're a very important troll, Len. That's why I'm here."

Len held his breath and gave a curt nod. "Alright then. I'm all about vigilante justice. If you remember, I told you the whole backstory of Inkton Welles, the superhero responsible for the hit on Ice Man. He's my inspiration. I'm more than qualified to handle whatever you've got planned." The troll's head was held so high, he appeared to look down his nose despite Granu's higher elevation.

Granu sighed. Now was the time to find out if Len could really be trusted. The plan was to present him the information and give him a few days to mull things over. She would stay away from her place while watching the camera she set up in her living room to see if the police showed up looking for her. If they did, she would know he betrayed her. If not, she would know he was on board. Withholding information of this kind was punishable by death in New Metta, so if he wasn't planning to join them, he would be an idiot to keep his mouth shut.

When she finished explaining the plan, Len sat on the edge of his chair, his eyes bright and wide, his hands folded in his lap in a failed attempt to hide the shaking. His mouth twitched into a slight smile that looked maniacal in combination with the rest of his overeager face.

"Do you know what you're saying to me right now? Do you know how huge this will be if we pull it off? I'll be the king of Nameless! I'll be worshiped as the genius I am. Finally!"

"Whoa, hold on there, Inkton Welles. I thought you would take some convincing. Don't you need a few days to think on it before you decide?"

"To become a legend? No way! So, when do we start?"

Granu shrugged. *I guess I won't have to hide away from my place after all*, she thought. "Right away. The guys are at Goron's as we speak. If you're sure you want to be a part of this, we can meet up with them now. But, Len, don't you want to take a moment and consider this? I mean, I'm asking you to risk your life." She trailed off as Len leapt to his feet and scurried around the room gathering his jacket, wallet, and keys. He was out the door before she could move to follow. What a strange little troll.

By the time Granu caught up with him, Len was striding down the wide, cavern street halfway to the tavern as fast as his stumpy legs could carry him. She still couldn't believe this was happening. How was it so easy to get everyone on board? Was everyone she knew a short conversation away from turning felon?

"Yo! Len! I knew it was only a matter of time before you two crazy kids were back together," greeted Kradduk, shouting across the bar.

"Shut up," growled Granu. Len grinned and put his arm around her. She resisted the urge to shove him off, opting instead for a gentle shrug. His arm fell away, and he gave a scowl which melted as he looked at Kradduk. Before anyone could say anything else, he clambered into the booth, making the larger troll move in and leaving Granu to take the seat near Fillig.

"I take it by your presence here that you're on the team," said Fillig, shooting Granu a questioning look.

"Sorry guys, but I didn't see the purpose in waiting a few days to see if he went to Bridge Protection or the police. He was eager to get started," she explained.

"So, who's the leader?" blurted Len as if unfazed by the conversation, his eyes the size of Granu's fist.

"Whoa there, slow down," said Fillig. "Everything we say at this point is strictly hypothetical."

But Len didn't slow down. "Everyone knows you can't have a super alliance without a designated leader. The Avengers have Captain America, the Ghoulknotts have Inkton Welles, the Rage Riot have Zelna Zoombig. Wait, you're Kradduk! TCB bigwig! You're an insider! Awesome!" His voice shook in emphasis.

"And you're Granu's special friend," replied Kradduk with a smirk. Len reached for Granu's hand. She batted him away, but he took no notice as he blabbered on at Kradduk like he was addressing Zelna Zoombig herself. "Your picture was in the Chronicle a few weeks back when TCB did that volunteer project clearing the river dam. And you're turning on them! Oh, and the way you handle the ladies..."

Kradduk's face contorted into an awkward smile, and Granu couldn't tell if he was flattered or frightened. "Right. Well, thank you for noticing. As it turns out, we do have a leader, and it's Granu," he said, directing the conversation away from the fan trolling. Len stared at Kradduk with his face suspended in open-mouthed, wide-eyed awe. When Kradduk didn't say anything else, he turned to Fillig. Fillig nodded.

"Her? Really? I mean, she was good for a meaningless day in the sack, but what makes her leader material?" Len's cheeks flushed and his eyes darted around the group.

Granu's upper lip pulled into a snarl. A low sound escaped Kradduk's lips, and a pink tinge spread through the whites of his eyes. Fillig put his hand on Granu's arm.

"She is brilliant, first of all," he said.

"You'd better watch yourself you measly cud-chewer," growled Kradduk.

"It's ok, Krad," said Granu, realizing how close her friend was to dismembering their computer whiz, who seemed utterly oblivious. She was growing accustomed to swallowing her pride where Len was concerned. Social graces were not his strong suit.

"And she is our cautious voice of reason. If anyone can orchestrate a successful hit, it's her," Fillig continued, his arm resting on Granu's and his eyes fixed on Kradduk.

Granu's muscles relaxed as she saw Kradduk's eyes lighten. Len looked her over.

"Brilliant, huh? Who knew?"

She snarled again. Fillig's arm steadied her once more. There would be little joy in killing a sad excuse for a troll like Len, after all.

"Well, if you're on board, you'll have to answer to her, and that's the end of it," said Fillig.

Kradduk nodded in affirmation, his eyes not leaving the smaller troll's face. Len still looked unsure, but he kept his mouth shut.

Granu cleared her throat. "In that case, the first order of business is a rock-solid plan. Then, we determine needed resources, agree on a backup plan should something go wrong, and decide where to convene when it's done. Oh, thanks, Dreatte." The grawback had appeared to refill their cups.

"Well, she definitely dives right in, I'll give her that," said Len.

"She can hear you," replied Granu, smiling as sweetly as she could. Len grimaced but put his head down.

When she was sure he wasn't going to say anything else, she continued. "The first phase is recon."

RECONNAISSANCE

F illig hated his job. More specifically, he hated his boss. Squeath was a blowhard who wouldn't be important if it weren't for his family's clout in New Metta high society, and even then, he'd never advanced past managing the demo department. With their rampant nepotism, swogs were nearly as much of an annoyance as the billys to a career-minded troll, achieving positions of power based solely on an artificial system of worth. Squeath was looking extra vile today with a vest stretched around his barrel of a torso and slacks that must be cutting off circulation to his polished hooves. He resembled a giant, over-stuffed sausage, with flesh popping out of every seam, perched behind his enormous desk. He slammed a folder of papers down in front of Fillig, the motion wafting his musk cologne around the room. Fillig forced his face to remain impassive.

"What's this?" demanded Squeath.

"What's what?"

"Fiiiillig!" Squeath's way of elongating Fillig's name was one more way the swog made him cringe. Sometimes it was a greeting followed by a fist bump, but this time, it was accusatory. "Don't play coy with me. Yesterday's reports on the demo job near 5th. They're chock full of details I specifically told you to omit. They're absolute crap. I told you to leave out any mention of the human crew you took into custody, so why did I read about a crew leader named Barbara from upstate?"

"It seemed relevant to the questions on the form."

"Damn the form. Fix it."

Fillig sighed. Squeath was constantly riding him about every little thing when he wasn't bragging about riding the secretarial staff instead. Once, Fillig thought to blend in by joking that if the swog were as good as he claimed, he would set his sights on the female trolls and swogs of the demolition team. There were quality ladies working demo. To his surprise, Squeath was offended.

"Have some respect. Those women deserve to be treated properly," he'd snapped.

"Unlike the secretarial staff?" asked Fillig, genuinely confused. His comment earned him a look of disgust. Imagine, Squeath disgusted by Fillig.

Fillig nearly choked on his Kid Piss when Squeath explained how molents and zimbles, while equals under the law of course, were really just put on earth for the pleasure of the higher creatures, to serve in any way they could. They were lucky to receive his attentions, so really, he was doing them a great service by elevating them to his status, even just for a quick throw in a broom closet. But trolls and swogs were worth far more, deserving the respect of their male coworkers. They were ladies, after all, and Squeath wouldn't put up with Fillig spouting off such machismo about those fine ladies, even behind their backs. Fillig had stood with his mouth open until the swog ran out of breath and outrage.

Then, as quickly as it appeared, the anger melted from the swog's face, and a big grin replaced his scowl. "At least they're not grawbacks though," he chuckled, "Amirite? Give me some!" He held out his hoof, and Fillig felt like he had no choice but to bump it if he cared for his career.

Fillig's stomach churned, and he'd nearly bitten off his own tongue. Never mind Squeath's shaky moral high-ground, Fillig had never heard such blatant bigotry. Sure, there were tensions between species, but nobody was openly speciesist in this day and age.

This day was different, though, and knowing his mission, Fillig was better able to control himself as he waded through the filth that was TCB. He smiled at his coworkers, joked with his underlings, and kissed the asses of his superiors. Today, he had a purpose. So, as Squeath laid into him about removing details from the reports, he nodded along.

"My mistake, sir. I will fix it right away. When I'm finished, there will be no trace of any humans." He gathered the folders from the desk and tucked them under his arm. "If you have a moment, Mr. Squeath, there is something else I'd like to discuss with you."

The swog motioned to a chair indulgently. Fillig nestled into it, now sitting an entire foot lower than his boss. He maintained his pleasant demeanor, however. Nothing would bother him today—not Squeath's superiority complex, not the rude comments, not even the covered window behind Squeath's desk likely installed there to intimidate trolls—because he knew that in a few short weeks, they'd all get what was coming to them. He cleared his throat.

"I've been thinking. It's been a while since TCB had a full structural inspection, and my team is sitting idle since there hasn't been any construction lately. I'd like to conduct a survey to ensure we are up to code and without any deficiencies. My over-attention to detail may be bad for reports, but it would be put to good use this way."

He knew Squeath couldn't deny the request. The swog was all about maintaining appearances, and a report like this would look great to the Figgs. It would seem as if Squeath were proactive, taking initiative to keep TCB safe. If Fillig did manage to find some structural concerns, Squeath could leverage the discovery to further his own career. After all, not every TCB manager had the foresight to fix problems before they existed.

"Great idea, troll. I'm glad I thought of it." He snorted at his own half-joke. Fillig had no doubt he'd take full credit, unless something went poorly of course. "You will begin at once, and I want a progress report by the end of next week."

Fillig nodded and smiled. This project would allow him to case the entire bridge, including the rooms adjoining the treasury, Bridge Protection's quarters, and the offices. When he found a serious defect in the northwestern quadrant, nobody would be suspicious since very few knew the true location of the room holding more money than all New Metta was worth. Fillig doubted Squeath was even privy to the sensitive information.

"Yes, sir. I expect the entire project to take no longer than two weeks in total. I'll get right to work."

Finding the defect would gain him some good will with Squeath, too. Fillig would make sure to include a few other fabricated problems in areas nowhere near the treasury just in case someone did know enough to become suspicious. Once the survey was complete, he was sure he could manipulate the situation so that he could oversee the *necessary* repairs personally.

In the meantime, he would photograph every inch of The Covered Bridge and create a blueprint which Granu could use for planning purposes. Fillig gathered his things and was moving toward the door when Squeath interrupted his thoughts.

"Say, Fil, you bag a piece of ass yet?"

"No, sir, but not for lack of trying." Fillig didn't care if it made him seem pathetic. Better to look like he was trying and striking out than to tell the swog how he truly felt and be ostracized.

"Keep at it! You take down enough human structures and competitor bridges, and they'll be lining up to suck your dick." Squeath stood to follow Fillig out the door, giving him a hard smack on the rear as they passed the threshold. Fillig winced. He was sure he'd have a hoof-shaped bruise in the morning.

Swogs in power was mind-boggling. Fillig thanked the Underlord the crass creatures didn't possess opposable thumbs, or they'd completely take over. Considering their dependence on others to complete mundane tasks, Fillig struggled to understand how they managed to control as much of the city as they did. It wasn't their brains, that was for sure. The swog keyboard was to blame for their business success at least. If Fillig could go back in time and eat only one creature, it would be the idiot molent who invented it.

"I'm sure I'll get some in no time." Fillig shot a sickly smile and held it while he walked down the stark white hallway. Squeath gave a squeal of approval and walked in the opposite direction. When Fillig was sure he was clear, he let his face fall and got to work.

His team was gathered in the break room. The brightest among them, a gorgeous troll by the name of Lyssa, lit up when he entered the room. Somehow, he'd find a way to ask her out before his life exploded.

"Hey underlings, gather 'round. We have a new assignment. Grigg and Overton, you'll be in charge of creating blueprints. Think you can handle that?"

In all, the demolition team was solid. They were mostly Vinkle grads who specialized in the particulars of destruction, and the two he addressed now both had minors in architecture. The rest were good with machinery, explosives, and planning. He explained the purpose and methodology of the survey to his team and broke them up into smaller groups—keeping Lyssa with him, of course—before sending them to the warehouse to check out the equipment they would need in the coming weeks.

12

THE SORE SPOT

Len answered another call.

"Ichtam Enterprises, where innovation meets affordability... Yes, of course. Let me transfer you to our exit team, and they'll get that handled for you."

It was another corporate manager dropping his account. Len sighed. He was great at getting them signed up, but keeping accounts was another issue altogether. Perhaps if the product came close to living up to expectations, he wouldn't get so many angry calls from cud-chewers with unrealistic expectations. This was a big one, too. He'd need to sign another two or three deals to make up for it.

Len knew he was meant for something more than this. It's why he got involved with Nameless, and it's why he was so eager to join Granu's crew. This heist was exactly what he'd been waiting for his entire life. It was his destiny. He would do something no hacker had ever done, crack TCB's system. His name would be known throughout New Metta as the mastermind, the genius behind the largest take of all time. Granu couldn't pull this off without him, even with Kradduk on the inside. Len was more than important, he was necessary, and in the end, he'd get the recognition he deserved. He would be wealthy beyond his wildest dreams, and Granu would see him for what he truly was: a real life superhero.

She would throw herself into his arms like raven-haired Figar in The Life and Times of Giants in Capes. They would live happily in infamy on the other side of the world, where they could hunt humans and snatch babies to their hearts' content until he grew sick of her presence. Then he'd eat Granu and find a female who appreciated him without seeing his genius in action, one who was truly worthy of him. Perhaps they'd have children of their own. He'd raise them to be superheroes like their pops. He quivered at the thought, a tiny grunt of pleasure escaping from his lips.

"Len, stop your perverted day-dreaming and get back to work." Ms. Mingle, a stern grawback with purple plumage and round, red-rimmed spectacles, was staring into his cubicle. "If I have to tell you one more time, you can kiss your cushy job goodbye."

Her squawking was what caused him to invest in noise-canceling headphones for the times he wasn't on calls. They currently sat on his desk next to an empty can of Kid Piss and a crinkled bag of Fleshy Chips. Cushy job. More like insignificant, mind-numbing waste of time and potential. When he was a superhero, this bitch would rue the day.

"Yes, ma'am. Sorry ma'am," he replied, fitting his headset back in place while casting a longing look at his headphones before swiveling his chair around to face the monitor, where a call log was displayed. He double-clicked on a line, and the phone rang in his ear.

A huge sniggle with wide eyes and a heaving chest cast a shadow over Len's desk in the fluorescent light, making Len swivel around once again.

"Who ate my lunch? Len, was it you?" Boggs blocked the exit of the cubicle, and the smell of his infected flesh made Len retch.

"I'm making a call, Boggs. Besides, I don't eat slop."

"Why, you insolent ass! I'll make slop out of you!"

A voice on the line answered "Crazy Towncars, how can I help you?"

"Yes, hello. This is Len Peat with Ichtam Enterprises. Are you the decision-maker for the company?" Len spoke over the booming sound of Boggs's tantrum and the squawk announcing the arrival of Ms. Mingle come to deal with him. Len couldn't see her around the mass of sniggle flesh, but for once, he was glad for her lurking. He may put on a brave face, but he knew Boggs could flatten him before anyone had a chance to notice the altercation.

"Is this a solicitor? We're on the no-call list," said the voice in Len's ear.

"Boggs, calm down and return to your cubicle at once," came the disembodied voice of Ms. Mingle.

"No, ma'am. Ichtam offers top-of-the-line services, and we only call companies who have expressed an interest in our offerings. It looks like a Mr. Gormun contacted us last year about internet access. Is that correct?"

As the secretary rifled through documents, Len watched the scene unfolding outside his cubicle with wry amusement. The sniggle's bottom lip protruded from his granite-like face as he stomped a foot, shaking the cubicle walls.

"But someone stole my lunch out of the break room." His objection was nearly a whine. He was like a huge slobbering babe.

"Back to work. NOW."

"Yes ma'am. I'm watching you, punk." Boggs feigned forward before thundering off down the hall. Len didn't flinch, and he didn't divert his stare until after the creature was long gone. Then, he pulled the plastic sealed box he'd taken from the break room out of a desk drawer and finished devouring the contents. Beef stew. It wasn't preferable troll fare, but it did the job of filling his stomach, and he couldn't resist baiting Boggs.

The person on the phone returned to say that they were no longer interested in internet service, but that they were in need of a phone company. Len seized the opportunity and, stashing the empty lunch container back in the drawer, launched into his pitch. By the end of the conversation, he'd replaced the account he lost earlier, even if it was with a smaller one. The night was still young.

Len was used to schmoozing to get his way. The youngest in a brood of six, he had to fight for food, attention, and just about anything else he desired. The only male and the smallest of the bunch, Len suffered at the hands of his bullying sisters until he was old enough to teach them a lesson. During wontog, he'd killed the oldest, Rowan, scattering her body parts all over the house as a warning to the others. It brought great pride to his parents, and the rest of the girls never bothered him again. They were downright pleasant, which was slightly off-putting for troll siblings, but it was a constant reminder of his strength. Whenever he doubted himself, he made a sudden movement toward one of his sisters and reveled in the fear glittering in her eyes. Every time one of those wretched females came around and treated him with respect, he knew his own worth. *Never underestimate Len*, he thought, *or you'll pay*. Of course, outside of the adrenaline rush of wontog, he didn't stand a chance against any of them.

Len's mother was the only one alive who knew what Len knew: that he was meant to be a superhero and that one day he'd fulfill his destiny. He couldn't wait until she heard about the first successful hit on TCB and discovered her son had pulled it off. He'd likely never see her again, but he'd find a way to ensure she knew it was him. What had his sisters ever accomplished? A brood of babe trolls, a job baiting human traps in the woods away from the city, a handful of other mundane milestones. Nothing. Nothing like he would.

He spent the rest of the day making calls and fighting the urge to quit his crappy job. Running phone duty for Ichtam wasn't exactly his dream gig, but it kept the internet on, so he suffered through by thinking of Granu waiting for him at the end of his shift. He managed to snag two more accounts, one for televisions and another for phones, before he logged out for the day, buzzing slightly from the Kid Piss.

Before he left, Len tossed Boggs's empty container into the urinal in the bathroom nearest his cubicle. Sniggles were notorious for their need to empty bladders frequently, so he knew the dirty cud-chewer would see it and go on an epic rampage. He snickered at the thought of the damage Boggs would do to the walls. Sure there would be a memo regarding repairs to the bathroom in the morning, Len packed up his supplies and donned his jacket. Nobody looked up to say goodbye as Len walked out the large, wooden doors and disappeared into the caverns of New Metta.

13

THE GRIFTER

Granu pored over the blueprints Fillig's team created, searching for any weakness in the structure. She was frustrated to find none; the bridge was rock-solid, constructed to guard its treasures as well as its secrets. In truth, it was a better vault than it was a bridge, with loose planks and knots frequently twisting ankles and flattening tires of vehicles crossing topside. The rickety appearance wasn't due to a lack of funds, however. It was a carefully constructed illusion to fool gullible humans, giving them exactly what they expected of a troll bridge while also providing a fortress to house a loaded treasury.

Every troll learned about TCB's influence in their underlings-prey relations courses in high school, so the note in Fillig's scribbled handwriting about TCB owning the only automotive shops within 30 miles was no surprise to Granu. However, the realization that the warped planks served many purposes, meeting human expectations while also offering another source of income—business for those shops—was. When he'd handed her the blueprints, Fillig had joked that he wouldn't be surprised if a secret team were employed to bang the bridge up every so often to keep the humans' wallets open as they shelled out massive amounts to repair busted tires and scraped under-carriages.

According to his notes, TCB also owned the rest stops and restaurants nearest the bridge, all the way to Clarksdale's outer limits, using the internet to hire and communicate with the human staffs. Humanity accepted trolls demanding tolls on the bridge, but underlings operating businesses topside would draw attention to just how pithy a human's existence was, a sad series of moments allowed to continue by the sheer good will of the neighbors below. That was Granu's opinion, though she always thought an uprising could be fun. But the Fairbax Government seemed to think keeping the food source content was more important than the revelry an uprising would bring. That meant letting the humans cling to the illusion of control and safety, happily reproducing to stock the population should rations ever run low.

Granu flipped through pages and pages of notes all detailing the power and reach of TCB, her stomach a knot of worms. Briefly, she wondered if she could get Kradduk to agree to pick another target, one that wouldn't leave every underling and human within fifty miles joining the trollhunt once the heist was complete. Though, how much would the humans be told? She doubted they'd be given more than a vehicle description and a number to contact should it be spotted. Even TCB wouldn't go against the Fairbax decree that humanity remain ignorant to the existence of New Metta. The prey didn't believe in the very underlings they worked for! They told each other terrifying tales of creatures beneath bridges as entertainment and to keep their children in line, yet they swore the stories were nothing more than folklore, even after handing their cash over to trolls as payment for crossing the bridge. If a human mentioned the existence of underlings in any seriousness, other humans ridiculed the offender mercilessly. It was truly a strange phenomenon, the lack of willingness to believe in the things right in front of their faces. Humanity was a stupid species as a whole. And that served Granu just fine.

The human FBI knew better, and she had no doubt the feds would be notified of a hit on TCB. How much would they help hunt down the perpetrators? Every underling knew the feds maintained a detailed record of the Underling Wars and a copy of the resulting treaty which placed Fairbax under the jurisdiction of the human government. Enforcement of the treaty would be troublesome at best, especially with the Underling Relations Division of the FBI kept secret from humanity. No, TCB's reach wouldn't extend to the feds beyond a general alert, so the humans, at least, wouldn't join in the hunt for the fugitives who'd robbed the place. *Well, that's something,* thought Granu, her nerves not soothed much.

She pushed on through Fillig's notes and blueprints, shaking her head. There were things here she was sure even Kradduk didn't know: notes about the shady comings and goings of executives, drawings of secret rooms nowhere near the treasury, used for Underlord knows what, and even a few photos of extensive surveillance equipment and the largest shredder Granu had ever seen. It seemed that TCB did everything they could to continue to operate outside the confines of the legal system and protect their mass quantities of wealth. Kradduk claimed that nobody knew all the secrets of the company, and Granu was sure she was only looking at the flies on the poo. Bartock Figg himself likely only knew the core information pertinent to running night-to-night business, despite his position as CEO.

The secrecy was what protected Fillig from suspicion as he ran his reconnaissance mission; everyone paid attention to their own cog in the machine, leaving others to do the same. In one short week, he'd managed to create detailed sketches of 80% of the building without a single inquiry into his activities. The structure of the Bridge itself was a deception, with two-stories of office buildings layered beneath the dilapidated topside, but that was common knowledge among underlings.

"I'm disappointed, really," Fillig had said to Granu one night. "I spent hours practicing my story in the mirror, and nobody will hear it. You'd think at least one Bridge Protection guard would wonder what I was up to, but no. They just nod and go about their business."

Granu told him to suck it up. The fewer people he needed to speak with the better, as far as she was concerned.

The blueprints didn't show a door to the vault, at least not in the traditional sense of a board covering a space in the wall which opens and closes with the twist of a handle. It was likely part of covering up the true location of the vault, in conjunction with the rumor mill constantly circulating incorrect information. Fillig only knew where to look thanks to Kradduk's intel, the source of which he would not divulge. Better to keep names out of it, he'd said, so that his source would be protected should things go wrong.

The vault was simply a void between reinforced concrete walls with trapdoors in the ceiling and floor providing the only access points. The ceiling trapdoor opened onto the topside of the Bridge, close to the west end, into one of the supply buildings. The supply buildings, positioned 50 feet from each other along the Bridge center, had gabled roofs protruding above the Bridge roof and brown doors marked 'Employees Only' leading to stairwells and supply closets.

Fillig's detective work had uncovered the door to the vault topside, but only after close examination had revealed a double-sided, locked door in one of the supply buildings. Its lock didn't match the others, and it was directly over the vault. However, using it as an exit point after the heist would be suicide since they would need to get to the end of the bridge to make their escape. The west end was still a solid 300 feet away, and pairs of Bridge Protection guards were stationed at regular intervals. Either they faced an exposed run, or they would plummet to their deaths off the side of the bridge.

It had taken Fillig even longer to discover the other trap door in the ceiling of the Bridge Protection offices since he initially didn't know one existed. He'd only gone poking around down there after the specific location of the vault and topside exit were confirmed. Those offices were normally bustling with activity. It was where reports were given, different shifts clocked in and out, and rule breakers were held in cells awaiting the arrival of New Metta's finest. Every Bridge Protection patrol consisted of two guards armed with pulse blasters, and at least 12 guards were in the offices at any given time, according to Fillig's notes. Granu frowned as she considered a number of plans, quickly eliminating each as she saw their weaknesses and pictured her crew as statuary dams in the river.

"Any new developments?" Kradduk approached the table with two flagons in hand. He must have noticed that Granu was empty. She'd been alone through the early morning hours aside from Dreatte bringing food and drinks. A few other tables had been occupied, and then vacated a while later, their inhabitants stopping in during transitions in their schedules. Granu hadn't realized it was already time for Kradduk to be finished with work. That meant that Fillig would be in soon too.

"Oh, hey. I didn't see you come in. Afraid not. The treasury is surrounded by cement walls. I'm not even sure how they get cash in and out. It's like a money prison. We're going to need a box man. I don't know if explosives are going to cut it."

"A box man?"

Granu sighed in exasperation. "You know, a safe-cracker?"

"Uh-huh," replied Kradduk. "Gran, have you been here all night? You look terrible."

"Gee, thanks. Is that how you pick up your dates?"

"I just mean maybe you should take a break, that's all."

A break. As if they weren't in the throes of planning a suicidal mission. Granu sighed again.

"Kradduk, there's no time for breaks. We need to get our plan solidified and executed before we grow complacent. Complacency will get us killed, need I remind you? Besides, I need the cash like yesterday."

"You know cash is not a problem."

Granu cut him off. She was sick of his blasé attitude about money. He hadn't had to worry about paying bills for so long, he'd completely lost touch with reality.

"For me, it is. Now, will you focus on these plans? How do they get the cash into the vault?"

Kradduk ran a stubby hand through his dark hair and hunkered down over the blueprints to look where Granu pointed. "The only thing I can figure is there's a secret room on one side with a slot in a wall. Fillig didn't draw anything like that?"

"Um, no. Damn TCB and their secret rooms! That may make another potential exit, though, so if it exists we need to find it. I wish you'd tell me how you know so much and how we can trust what you do know."

"I have access to files that most don't. My job is to keep TCB clear of any federal attention, and it's not easy most days. Any days. That's all I can say."

Granu gasped. The feds had attempted to smoke out all the known cities in a coordinated attack during the Underling Wars. Unfortunately for the humans, only 5 cities of nearly 250 were known, and the creatures had banded together. It didn't go well for the humans. Allowing the feds to place Fairbax under human jurisdiction was nothing but a political maneuver to keep the food source intact, and they all knew it.

A loose alliance resulted, founded on the knowledge that at any given moment, hoards of trolls, swogs, sniggles, and the like could annihilate existence as humanity knew it. Now, the only time the feds dared to interfere in underling matters was in situations that could escalate to affect human lives. Spooking the food source would jeopardize the alliance, not to mention underling existence.

"They're really doing things that would get the feds' attention?"

"Seriously, Granu, you are so smart in so many ways, but sometimes you're plain naïve."

Granu scrunched up her forehead and raised a portion of her upper lip, showing a sharp canine. Her patience with all the members of her crew was running thin, but Kradduk was the only one with whom she was comfortable expressing herself.

"I mean no offense. I think it's cute."

"Cut the condescending bullshit. How could TCB be a threat to the humans? What could they possibly do that would bring the feds down on them?"

"Oh, Granu. All manner of things. Have you ever heard the myth of the grawback Icarus? Or the human story of Babel? Whenever any entity grows so great it thinks itself above the law, it pushes on dangerous territory. It's not only underlings that TCB controls, and it's my job to ensure the feds remain blind."

"Sometimes, you're a little frightening," said Granu.

"I know."

A long moment passed before Granu decided it was better to let it go. They had too much to worry about that didn't involve ending life as everyone knew it. Though, if they failed, it would likely have the same effect for her little crew of unlikely criminals.

"Fillig should be surveying the area around the vault next week. I didn't want him to seem too eager and tip them off that he knows what's there."

Kradduk nodded. "It makes sense, but nobody seems to be questioning his little survey job yet."

"Still better to be safe. A drop-off room makes sense, I guess. It's not like anyone's been seen using the trapdoors with any frequency, or others would know about them. And they do need a way to get the cash in." Granu took a pencil and drew a question mark on the blueprints over two potential locations adjacent to the vault. "Assuming we can get in, we still need an exit strategy. I don't see how either of the trapdoors is an option. One comes out on top of the bridge, and the other would deliver us straight to Bridge Protection."

Kradduk shrugged. "Why can't we blast our way out?"

"That might work to get in, but the room is too small to use explosives to get out. We'd blow ourselves to smithereens." Granu jotted a note to ask Fillig about explosives.

"Oh. See Gran? This is why we need you. I'd have gotten the money then blown it up along with myself." Kradduk grinned. "What about going out the way we come in?"

Before Granu could remind Kradduk that they hadn't settled on a way to get in, Fillig joined them after his night of covert ops. He broke into the conversation without bothering to find out what it was about."Hey gang! I'm in love."

"Not again," sighed Granu. "Aren't you supposed to be working and, you know, not getting us all killed?"

"Oh, I am. Here's my report." He smacked a folder with detailed sketches of another part of the bridge and another stack of notes to accompany it down on the table but didn't waste time explaining it. It was nowhere near the vault.

"She's absolutely amazing. She's on my demo team, and she's the smartest female troll in New Metta, bar none." His hand emphasized his words until he noticed the scowl on Granu's face and dropped it to his lap.

Dreatte brought a basket of baby toes and set it down in front of Kradduk, who grunted in thanks.

"So she's got a fat rump?" he said, chewing noisily.

"As Granu so kindly reminded us a few weeks back, not everything boils down to looks. But, yes. Yes, she does. Her name is Lyssa. Isn't it beautiful?" Fillig's lips pulled back, exposing perfectly filed canines, a blush coming to his cheeks. His dark eyes twinkled as he bit his bottom lip.

"So, is this Lyssa going to take your name?" asked Kradduk. "Lyssa Schist? Ugh."

"Hey, you're one to talk. And no, she's progressive. I think she'll hyphenate. Lyssa Tuff-Schist."

Kradduk snorted. "Yeah, that's much better."

"No. Oh no. Not now. This is going to get in the way of the mission, I just know it," said Granu.

"Listen to the task-master over here. Life is about more than our criminal activity, Granu. But, of course she's not. I want to bring her in on it," said Fillig.

Granu shot to her feet, rattling the table. "Absolutely not! Are you mad? It's not the QuickBite we're talking about robbing, it's—" She cut herself off, realizing how loud her voice was in the busy bar. Half the place was looking at her. She sat back down and continued in hushed tones. "You know what it is. It's dangerous."

"I know. I was afraid you would say that, so I kind of already told her." He winced as he spoke, his voice raised at the end like a question that wasn't, and his eyes fixed on the puddle on the table.

Before anyone could react, Granu shot up again and swung her fist into Fillig's nose. Blue blood spurted all over the table. Kradduk snatched his grog away just in time to save it from the spray.

"What in the heaven was that for?" Fillig spat as he thrust his chubby hands over his face to try and contain the bleeding. Dreatte appeared at the table with a fist full of napkins and a grin.

"I always thought it'd be this one that got the bad side of you, Gran," she said, nodding her head toward Kradduk.

"You know you deserved it," said Kradduk. "It's one thing to bring a female home and then send her packing when you're done. It's another to divulge all your innermost secrets. The only thing worse is marrying her and siring grubby little offspring."

Granu ignored both comments. "You're always doing this, bringing females to everything we do. But this? This isn't some party for her to ruin like you ruined Gramp's birthday, this is serious and dangerous."

"Hey, now, Mena could have been the one!"

Kradduk shuddered. "Fillig and Mena. Fillamena. Ugh. I mean it was better than Fillani if I have to rank them, but neither was tolerable for any length of time."

"Oh! Thank the Underlord Fillani didn't last! That was a train wreck, only good for the entertainment of watching them fight. Didn't you start taking bets on the outcome of the fights, Kradduk?"

"I did. I was sad when they broke up. I made good money that way. It helped that Fillig never won."

Kradduk had a way of making Granu's anger dissipate. She laughed, the sound a bright contrast to the guttural, grunty laughter of her male cohorts. Then, her face tightened again. "But, that's my point. Mena wasn't the one, Dorani wasn't the one, and it's doubtful that this one is either. You've endangered us all for another one of your floozies."

Fillig cut Granu's rant off by bolting upright, flashing his best smile despite the blood still pouring down over his lips, and motioning to the door. "There she is. Everyone, meet the incomparable Lyssa. Isn't she sublime?"

Granu snorted and Kradduk groaned in pleasure as they watched her cross the room.

A female taller than Granu by at least a foot, with red hair and black eyes sauntered toward them, weaving between bar patrons and stools. She did indeed have a perfectly plump rump, which caught the attention of every male in the tavern. When she laid eyes on Fillig, taking in the blood still pouring down his face, her teeth bared. "Who did it?"

"I did it. Want to make something of it?" asked Granu.

Before Lyssa could reply, Fillig jumped in. "Lyssa, this is my best friend, Granu."

Lyssa's snarl melted into the sweetest smile Granu had ever seen. White teeth surrounded by soft lips created a perfect contrast to the troll's sublimely wrinkled, sagging skin. Her black eyes actually sparkled. She was troll beauty personified. "Ah, Granu, right. Since you go back so far, I don't think I do. I'm sure he deserved it. Some trolls have a habit of getting on our bad sides," she said, giving Granu a conspiratorial wink.

Great, thought Granu, *she wants to be best friends.* Granu much preferred the snarling beast to the gentle kitten, especially if she was saddled with the troll for the heist. The fierce creature, she could use.

"I've heard so much about you," continued the newcomer as if her beau wasn't bleeding through half the napkins in the bar. Everything on the table was covered in blue spatters. It wasn't uncommon for a troll to throw a punch, and troll noses tended to bleed disproportionately to the damage done, so nobody in the tavern took notice of Fillig's blood or Granu's momentary stand-off with Lyssa.

"Funny, I was just hearing about you for the first time," replied Granu, narrowing her eyes. She suddenly felt trapped between Kradduk's thick thigh and the wall. It was a small space like the Bridge Protection cells Fillig drew on the blueprints, suffocating and tight. "I need some air."

Kradduk moved out of the way, standing to address Lyssa and letting Granu slip by as he took Lyssa's hand in his and raised it to his lips. "You are beauty in the flesh. I am Kradduk." He pressed his wide mouth her hand, and Granu rolled her eyes.

"Watch it or your face will match mine," growled Fillig, staring down Kradduk as if he'd stand a chance of winning that fight.

Kradduk laughed at Fillig's bravado as he returned to his seat. Lyssa squeezed in next to Fillig. Granu, reluctant to leave the two nitwits with a troll that looked like *that*, reconsidered her walk and stood by the end of the table, leaning against the wall as she struggled to command an air of callousness. The space was thick with thoughts and glares, though Lyssa seemed oblivious, smiling and fluttering her eyelashes. Nobody said a word until Dreatte brought a round of drinks. When Len arrived moments later, they were just beginning to poke at small talk regarding the humidity in the caves this time of year. Len tried to get Kradduk to move to the empty space inside the booth, and, failing, resorted to snagging a chair from an empty table nearby and pulling it to the end of the booth. He sat, straddling the backward chair and staring intently at the newest addition to the group.

Lyssa chattered. "Did Fillig tell you that I head one of our destruction teams? Well, I got my masters from Vinkle. Isn't that where you went, Granu?" When she got no reply, she kept on talking cheerfully about herself and work, Fillig hanging on her every word. Kradduk asked questions. Len, giving up his ogling, typed maniacally on his laptop, and Granu just stood, waiting.

Finally, when there could be no more meaningless drivel, Len looked up from his screen, pinned Lyssa with a steady glare, and blurted out, "What do we know about her anyways? Why is she here?" Granu thought she might just kiss him again.

"Len," gasped Fillig. "I'll thank you to be more respectful."

"Um, no. This is bigger than your damn hard-on. I thought Granu was the leader, and I seriously doubt she signed off on divulging our plan to this outsider, but I can tell by the way she talks she knows something. You do, don't you Lyssa? Don't play stupid. I see right through you. Granu, did you say he could tell this trollop?"

"Nope," replied Granu over the loud protests of Fillig. Lyssa appeared nonplussed. At least Fillig's misstep got Len to embrace

Granu's leadership. Now, they just had to make sure it didn't sink the entire mission.

Lyssa's eyes widened and shimmered. "I didn't mean to cause any problems. In dear Fillig's defense, I didn't really give him a choice. I caught him snooping through some files he had no cause to, and it was either risk it and confess to me or be taken straight to Squeath. He didn't tell me about you lot until I agreed to help." Her bottom lip quivered slightly.

"And why did you agree to help?" asked Granu.

"Oh, a million reasons. Because I despise TCB, I love money, and I think this guy here is pretty damn cute." She flashed a smile. So much for the tearful damsel routine.

Granu rolled her eyes as Kradduk fist bumped Fillig. Both female trolls snapped, "Don't do that," simultaneously.

Fillig looked like he might implode from sheer happiness. "See! You'll be best buddies, hunting humans outside the boundary in no time."

"Don't forget the manicures and tickle fights," added Kradduk. Len perked up at that.

"Don't bet on it," replied Granu.

Lyssa shrugged. "I don't know about manicures and tickle fights, but I would love to go hunting with you sometime Granu."

"Where do you find these girls?" asked Granu. You didn't go hunting with just anyone, and Lyssa offering it up was either a sign of the troll being far too trusting or extremely manipulative. Granu couldn't tell which just yet though she hoped it was the latter or they were all screwed.

"Granu, be nice," said Fillig. Lyssa didn't seem the least bit affected by the cold reception. She smiled, in fact. What an odd creature. Smartest troll in New Metta? Granu seriously doubted that.

"We need code names," said Len in a quick change of focus. It broke the tension.

"This isn't a movie," said Granu.

"Well, we can't go around talking about running a heist on TCB in cool moonlight, now can we?"

Granu sighed, and Kradduk smiled.

"For what it's worth, I think he has a point," said Lyssa.

"Great, now she's little miss criminal mastermind," said Granu. "Fine, come up with some code words for the plan, but you won't be giving me some silly name like your comic book characters."

"What about calling TCB the Intergalactic Base?"

A chorus of groans met Len's suggestion.

"What? Too long? How about the Death Star?"

Kradduk put a hand on Len's shoulder and shook his head. "Let's just go with the Big Taco."

Fillig snorted his grog and Granu grinned.

"Ugh, so what are we going to call the plan, Taco Tuesday? And heist day the Taco Stand? Utterly ridiculous. You plebeians sicken me," said Len.

"Nah. The vault would be the taco stand, of course," said Kradduk.

"That makes even less sense. Why would a taco stand be located inside a taco? How you morons have the nerve to make fun of me is incomprehensible." Len's cheeks were pink.

"You know what?" said Granu, ignoring Len's outburst, "The Giblets concert is coming up. Let's plan to pull this off that night, then we can just talk like we're going to the show and we're grabbing chow beforehand."

"Oh, I love the Giblets!" exclaimed Lyssa.

"And I love tacos," said Granu. "As long as we're stuck with Miss Perky here, let's get to work. We need to get the details ironed out if we're all going to survive this. Fil, do you think we could use explosives of some sort to get into the vault? It's either that or hire a box man."

"A what?" asked Fillig.

"Oh, never mind," replied Granu. "Would explosives work?"

"Oh, Filli-bear, we could use PODs," interjected Lyssa, bouncing in the booth.

Fillig grinned. "That just might work! They're small enough to carry in, and their tech keeps the explosions well-contained so they wouldn't take down the entire bridge. We would still need to keep a safe distance, though. Maybe 50 feet if we get the minis."

Granu resisted the urge to gag at Lyssa's pet name for Fillig, and jotted mini PODs into the margin of her notebook.

"Ok, great. That settles getting in, but we'll still need to discuss an exit strategy. The explosion will bring Bridge Protection down on us, even with my distraction."

"Let's stick a pin in it," said Fillig, drawing ire from the rest of the table.

"TCB is getting to you, man," said Kradduk.

There were nods all around except from oblivious Fillig, who was staring at Lyssa like she was a bowl of entrail ice cream. Len buried his head back in his laptop as Granu continued the planning session.

"Kradduk, any idea how many TCB employees work at a time?"

"No, but I'm sure I can find out."

"Can you also find out how many are likely to give us trouble? I mean, I doubt the custodial staff is paid enough to risk their lives tackling us, but I want to make sure we know what we're up against."

"On it, boss," he said before calling to the server as she passed the table. "Dreatte, can you bring me a big basket of fried fairy wings?" Dreatte nodded and disappeared into the kitchen.

14

THE PLAN

Granu spent the following weeks teetering on the verge of pulling the plug on the operation but never quite bringing herself to do it. Every time she steeled herself to talk to the others about ending the craziness, something happened that yanked her back into the game. The first time, Goron's lost electricity the very moment she opened her mouth to form the words. The next thing she knew, she was detailing specs of where a getaway car would need to be located based on different potential exit points. The second time she planned to pull out, Fillig got caught up at work and didn't make it to the tavern for their usual meeting. The third time, just as she was about to broach the subject, a group of frat trolls approached the table with a flier about a manure collection they were conducting. The goal was to fill an entire cavern with excrement then use catapults to bury Mehgut Mountain, a gorgeous land that served as home to billy goats.

"This will be our coup d'état," said one troll, wearing a maroon and gold Vinkle U sweater and flip-flops.

"Uh, I'm not sure what that means, but it'll be a solid blow for sure. I've already got the owner of Goron's on board with collecting from here, no thanks to that molent bastard behind the bar." The second troll was blond with pronounced cheek bones. Somehow, he appeared tan. It must be that new leather conditioner rich trolls were slathering on these days.

"Yeah, I can't believe he called this dumb. It's pure genius. The billys will never see it coming," replied the first.

"So, you want us to do what?" asked Granu.

"Take one of these collection bowls and drop it in your toilet. When it gets full, take it to one of the designated collection sites. Here's a map." The blond troll held out a map with red circles marking many different caverns throughout the city.

"Um, ok, but you don't think the billys already know about your plan? You know the old proverb 'Think a troll has a secret—'"

Everyone chimed in to complete the line, "—know a goat will rut it out."

"Yeah, lady, we all know how it goes, but we've kept this one close, you know? There's no way they could possibly catch on. So far only me and my boy Brett here know about it."

"And everyone in this tavern. You're talking openly about it in a public place, remember?" Granu rolled her eyes.

"My gran says the feud started when the billy goat president had his family eaten by a troll named Beecham. Now, they spy on anyone descended from that troll. We're not, so they don't care about us," said the blond troll.

Sick of dealing with them, Granu nodded sagely and took a bowl and a map to make them move on to the next table. Like catapulting shit at a mountain would do anything to curb the Billy Goat Blight. Kradduk glowered at the loitering trolls, his look sending them scurrying away with grunts, snarls, and sideways glances. Granu wished she were more intimidating so idiots like that would leave her alone. By the time the distraction was gone, the moment to kill the plan had passed. Finally, she decided that it must be fate. She must be destined to lead this lot in the most foolish escapade in history. So, she focused on planning, wondering if she'd ever come to her senses.

"Billy goat president, to think," scoffed Kradduk.

Fillig nodded. "Yeah, everyone knows the feud started with three goats trying to cross the bridge without paying the toll. Everything's about money in this world."

"What? No. The feud started because the billys took offense to our presence in the canyon. It's a turf war. Don't you read your history books?" Kradduk's expression was one of glee at catching Fillig ignorant on a topic he could speak to. It was a rare occurrence.

"Are you really claiming to be more scholarly than I?" Fillig's chest puffed up. "If it's a turf war, why do they only target trolls? Huh, smart guy? The city is filled with other underlings."

"Guys, calm down. Who really cares how the feud began? We need to get to work." When Fillig and Kradduk settled, Granu added, "Besides, it all started over a torrid love affair."

The table erupted into a heated discussion about the origin of the Billy Goat Blight and political wars between goats and trolls. When Kell walked by, he rolled his eyes.

"Are you lot really arguing over the feud? I've worked in bars my whole life, and every troll thinks he knows the real story, but I'd wager my savings account that not a single one of you idiots got the right of it."

"Hey, there! Watch it," said Granu. Kell shook his head, tossed a bar towel over his shoulder, and left them to their bickering. They argued through the rest of the day, eventually heading home for some shut-eye with little planning accomplished.

The following night was supply night. Granu used Kradduk's cash to buy a stack of tickets to the Giblets concert in case they needed a cover, then took the opportunity to sleep in while the rest of the crew completed their work nights. It was nice to shut off her brain for a while. When she arrived at Goron's in the early evening, everyone was already gathered around the table.

"Good evening lay-about," said Kradduk, standing to let her scoot into her normal seat. Fillig and Lyssa sat opposite them, and Len had his usual chair pulled up to the end of the table.

"So, did we settle the great Billy Blight debate?" asked Granu.

"Well, we're clear it wasn't some love affair, you twisted little imp," said Kradduk.

Granu shot him a dirty look at his reference to her stature but decided to let it pass. "Fillig, how's your search of the Big Taco? Did you figure out how they get the cash into the vault?" she asked.

"I'm not sure how effective talking in code is if you're so obvious with the rest of your words," answered Fillig. "But, yeah. I never found the drop-off room Kradduk told me to look for, and that's because there isn't one. But there *is* some kind of a drop slot in the Bridge Protection Offices. It must be where the cash goes—into the wall. The toll takers would think the vault is attached to Bridge Protection, but we know better, so I got to thinking about how it gets all the way to the vault on the other side of the building. I've been stumped all week, then it hit me! Some kind of conveyance device! The cash moves through the wall all the way to the vault! I'm not sure if it's a belt or a mini motorized vehicle, but that has to be it."

Fillig looked around and seemed disappointed when nobody cheered.

Granu's tone was thoughtful. "The idea isn't to disguise the entire taco but to taco anyone tacoing in. Is the taco large enough for a troll to taco through?"

"Ok, you need to cut that out right now," said Kradduk.

Fillig seemed to get her question, though. "Not even you could fit, my dear. We could possibly get a camera in there, but there must be security measures to ensure that even molents can't squeeze through that way. Otherwise, that group of them that tunneled in would have thought of it, I'm sure. They came closer than anyone to actually robbing the place."

"A camera? That might not be such a bad idea if we can find a safe way to pull it off. It would serve us well to get a look inside the room. Kradduk, add a tiny camera to the list. Len, I'll need your technical expertise to help me devise a plan to get a feed from the room to my laptop. Kradduk, you start thinking of a way to get access to the drop-box so we can plant it."

There were nods and grunts all around.

"Ok, do we need anything else?"

The plan for the heist was simple. Kradduk made the point that the more complicated the plan, the more room for complications, so they'd worked to devise the most direct course of action possible: blast their way in and leave through the door in the floor. If Granu's distraction was successful, Bridge Protection's central office would be empty while the forces were wrangling the wontog-raging teens. If it was unsuccessful, they'd be overrun by TCB forces as soon as they opened the door. It was dangerous, but it was the best they had.

The getaway car would be stationed at the west end of the bridge topside, a move that would be completely unexpected by Bridge Protection. It only made sense that trolls cleaning out TCB would go to ground, so tearing off into the bright sunlight would all but ensure their escape, if they could get that far.

"Mini PODs, duffel bags, top-grade sunsuits, pulse shooters, smoke bombs, and a pair of nards the size of New Metta," listed Kradduk, adding the last item in his unnervingly neat handwriting. "Nope, I think that about sums it up."

Lyssa popped a bubble she'd been working on for some time and only appeared to be half listening. Underlord, Granu wished that troll would step out into the sun before this all went down. Fillig nodded along, but his gaze was settled on Lyssa's breasts, which sat on the table like it was made to shelve them; her low V offered a view not much different than that of the canyon from the top of the bridge. Len was typing something on his laptop as usual, and Granu was sipping on grog, pretending to have it all together while once again considering the best time to tell the lot of them that she was pulling out.

"Where do we even get those things?" asked Fillig. "It's not like there's a specialized store in every cavern specifically stocked for the criminals among us."

"Oh, don't worry, I've got a guy," said Kradduk, winking.

"Don't wink at me, it's creepy. Is this guy like your tie guy or your meat guy or your fruitcake guy? Don't get me started on your fruitcake guy."

"All you need to know is I've got a guy," said Kradduk, handing Granu a folded sheet of paper. An address was printed on it in Kradduk's elegant hand.

"Ick. No respectable troll should write like this," said Granu, inspecting the paper. "Well, this isn't shady in the slightest."

Kradduk grinned. "Just knock on the door four times, no more or less, and tell the doorman you're looking for Shorty."

"Shorty?" asked Granu, looking askance.

"Yeah he'll know what you mean." Kradduk hunched over the table in a conspiratorial way that failed to put Granu at ease.

"How will he know what I mean if I don't know what I mean?" she asked. "Why don't you get the supplies yourself? He's your guy."

"I work for TCB, Gran, I can't be seen talking to his sort. Besides, my guy has a thing for the ladies. He'll give you a better deal."

Granu sighed and pocketed the paper. "His sort, huh? What sort is he?"

At Kradduk's silence, she sighed. "Well, I guess that means you're with me, Lyssa. And here I thought this couldn't get more awkward."

Lyssa smiled. "Great! I've been hoping to get a chance to hang with you, Gran."

"Don't call me that."

The insufferable female continued on as if Granu hadn't spoken. "You know, I was thinking, won't the duffel bags make our escape difficult? And I don't know about you, but I'm pretty sure there's more than four duffel bags of cash in that taco stand. I think we need some other way to get it out."

Granu's mouth twisted and her eyes narrowed. She hated to admit it, but Lyssa was right. It was the first useful thing the troll had said since they brought her on board. Granu got her wits about her then began to think aloud.

"With four able-bodied trolls inside, we have the strength to carry more, but we'll need our arms free in case we're overrun when we drop into Bridge Protection Central," she replied. "We have no guarantee there won't be an ambush waiting for us down there."

"My thoughts exactly! You're so smart! It's no wonder you're in charge." Lyssa twisted her red locks around her finger in a way that contrasted with the keen shine in her black eyes.

Granu thought she detected a note of sarcasm in the other troll's voice, but she didn't have long to think on it before Fillig piped up.

"How about carts? We could roll it out."

Granu shook her head. "No, our exit is through a trapdoor. Whatever we use has to move with us."

Kradduk cleared his throat. "What about straps? They sell those cross-bodied, notched ones at Knickers. You know, the kind you use to hook a mate to the bedpost or ceiling?" Kradduk looked around expectantly, as if everyone would know exactly what he was talking about. They didn't. Blank, confused, and disgusted looks met him all around. "Oh, don't act like none of you like it dirty. It's not my fault you can't find willing partners."

"Disturbing mental image aside," said Granu, "that might actually work. Large duffel bags with carabineers on each end to hook to the straps could let us haul two bags each on our backs. We could carry some as well and abandon them if we need to fight our way out. Good thinking."

"And I bet my guy could make some duffel bags with pulse deflective material to protect our backs if things get ugly," said Kradduk.

"What, exactly, does your guy do?" asked Fillig, who hadn't stopped staring at Kradduk with narrowed eyes since the strap comment.

Kradduk's face was the image of innocence as he sipped his grog and shrugged.

Granu stood. "Alright then, Lyssa, with me. Fillig and Kradduk, you are on sex shop duty. Get the carabineers while you're at it. Len, um, just keep doing whatever you're doing." Len gave a barely perceptible nod as the rest of the crew disbursed.

15

THE BOOBY TRAP

The passage was dark, ominous, and narrow, and it felt even more so with Lyssa prattling on about one thing or another. It seemed like the troll had a switch; either she was talking or she was spacing out, there was no in-between. Water dripped from the stone above, sending a chill down Granu's spine every time a drop made contact with her scalp.

While most passages in New Metta were wide enough for three sniggles to navigate side by side, this one barely accommodated two trolls walking single file. Granu didn't understand how Lyssa wasn't the least bit anxious in such tight passages, but then, she didn't understand much about her companion.

Currently, the redhead was going on about Grimes Measley and how gorgeous he was in the recent book-to-movie classic, *Grinding Stumps*, wherein he was tortured for years before falling for his captor and living happily ever after. Granu wasn't one for romantic comedies. They made her sick, but not in the good, just-licked-a-mold-spore-pop way, more in the eye-rolling, Fillig-may-have-found-the-love-of-his-life-again way.

"Uh huh, yep, I know, right?" She muttered platitudes as they pressed along the passage. They had to climb over a pixie-dust-snorting junkie troll. He grumbled something offensive but didn't bother to so much as roll over as first Granu, then Lyssa, scrambled to get stumpy legs over his hulking mass. He smelled like almond milk, that vile human concoction Kradduk brought from his last trip topside on official TCB business.

"Ick! You'd think he'd find a place to do that in private," squawked Lyssa with a look of disgust.

Granu huffed. "Come on, princess, let's get a move on. I want to get this over with as soon as possible."

Finally, they reached the address on Kradduk's crumpled paper, knocked four times, told the large troll at the door they were there for Shorty, and were admitted through the back door of a cavern that reeked of something unidentifiable. The acrid stench made Granu's eyes water. The metallic, hammering sound of a machine echoed through the space in a way that could only mean there was a much larger cavern on the other side of the tan double doors.

Where in the Underworld did Kradduk send me? thought Granu.

The doortroll didn't invite them any farther than a tiny, cramped room with tan, scuffed walls, an overstuffed green sofa, and a wooden desk tucked into a rocky alcove. Something brown stained the grout of the tiled floor. He grunted before disappearing through the swinging doors, and the visitors took that to mean they should wait. The swiveling, wheeled chair looked too small to be comfortable for anything larger than a grawback or molent. Granu attempted to consider all potential outcomes of this meeting, but nothing could prepare her for what walked through the door.

She nearly choked on her own saliva. A human. Here, in New Metta, among all manner of humanivore species. He was pale with dark circles beneath half-closed, bloodshot eyes. He wore baggy jeans and a tie-dye shirt, his hair hung in oily clumps, and he smelled of something wholly organic, detectable even through the chemical stench of his surroundings. Granu's nose hairs recoiled in protest.

"Ladies! I'm Shorty. I hear you have need of some materials," he said, skipping pleasantries and casting an appraising gaze Granu's way.

Granu and Lyssa both stared at him in silence. His baggy clothes made him look skinnier and bonier than he was. Despite his sallow cheeks and disgusting smell, Granu's stomach growled. Lyssa licked her lips.

"I take it I'm not what you expected? Yeah, man, I just don't really fit into society above ground. Needed to get off the grid, you know? So I set myself up nice down here with this little leather operation."

"Leather? Like, unicorn hide, makes a great sofa leather?" asked Granu. It was not what she expected; though, if pressed, she wouldn't be able to explain what it was she expected. Something illicit at least.

"Yep, tasty steaks, sex juice, and furniture. The unicorn truly is a marvelous beast when you know how to harvest him right. Otherwise, he's just a stupid cud-chewing pack animal. You'd think with the horse being so smart, old cousin unicorn would be able to tell his tail from his testicles. But alas, not so. Where did you think you were?"

"I honestly had no idea. This isn't the kind of thing I normally do." Granu shifted her weight from one foot to the other and looked at the ground as she continued, "I don't mean to be rude, but nobody tries to, um, eat you?" At that, she looked up and met his gaze, her eyes dilating.

Shorty didn't seem to notice. "Nah, man. Everyone's pretty cool to me here. It pays to know how to procure items that others need, a skill I am most adept at it seems. Besides, old Magna wouldn't let anyone mess with me, and nobody messes with Magna."

"The troll who answered the door?"

"Yeah, man. He's my life partner, the yin to my yang, the cheese to my macaroni. Do you want to shoot the shit all night, or do you have some business for me? I've got a lot going on, you know." Shorty motioned to the room beyond the double doors.

"Um, yeah, right." Granu tried not to show her shock at a human mated to a troll as she swallowed her desire to turn him into a snack. She handed over her list, and Shorty perused it for a moment, nodding and grunting.

"Yeah, I can acquire or fabricate most of these. Not the sunsuits, mind you, since they're so regulated by the feds, for good reason, I'm sure you know. But the rest is in my repertoire, if you will. As far as the weaponry, I'll need you to come with me. But first, Magna's gotta make sure you're clean." He yelled, "Yo, Mag, could you kindly search these babes for me?"

The large troll with black eyes set closer than even Len's and the most enormous nose she'd ever seen emerged from the swinging doors with a loud thump. His facial proportions made him appear dim-witted, but his size should guarantee him a more suitable mate. Heaven, a molent would be preferable to a human. How did he resist the urge to take a bite out of Shorty? Granu's mind reeled as Magna nodded his head to indicate that they should stand. He gave them a thorough pat-down before grunting to Shorty and disappearing again.

"A troll of few words, huh?" said Lyssa. "A commendable trait in a mate."

Granu cocked her head to the side. Fillig certainly didn't fit that description, though few trolls she knew did.

"This way." Shorty narrowed his gaze at Lyssa before leading the way through the doors and into a large open space lined with metal scaffolding that created a second, balcony style story around the perimeter. True to his word, unicorn hides were being stretched and pounded by a large machine in the center of the space, creating the hammering sound Granu had wondered about. A dozen or so workers wearing white aprons and masks moved hastily, attending to some duty or other in various parts of the cavern. The smell was nearly unbearable, and Granu figured it must be some chemical they were using to cure the hides.

As if reading her mind, Shorty said, "You get used to the smell. It's an acquired redolence, if you will."

The trolls exchanged a look as Shorty stopped in front of an elevator with a number pad protected by key access and pulled the chain from beneath his colorful shirt collar. A tiny piece of metal was attached. He fit it into the keyhole, entered a code into the keypad, and they rode to the top floor.

Unlike the space below, this room was smaller, with a ceiling too low to allow a sniggle access and many alcoves overfilled with various items stacked on shelves and stuffed in bins. Equally overloaded, large metal upright shelves dominated the open space of the room. It resembled a hardware store with a much broader selection of apparently random items. They followed Shorty down an aisle with hooks, bins, strange plastic discs of many colors, and packages of back scratchers with tiny wooden hands. Granu cast a sideways look at Lyssa, but the redhead was watching Shorty's back with a ferocious gleam in her eyes. She hoped she wouldn't have to tell Kradduk that Lyssa ate his supply man.

"You're welcome to look over the things here and grab what you need after we visit the playroom," he said.

"Um, ok, thanks," Granu replied. She didn't like the tone he used to reference the playroom.

It was a locked cage filled with shelves bolted to chain link walls, and it contained the largest assortment of weaponry Granu had ever seen. She and Lyssa stood in silence as Shorty described the array of pulse blasters displayed on a peg board on the back of the door, the smaller, hand-held models. Everything from finger blasters to fully automatic rifles was accounted for in the small space. Granu even saw a sniper blaster propped against the far chain wall. She didn't want to think about where that thing would end up or what situation she and her ever helpful comrade had gotten themselves into as they nodded along with detailed descriptions of each weapon. When he finally finished, she chose four lower-powered blasters sized perfectly for troll hands and handed them to Shorty.

"I think these should do just fine."

"Solid choice. Right on. You ladies know your shooters."

Granu wondered if he was humoring her or if she'd been lucky enough to choose quality weapons. He packed the blasters in a leather case along with the four mini PODs Granu described, then accompanied them through the rest of his shop.

What first appeared randomized made much more sense upon further investigation. There was a section for scaling equipment, a section for weapon accessories, a section for tracking devices, etcetera. They chose a sturdy rope, because Granu thought it was always wise to take a rope on a mission of this nature, then described the camera they needed without getting into too much detail about its purpose.

"Hm. Sounds like you could use our pen spy eye. See this little bugger? It looks just like a run of the mill ink pen, but there's a tiny camera here. It won't get you the clearest picture in the dark, but you should be able to make out general shapes of things. If you need to know someone's eye color, it's probably not for you."

"No, that sounds perfect," said Granu.

"Right on. How many you need?"

"Just the one."

Shorty added the pen spy eye to the bag before taking them back to the elevator and back down to the stinky, light colored room. He sat in the swivel chair, pulled out a calculator, and typed in a series of numbers.

"It will be 2400 bucks for the blasters, PODs, and camera and another 1300 for the bags," he said.

Granu's eyes widened. "What? That's outrageous! We don't have that kind of cash!"

"Sorry, lady, but I gotta make a living here. I take BitCoin, if that helps."

"How about this," said Lyssa, fluttering her eyelashes and interjecting before Granu lost her temper. "We do the job then pay double for the goods."

"What do you take me for? I know you'll never come back. I'm an easy-going guy, not a fool. My man Kradduk told me you'd have the cash. You'll pay for the goods now, or Magna will deal with you." Suddenly, Magna appeared at the doors, as if he'd been listening to the entire conversation while waiting for the right moment to burst in. The giant troll bent his fingers back to crack his knuckles.

"Now, we can be civil," said Granu, counting to ten in her head and shooting a warning look at her partner in crime. Kradduk had sent them with 3000 bucks, and she was sure she could get Shorty down if she kept her temper. He was just a stupid human. "We do have cash on hand, but we can't afford the prices you're demanding. Is there some arrangement we can make?"

"Well, now we're talking. Magna, honey, could you wait inside? I have some negotiations to see to."

The troll stared at Shorty for a moment, his face showing no emotion, before grunting and turning on his heels. The doors banged into the wall as he pushed through them.

"An agreement, you said a moment ago? You're both so lovely, I think we can work something out," Shorty said, flashing a yellow grin. Granu and Lyssa exchanged an uncertain look. "I love my husband, don't get me wrong, but I have other, ahem, needs. And you're just so incredibly lovely. I'll cut the price in half for certain services if you get my meaning."

"No way! I'm no prostitute!" Granu stood, green eyes ablaze and teeth bared. Perhaps she could devour this asshat before Magna made it back into the room.

"Calm down, I just want a look," he said. "Like I said, I love my husband."

"You sick son of a bitch." Granu growled deep in the back of her throat. Lyssa put a hand on her arm.

"Gran, he said a look. How about this. You cut the price in half and we pay half up front, half after the job if we give you the look you want."

"Speak for yourself!" Granu was seeing red, and she was seconds away from eating this perv, beastly troll husband or not.

"Those are my terms. Show 'em or get out."

With no fanfare, Lyssa lifted her shirt, showing off two sagging boulders with nipples the size of Shorty's head. He made a disgusting sound of pleasure, and Granu was sure his hand was in his pants, though she couldn't see it beneath the desk.

A second later, he was looking greedily at her. "Now you."

Granu was shaking with restraint. "Can't she do it twice?" she said through clenched teeth.

"No. I like your green eyes, and I can tell your tits will be round and firm."

We're in too deep to tank the plan over this cud-chewer, thought Granu. She took a calming breath. Groveling was not her instinct.

"I know you're human, so you don't know any better, but round and firm do not make attractive troll breasts. I'm not attractive. Lyssa, on the other hand, is troll perfection, so you'd be better to take another look at her."

"Aw, thanks Gran! That means so much to me! And you're pretty too!" Underlord, Fillig was wrong when he described Lyssa as brilliant. She was dumber than a unicorn.

"I don't know if you've noticed, but I'm not a troll, baby. I like what I like, and I like you. Now get on with it. I have work to do." He licked his lips as his arm moved up and down, and it made Granu's stomach turn. It was this or eat Shorty, and Granu knew she and Lyssa couldn't get away with the supplies, not with Magna on watch. They would return to Goron's empty-handed. If she thought that would deter Kradduk, she'd take the chance, but she knew better. She wasn't about to let Kradduk kill himself taking down TCB alone, even if it was his fault she was in this situation. She did as Shorty asked.

Afterwards, he took a few minutes to himself as the trolls settled back on the couch, Granu doing her best to keep from thinking about what was happening behind the desk. Then, he called Magna back in to oversee the exchange of cash. The hulk stood in the corner, his arms crossed over his chest, and his eyes facing forward.

An hour later, Lyssa and Granu entered Goron's with the leather bag.

"Utter a word, and I'll eat you for breakfast," muttered Granu under her breath as she and Lyssa approached the already assembled group.

"Our trip was great, how was yours Granu?" asked Kradduk with a grin plastered on his oversized head.

"Go out in the sun."

Kradduk laughed as Len and Fillig looked on in confusion.

"Tell me why you couldn't be seen entering a leather shop?" asked Granu, still seething.

"Oh, I could, I just thought you'd enjoy the trip more. How's old

Shorty doing? Did he give you a good deal? He quoted me 1000—1200 for the lot depending on your weaponry choices."

"You son of a cud-chewer," growled Granu.

"He was really nice and appreciative of our business," said Lyssa, handing Kradduk the few bills they had left. "Here's your change."

Kradduk didn't stop laughing for the better part of the hour, and Granu didn't stop staring at him, dreaming of ripping out his perfectly saggy throat.

16

A CLOSE CALL

Do you think it's too much? Do you think it's too early? I don't want to scare her off."

"Fillig, you need to calm down. Yes, it's too much. Everything you do is too much. For some reason, this girl likes you, but I suggest you lay off the grand gestures at least until after we pull off the, um, concert." Granu was sick of Fillig's mooning, but it was nothing unexpected. If he liked a female, he threw everything he had into courting her.

"That's all you care about, the *concert*." He leaned into the word.

"Hey, I didn't want to be dragged to this concert in the first place. You and Kradduk were going to get yourselves killed if not for me. We all need to have our heads in the game if we're going to take on the taco stand. I've accepted the distraction that is Lyssa, not that I had much of a choice. Now, you need to keep your wits about you and focus on your role in all of this, not be mooning over some girl."

"My wits are just fine, and hers are unshakable. If you haven't noticed, she's a very driven troll."

Funny, to Granu she seemed distracted and, at times, downright dim. She wondered how Fillig always managed to see good in others, even when it wasn't there. It was an annoying personality trait of his. She continued to stare at him until he broke.

"Yeah, ok. You're right. Sorry, Gran. I just don't want to disappoint her. What if she expects grand gestures?"

Granu sighed. "Every time you fall for a girl, and that's often, you go a little off the deep end, Fil. Most trolls expect their mates to be self-serving and less, well, like you. I guarantee you, she doesn't want or expect grand gestures. If she's like every troll I know, she wants a fierce mate, not a thoughtful one."

Maybe one day he'd find the perfect mate, someone who appreciated his efforts, but to assume every female wanted to be pampered was not the way to live long enough to find her. Among sun-avoiders, sentiment equated to weakness. Most of Fillig's dates ended up trying to eat him. One day he'd be going on about how amazing the new girl was, and the next he'd come to the tavern with fresh scars and sad, puppy dog eyes, playing "Lonely Love Feast" on the jukebox and drowning his sorrows. Granu was worried that one day one of his mates may succeed in ending his search for true love with a fatal wound, but it would serve him right. She'd been telling him for years what female trolls really want, but he insisted on ignoring her and carried on trying to woo them like a human would. It was disgusting.

"Are you sure, Granu? I don't want to lose her."

"Fillig, trust me. The roasted infant is enough. If you fill her apartment with crispy babies and dried weeds, you will drive her to aggression. And if she's not into you anymore, what keeps her from going to Bridge Protection and spilling all our secrets? You will not get me killed over a mate."

"Your priorities are really screwed up, Gran."

"Excuse me for putting my existence over your love life. Just keep your romantic side in check until after the heist, got it?"

Fillig's shoulders slumped. "You're the boss."

Granu was relieved he didn't call her out for not using the code. It was enough that she was thrust into the role of boss, she didn't need her crew jumping on her every misstep, especially when they were the ones endangering the mission. She glanced at Fillig, who was slouched in the booth over a flagon of grog.

"Cheer up. She's into you and acting like a proper troll isn't going to screw it up. Now, go get some work done. We need to figure out where to plant the explosives along the wall of the taco stand, and we need details about the cash drop process so we can get eyes on the inside. We've only got two more weeks."

"Can you stop calling them explosives? They're Portable Obliteration Devices. PODs. You sound uneducated calling them explosives."

Oh, Underlord, here we go, thought Granu. A defensive Fillig was a displacing, condescending one, and discussing his failures in love always made him defensive. When Granu refused to take the bait, biting her lip instead of escalating, he stood abruptly and snatched his sketches off the table. He shoved them into his briefcase in a messy wad and made pointed eye contact with Granu before turning on his heels and storming out, leaving her to pick up the tab with the rest of Kradduk's loan.

She watched him go, shaking her head. Poor sap. He may think himself trollish, puffing up with anger, but he actually resembled a juvie throwing a tantrum over being told he couldn't eat a wayward toddler near city limits.

In truth, she was happy to be left alone for a while. She still had some details to iron out, and planning a heist was nearly impossible with Fillig's incessant whining. He only served to remind her why she was leading this cobbled-together group, because without her, they would end up dead; Fillig with his throat ripped out by a would-be mate and Kradduk by walking into the sunlight assured of his own invincibility. Between Fillig's love life and Kradduk's inability to take anything seriously, the pair had no chance. Now, Granu was down to two weeks, not nearly enough time to plan every single second of the heist. She needed the money now, and any delay only served to elongate their period of vulnerability. They were like sitting unicorns, vulnerable to discovery, ripe for execution at any moment. Even if she did have the luxury of time, there was sure to be some variable, some tiny detail she forgot to plan, that would pop up at the last minute.

That was the way with anything important—you could only chart it out so much before you began to drive yourself insane.

A troll-run heist at midday coupled with a topside exit would give them the element of surprise. Most attempted hits on TCB occurred at night, when Bridge Protection most expected it, because all underlings had low sun tolerances of varying degrees. Since sunlight meant death to trolls, they were the most vigilant of all sun-avoiders. While a grawback might lose some color in his plumage and a molent would be indefinitely blinded by the sun, a troll would be dead right where she stood should even the slightest ray penetrate her coverings.

Once, New Metta had to send a clean-up committee to remove a dam of dead, stone trolls from the river because water was flooding the lower tunnels of the city. These days, death by sun was rare since modern trolls had more sense than to leave the caverns during daylight hours, but it still happened every now and then. Sometimes a troll would be caught out too late, sometimes he'd wander into the canyon to end his suffering, and sometimes, someone would leave him out there tied to a rock.

Even if they thought to pull off a hit in the day, trolls would be expected to go underground, and doing so would mean inevitable capture since there was no way to leave New Metta through underground means. Why there wasn't a subway connecting the city to others was a complete mystery to Granu, but Kradduk claimed it was TCB's influence that kept anyone from building it. The bridge provided passage for underlings as well as for humans, after all, and if TCB hated one thing, it was competition.

And that's exactly why Granu had to make her move with the sun shining overhead. The search would be focused underground, but her crew would be long gone, traveling down the highway in a van with blacked-out windows. It was risky and never done, mostly because trolls who relied on window tinting didn't return home, but it was exactly the kind of crazy scheme they needed in order to succeed. Besides, Kradduk had a tinting guy.

Kradduk was busy scouting TCB's resources for appropriate sun protection suits, the most important element of the plan. Without them, they couldn't get to the van to test out the tint job. TCB had access to cutting edge technology, and he claimed the irony of stealing their means of escape from the target would be sweet. It was bold, if not foolish, but if anyone could talk himself out of a tight situation, it was Kradduk.

Meanwhile, Len was still working on a way to hack TCB's security system, and Fillig was still mapping every nook and cranny of the facility. Lyssa was schmoozing Squeath, gaining more and more trust so that when the day arrived, she could keep him in line and dispatch him easily. And Granu, the fearless leader of the crew, was sitting at Goron's, downing another flagon of grog.

She burped loudly, earning appreciative glances from three trolls and a swog, but none came to talk to her. It was her bright green eyes, she knew, that put them off. Her laptop was open on the table in front of her, and she had piles of journals scattered haphazardly around her when a Bridge Protection squadron came in to grab a bite. They settled at the table next to her corner booth. Granu fought the instinct to snatch up her belongings and run, sure that a quick, loud departure would draw their attention more surely than a quiet one. To her horror, a gorgeous troll with silver tresses and the build of a cement mixing truck made eye contact then got up from his seat to approach.

"Hey there, mind if I join you?" he asked, wrinkling his snout in a flirtatious gesture as a black lock fell in his eyes. He pushed it back with a fat palm.

"Um, sure," replied Granu, her eyes darting to her computer screen. She quickly shut it with a thud then met his eyes.

"I'm Henson."

"Granu." She flashed her most attractive smile. Hopefully if he noticed her staring at his uniform, he took it to mean she was into official males. He must be suspicious of her though, or why else would he be giving her the time of night? The troll was nearly hotter than Kradduk.

"You have a contagious smile, Granu. You should use it more."

She'd forgive him for the awful line if he would just go away. "I use it when I feel the need. It serves me well."

The troll laughed. "Whatya got there? Work?"

"Um, yeah. I teach, and I'm grading papers on my break," said Granu, grasping for a plausible lie. Yep, he was onto her. He had to be. He smiled, and the smile touched his wide-set, tiny eyes.

"Good with little trolls, good to know. Let me buy you a drink?"

"Oh! I really shouldn't. I have to get back to the young ones soon, and I've already had a bit, but thanks."

Henson frowned. "You can be honest with me. You don't find me attractive?"

"Oh, I do. I really, *really* do." Granu bit her bottom lip and swallowed hard. "It's just a bad time for me right now."

The troll sighed. "I guess I'll rejoin my friends then. I thought you might be up for a good time, but it seems you're a bit of a workaholic. No fun at all. See you around."

Granu smiled, trying not to let the relief show in her face. She was sad to see Henson's black eyes and thunderous derriere go, but even if he were truly interested in her, the last thing she needed was a Bridge Protection officer nosing around. Besides, he was a bit full of himself.

After what she deemed an appropriate amount of time for a break from work, Granu packed up her notebooks and laptop and left without a glance at the table of officers, though she could hear their banter and laughter. She didn't want to spend another moment in their vicinity, even if they were only letting off steam after their shifts. As she left, a pair of swogs pushed past her, one enormous and the other tiny. Shit. It was Big Pig and Little Pig, come to join their coworkers. Forgetting her relaxed exit strategy, Granu bolted.

There was a coffee house down the street, a dark little place that served teas and coffees from all over the world. A grawback strummed a guitar in the corner—a soothing folk song about a cholera outbreak called "Down by the River"—and a mural of a village ransacking adorned the long cave of the room. Shadows marked nooks and crannies where benches and tables were crammed, and plush, velvety material in reds, purples, and golds covered everything. Granu climbed down a short staircase in the middle of the long, narrow cavern to take a table in the very back. She didn't expect anyone to bother her here.

She flagged down a server, a smallish zimble with piercings in his striped ears and long snout, ordered a pot of grainy brainy brew, and got back to work.

17

THE BREAKTHROUGH

Eureka!"

Everyone in the surrounding cubicles jumped at the sound of Len's high-pitched proclamation. It was louder than he intended, but he didn't care. He did it! He finally found a path into TCB's bleeding edge security system, a tiny bit of code he could manipulate. The newest thing wasn't always the most reliable, at least not in tech.

The encryption he ran on his work computer, a trick he'd picked up from his work with Nameless, kept the IT department from noticing his activities, and he'd made enough calls to fill his work log for the week. Two sales and a handful of follow-ups should keep Ms. Mingle off his back for at least a few days, buying him the time he needed to focus on his true work, his masterpiece, the work he was doing for the Five.

When he'd first used his nickname for the team, Kradduk had guffawed and Granu had looked at him like he just sprouted horns, so he refrained from using it aloud. The Five. It was sleek, elegant, and lacked the ridiculous factor prevalent in other superhero group names. And he, Len, was the master spy of the Five, a highly advanced crew of hardened criminal geniuses with special talents. Well, maybe that last part was a stretch. Granu might laugh at it, but Len had heard her refer to the crew as the Five at least once since he'd introduced the name.

The Five. He said it under his breath before realizing that other creatures could hear him and looking around frantically before coming to the conclusion that nobody cared. Then, he shifted focus back to his discovery.

Len stared at his monitor straight into the office of the VP of Operations at TCB, Dammon Rupp, brother-in-law to Bartock Figg and Kradduk's immediate supervisor.

Len had successfully hijacked the most advanced security system in New Metta, utilizing a cloaking script that would limit his imprint if the breach were discovered. Kradduk's boss was in the act of nailing his assistant against the wall, her stubby molent limbs contorted into unnatural positions that couldn't possibly be ergonomic. Dammon grunted and sweat and cussed and thrust as the poor creature made high-pitched sounds of pleasure that were too forced to be genuine.

Swogs. All they did was screw and brag, neither skill seeming to gain them any business acumen. It must be their complete lack of compassion that gained them positions in power, Underlord knew it wasn't their brains. Kradduk spoke highly of this particular swog, but, to Len, he seemed the same as Fillig's boss and all the others.

Not at all like him. Len had only ever been with one woman, and only she held his heart. He couldn't wait to show her what he'd accomplished, a feat no other being in New Metta could pull off. The program he'd designed was clean and efficient, beauty to rival the green of her eyes, if only she knew enough about technology to recognize it. Len looked around one last time to ensure none of his coworkers were able to see his monitor as he hastily closed the program.

Just then, his boss rounded the corner. What fortuitous timing. She stood behind him, her red-rimmed spectacles sliding down her orange beak.

"Ms. Mingle, you're looking lovely today. Did you get your feathers tipped?"

"Save it, troll."

Len shifted in his chair but met her giant, brown eyes with the most blank expression he could muster. "What can I do for you?"

"Explain how you're able to make sales when every time I come by, you're wasting time," she said.

Len realized that when he closed the program he wrote to hack TCB, a game of Mind Warp was left on his screen. Little humanoid figures flashed on and off as a weapon resembling a pulse blaster hovered over them.

"I work in bursts of genius?"

"Hm." She paused and stared at him as if waiting for him to break, but Len kept his mouth shut and his eyes wide, the picture of innocence. "Well, you're wanted upstairs."

The grawback turned and led the way through the halls. Boggs snickered when they passed, a bit of snot flying from his nose and hitting the desk in front of him. Nobody went upstairs unless it was to be reprimanded. The dim-witted sniggle muttered something that made him giggle harder, earning a stern look from Mingle, but she didn't slow her pace. Len wondered whether Boggs was truly worth the space he occupied.

Fluorescent lighting gave the wide hallway a sickly, yellow glow despite the pale blue carpet. It was the most probable source of Len's numerous headaches, though they could be attributed to many things: the dull colors, the bright screens, the sickening scent of flowers that grawbacks and molents insisted on infusing cleaners with, making everything reek of springtime, the most foul of seasons. How could any creature on earth find the smell of live flowers appealing?

Perhaps that's grounds for a lawsuit, the constant subjection to noxious chemicals, he thought as he followed the fanned feathered tail of his boss and did his best to push the smell from his sinus cavities.

Ms. Mingle stopped abruptly in front of Hampton's office, and Len nearly ran into the back of her. Her feathers poked through the material of his pants.

"Do you mind?"

"Oh, sorry." Len took a step backward.

His heart dropped into his stomach as she rapped on the door, her taloned hand balled up in a fist. Hampton was head of HR and not a creature to take lightly. He was a carpoid, a species so rare they made passersby stare on the rare occasion they stepped out in public. Brown spines on his back and orange gills on his neck made for an intimidating sight. Very few carpoids existed in all of Fairbax, as far as Len knew. He had never seen one, including Hampton, outside this very building. Perhaps Hampton was a supervillain donning a disguise that he shed when he left the office. It was the only plausible explanation. Whatever he was, Hampton was fierce. His hard eyes moved from his computer to gaze at Len who stared with open defiance as he awaited his fate.

"That will be all, Ms. Mingle." At Hampton's dismissal, the grawback ducked her head out of the room, leaving Len alone with the freak of nature.

"Two sales in one day. Five this week. Impressive, Mr. Peat."

Len swallowed, his face relaxing. "Thank you, sir. It's been a good week." He did his best not to stare at the orange spines protruding from the man's head and found himself looking at the gills instead. Quickly averting his gaze, he settled for a brown splotch on Hampton's forehead.

"Our IT department tells me that they can't access certain files on your computer. Mind telling me what that's about?" Oh, there it was.

"It's, um, well, you see, I was just going to—"

Hampton let out a low, rumbling laugh at Len's discomfort.

"Whatever it is, your numbers have increased dramatically in the past couple weeks, so I can only assume that it's a system for landing sales. While I'd love to harness that particular ability, I understand your desire to preserve your edge, and I admire your tenacity in doing so." Hampton's multiple chins wobbled when he spoke. "Since you've managed to outsmart my IT department entirely and I doubt you'll be divulging your secrets without some kind of recompense, I'd like to access your skills from another angle. Do you understand what I'm saying?"

"Yes, well, no, not exactly."

"I'm promoting you."

Len let out a sudden breath. "Oh, wow, thank you, sir." His eyes snapped to connect with the carpoid, and he immediately regretted the move. Of all the man's features, his orange, horizontal irises were the most disconcerting. Eyes were clues to a troll's intentions, and black and brown eyes could be read easily. Other colors were just unnatural. Except for Granu's, of course, they were beautiful. Hampton's were plain creepy.

The carpoid didn't seem to notice Len's predicament. "I do, however, expect that you will be using your skills to inspire others to increase their numbers as well. Oh, and if any goats show up as a result of this promotion, their actions reflect on you."

Len's mouth dropped open. Mentioning the Blight so openly could be an HR nightmare for Ichtam, even if they were known as an old-fashioned company. And to hang the actions of the billys on the targeted troll was not only incredibly politically incorrect, it was unheard of in present times. Ichtam didn't have the resources of TCB or Kradduk to hush their indiscretions either. Len snapped his mouth closed with a pop before returning his stare to the brown splotch and nodding. He briefly considered a lawsuit, but he didn't plan on sticking around to see it through, not with the Five about to make their move. So, he listened patiently as Hampton outlined his new duties.

A promotion. Perhaps Len's luck was changing. Ms. Mingle was going to be irked to report to him, and Boggs would be downright furious.

"Excuse me, Mr. Hampton, but does this give me any hiring or firing abilities?"

Hampton chuckled from deep inside. "Eager, are we? Ultimately, those decisions belong to HR, but we will definitely be open to your recommendations."

Len grinned at the thought, but ultimately decided it would be in poor taste to push the issue. Hampton finished up his spiel, set out a stack of papers for Len to sign, which included the typical Troll Equality statement denouncing any discrimination in regards to the

Blight. Len bit his tongue as he signed his name. When the meeting was complete, he shook Hampton's webbed hand and walked himself out.

Had this promotion occurred weeks ago, Len would have celebrated, but now he felt weighed down by it. Worse, he needed to come up with a unique system to increase sales, some sure-fire way to get others to perform as well as he did, or Hampton would become suspicious. The last thing he needed was Hampton bringing in someone who could crack Len's encryption. The Five would be destroyed. He left work feeling as if he might spew at any moment.

18

THE HOLE IN THE WALL—PART II

The group reconvened at Goron's just after sunrise. Granu was still jumpy from her earlier encounter with Bridge Protection, no matter how complimentary said encounter was, and Len was sulking.

"What's your problem?" asked Granu, tossing him a moldy roll when he raised his head. He caught it and tore a bite off with a growl before spitting it out.

"Pah! This is what food eats. Don't you know I'm a carnitarian?" he said, banging the roll into the table and squishing it flat with his stubby palm. Granu cocked her head to look at him sideways and said nothing. Len sighed. "I need help. I mean, I know I can figure it out since I am a genius and all, but I could really use some input here if any of you lot have any."

"What are you blubbering on about?" asked Granu.

"I got a promotion."

The words hung like lead in the air. Kradduk and Fillig both kept their heads low, Lyssa's eyes went wide, and Granu shook her head. It seemed like the hits kept coming. The last thing the crew needed was an appearance from the billys.

"And not only that, I need to design a program to increase sales at Ichtam. It's either that or have our operation discovered."

"In what world do those things correlate?" asked Fillig from his spot in the booth facing the corner.

"In the one where encrypted files were discovered on my hard drive and in order to protect them, I need to create something believable quickly, before Ichtam brings in security experts. In that world."

"Why don't you just scrub your hard drive?"

Len stared at Fillig with raised brows and pursed lips. "Aren't you just the smartest troll in smarty troll town. You think I didn't think of that? Of course I didn't leave sensitive information sitting on my work computer, but then what do I tell them when I have nothing to show? What if they get the police involved? Nothing is ever gone forever in tech. There are underlings who can retrieve files even after they've been erased. Heaven, *I* can do that."

"They'd need a warrant for that. And on what grounds? You've done nothing illegal. Yet. I think you're just jumpy," said Fillig.

"I'm not just jumpy. I hacked into the Big Taco today. I watched that filthy swog boss of Kradduk's, Dammon Rupp, pound a molent girl in his office. How that even works, I don't know, but she seemed to enjoy herself, or at least pretend to."

Fillig wrinkled his nose in disgust as Kradduk laughed. "Enjoy the show?"

Granu ignored him. "You did it? You broke through? Why didn't you lead with that, you wonderful computer magician? Oh, I could kiss you!" she cried.

"Oh, well, I mean, if you want to," stammered Len, his cheeks flushing and a smile toying at the corners of his mouth for the first time since he'd arrived.

"It's an expression, you genius you." Granu punched him in the arm. This was the development they'd been waiting for, the key to pulling off the heist of the century. Len rubbed his arm where she'd made contact but continued to smile.

"Cheers to Len, our ticket to a new life," chimed Kradduk, and everyone raised a flagon.

"In light of current circumstances," said Granu, grinning like a babe on her first hunting trip, "if Len feels that he needs our help, I think we can spare a few minutes to discuss his problem. A little paranoia is justified in this case."

There were nods all around. Granu continued. "Len, what have you got so far?"

"Nothing. Nothing I've come up with has any measurable results in sales, according to my simulations." He thumped his forehead down on the table, his momentary glee gone.

Granu thought for a moment. She nearly pitied the hapless troll. He finally got the recognition he craved, only to be fearful of a billy appearance and desperate to contrive a believable sales scheme in order to maintain his cover. "What about a program that scans your database for previous clients so you can work on repeat orders?"

"We already have that. What is this, the two-thousands?"

So much for feeling bad for him.

"Hey, there's nothing wrong with the oughts. I did some of my best trolling for females then," said Kradduk.

"Yeah, Krad, the rest of us were kids then. I went into wontog in '08. Len, were you even born then?" asked Fillig.

Len nodded but didn't add to the conversation, instead pounding away at his laptop as he ran more simulations.

"Granu was probably listening to the Screaming Pubes and making out with their posters." Kradduk pressed his arm against Granu's playfully.

"Hey, I didn't listen to that crap," said Granu, a deep blush revealing the lie. "Can we get back to work on Len's problem now?"

"Yes, thank you," the small troll replied, squinting as he stared at the screen.

"Alright, alright, how about something that dials for you so you don't have to do the legwork?"

"Kradduk, really? I think Fillig is right. Maybe you should sit this one out," said Len, shaking his head.

Granu laughed. "Oh, here's an idea. Ichtam targets companies, right? So, you're cold calling receptionists. What about a program that pulls the names and phone numbers of the CEOs, Presidents, and Vice Presidents. You know, the ones who actually make the decisions? That way, you're skipping the gatekeepers."

Len looked into her eyes for an extended moment, pupils dilating as if he saw her for who she was for the first time. "Granu. That's it. That's brilliant!" He began furiously typing. "I guess you are intelligent, after all."

Granu cast him some serious side-eye. "Um, thanks?"

"Now that we put that pressing matter to rest, can we work on our plan for TCB?" asked Fillig. "You know, the reason we're here?"

"Yeah, let's get to work," said Lyssa, who'd been peering over Len's shoulder at his terrible handwriting. "I have a hair appointment in the evening, and I'd like to get some beauty sleep first."

"You're already beautiful," said Fillig, eliciting a groan from both Kradduk and Granu. They met eyes and grinned. Len kept typing as he reached into his bag with his free hand.

"Oh, yes. Well." Len tossed a flash drive across the table to Fillig. "Here. You can watch their footage with this. Don't lose it. It's a full day in the life of a VP at the Big Taco."

"You only just now thought to share this? Damn, Len."

Kradduk laughed. "Does that get your panties out of your ass, Fil?"

"Shut it."

"So, where does that put us?" Lyssa wore a bored expression but seemed to be all about business. It struck Granu as strange. Something about that troll just wasn't right. One minute she played the absent-minded, shallow, pretty redhead, and the next she seemed focused and calculating. Which troll would she be on heist day?

"Len is a genius who broke into the Big Taco's system, making our trip to the Giblets concert possible, and Fillig is pouting over something," replied Granu in response to Lyssa's query.

"Yep, that about sums it up," said Kradduk.

"Nobody likes a grumpy face, Fili bear," Lyssa took Fillig's cheeks in her hands, shaking his head back and forth as she enunciated each word.

"Get a room," said Kradduk. "Really, I have one on permanent reserve across the street at Le Dump if you need it."

"What's wrong with you?" asked Fillig as Lyssa giggled. Kradduk stuffed the key he'd offered back in his pocket.

"Hey, you never know when you're going to need a swanky hotel room! And you could have just said 'No thanks Kradduk. Nice of you to offer Kradduk.'"

"I hate to break up the love fest, but Lyssa, have you and Fillig found any weakness in the walls around the vault?" asked Granu.

"There isn't one," grumbled Fillig.

"That's not technically true," said Lyssa. "I've been working Squeath, and I think he's about to tell me something big about the taco stand. He doesn't know that I know where the money is, mind you, but he's been trying real hard to get in my pants, and he's been talking about a big project to make the Big Taco safer. I told him I'm pretty sure it's the safest structure in New Metta, but he hinted at some kind of weakness. I'm pretty sure I can get him to give me the job of shoring it up, whatever it is."

"But I'm your supervisor!" interrupted Fillig. "If anyone should be trusted with that kind of knowledge, it's me. Besides, how does he know about a weakness that our team hasn't discovered yet?"

"No idea. Sorry, babe, but I have some assets you can't hope to match. Squeath is a pig, and I plan to use that to our advantage. Besides, it's not like you're building a lasting career. We'll be out of there within the month, so what do you care?"

"I care that he's sniffing around you like that, especially after reading me the riot act about how the demo ladies are off-limits. And it's principle. You shouldn't be given preference just because you look good."

"Oh, honey, I talk a good game too. This will be over soon, and we'll be filthy rich living in the mountains feasting on inbred humans in no time."

"Is that what crawled up your ass?" asked Kradduk. "You're jealous? Cuz, you've got to grow a pair."

"I have a pair bigger than yours. Care to compare?"

"Somebody get this troll a drink before he puts his hairy nards on the table," replied Kradduk. He grinned at Lyssa, "Is he telling the truth?"

"We haven't gotten that far, thank you for leaping over the line once again," replied Lyssa with a nose crinkle. Granu glowered. Since when did Lyssa banter with Kradduk?

"So THAT's the problem. Gotcha." Kradduk winced.

"Ignore him Fillig. Not every troll cares so much for such base things," said Len, looking up from his notebook. Lyssa fluttered her over-sized eyelashes in his direction, a smile toying at the corners of her mouth.

Granu chuckled uncomfortably. "Kradduk, Fillig, have either of you discovered how to access the Big Taco's high-end sunsuits?"

"About that," said Kradduk, "We underestimated security. It would have to be an entire concert of its own. They're locked down tight, and only those with custodial clearance can access them."

"How hard is it to get custodial clearance? Shouldn't you have access to any area some custodian does?" asked Granu.

"That's a part of the Big Taco's security protocol. Employees can only access areas necessary to complete their assigned tasks. There are programmed keys for each section. I only have access to the executive areas. I can't even go to the bathroom on level 1."

"But Fillig had free run to case the place!"

Kradduk nodded. "Because that was required for the task he was performing. Hey, Fil, you didn't happen to snag some sunsuits during your search, did ya? I'm pretty sure Bridge Protection would have discovered them missing by now, and we wouldn't be alive to have this conversation."

He had a point. Perhaps stealing the suits from TCB was a foolish idea. Granu kicked herself. Of course it was a foolish idea, it was Kradduk's.

"Well, I don't plan on conducting two concerts at the most heavily guarded structure in New Metta," she said. Then it hit her. The perfect place to snag high-quality sunsuits. "Hey, Fillig, what about the quarry? Your coverings when you worked there must have been top-notch. I mean, as far as I know, only your head is made of stone."

"Hilarious. Well, they're not guarded, but they are locked up at nightfall since nobody needs to stay safe from moonlight. They are high grade, probably the best in the city. But most of the quarry is tented when we work as a double-precaution. I don't trust *any* coverings in direct sunlight."

"Well, for our plan to work, we're going to have to, and if they have the best, you've got to get them."

"How am I supposed to do that? I didn't exactly leave on the best of terms. I'm not even sure how to get in to snag them without arousing suspicion."

"That's what you hired me for, the planning," said Granu. "We'll go over your next assignment in a bit. You can't start until the sun goes down anyhow. You can't exactly waltz in with no protection in the middle of the day."

"Hired you? Is somebody paying you?"

Granu smirked. "You will when we clean out those sons of goats at TCB."

"And, might I ask, what next assignment are you talking about? I'm not going back to the quarry," replied Fillig, pinning Granu with a dubious, but fiery, glare that promised a challenge.

"I said later."

"Dreatte, where are you with the next round?" he called. "I feel like I'm going to need a drink for this."

Kell appeared at the table. "Hey guys. Drea isn't feeling well today, so she went home. I'll try and cover you, but I'm on the bar, so it might be easier if you come up for whatever you need. Did I hear someone say they wanted tacos?"

"Um, yeah, me," blurted Granu as Kradduk and Fillig both said "No" far too loudly.

"Alright, then, one order of tacos. Toddler?"

Granu nodded and forced a smile.

"You've got the whole place to yourself all day?" asked Fillig.

"Seems that way. It's alright, though, I've got the skills. I'll be right back with your drinks." The tattooed molent returned to the bar to fill up some pitchers.

"Could you be any more obvious?" barked Granu. She looked back and forth between Kradduk and Fillig. They both shrugged. Len snickered.

"*Anyway.*" She emphasized the word and stared at Kradduk. "I've located eight juveniles who should be entering wontog within two weeks. As the day approaches, I should be able to smell which are the closest. I figure I'll bring some who aren't as well to add to the confusion. A typical field trip is around fifteen, and maybe I can sniff out another one or two nearing the change before the concert. We'll enter the main gates, go through security, and embark on the tour. Kradduk, have you positioned yourself as tour leader?"

"You know it. I fudged some documents after getting myself in trouble for some misappropriations."

"What? You're supposed to be lying low!"

"Well, it wouldn't be believable if I asked for tour guide duty, but as a punishment, nobody questioned it. I start my new duties on Monday. Though I'm really not going to like working daylight hours. Ah, the things we do for money, glory, and sweet, sweet vengeance." Kradduk cracked his knuckles and leaned back in the booth.

"You're a little scary sometimes," said Fillig, and Len nodded in agreement.

"So, I hear."

"Alright, so as soon as we're in, Len will take over the security system. Have you found a way to mute the alarms?" Granu continued.

"Not yet, but now that I've broken in, it shouldn't be much. I simply need to alter their programming and hijack the codes that communicate with the alarms and cameras. I should have that figured out by the end of the week or so. I managed to duplicate their security protocols so I can run accurate simulations."

"Great. It seems like we are on track. Are we all set to send the camera in tomorrow night?"

"As set as I'm gonna be," said Kradduk. "I've befriended a toll-taker named Zet. We've been having midnight snack together all week, and he brings his deposit with him in a bag. I think I can clip the pen onto the bag, but whether he notices it or not is dumb luck. Worst case, he sees it and wonders how it got there. He's a nice troll, but not the brightest. He wouldn't think to dissect it."

"Ok, then. Great work. Maybe we won't need your intel from Squeath after all, Lyssa," said Granu, fighting to hide the satisfaction from her voice. Anything that undercut Lyssa's contributions without hurting the cause made Granu giddy. "Len, do you have the pen's camera set up to display on a laptop?"

Len gave Granu a look dripping with disdain. "Of course. Any idiot could do that."

"Sorry, but I've got to check on all loose ends. Lyssa, report in if you get anything remotely useful, and the rest of us will just wait it out. Who's hungry? I'm dying for some fresh meat. I wonder where Kell is with those tacos."

"I've got a date," said Kradduk, "but it shouldn't last much longer than it takes to walk to my place and back if you know what I mean."

"Really? You're bragging about how fast you can get off?" said Granu.

"Hey, I'm all about efficiency." He put on his jacket, tipped his hat, and headed for the door.

"There's the Kradduk we know and love," said Fillig.

"I'm heading home for some shut-eye. Catch you trolls tomorrow." Lyssa kissed Fillig before heading out. Len remained seated in the chair at the end of the table as Granu instructed a miserable Fillig on how to get back into the quarry to steal four sunsuits; Len wouldn't need one as his presence would be remote. The van should be shielded enough, and if it wasn't, they'd all be toast anyways. Half an hour later, they added a unicorn rump roast with blood gravy to the order.

19

DAYLIGHTING

Fillig was pissed. He'd spent much of the morning with Granu as she concocted the worst plan in history, and after grabbing a few hours of sleep, it was up to him to execute it. He navigated the passages leading toward the quarry, muttering the entire way about being forced to beg for a job like some half-beaten man child. His stomach did cartwheels the entire way.

I work at TCB. I don't have time to daylight at the quarry while putting in full hours at the most prestigious company in the city. Besides, I'm better than all these idiot cud-chewers slaving away to provide limestone for our toilets, he thought. He'd agreed to let Granu take the lead on this heist, however, and this was her directive. The sunsuits were vital to the plan, and the quarry had the best available. Without this piece of the puzzle, they'd be turned to stone as soon as they got their hands on the cash, or worse, they'd be picked up by Bridge Protection trying to get into the caverns. Still, the importance of the mission didn't make this any easier.

The blue-lit passage widened before making a 95-degree turn, the minimum required angle for exterior facing entrances, and opening into the canyon. The river was still two hundred feet away, gurgling as it flowed over rock, but the stones beneath his feet were smoothed by hundreds of years of water flow before the supply shrank. It was tightly packed, making a perfectly safe walkway so long as the sun was down. The moon overhead illuminated the canyon and reflected off the statues of trolls who'd been caught outside when the ball of fire rose, their faces forever contorted into screams of agony. It was quite beautiful. He made a mental note to bring Lyssa back for a midnight picnic before they had to leave town, a romantic thought that brought a momentary smile to his face until he remembered his purpose.

Fillig trudged on for another mile and a half before the too familiar fence loomed ahead, making every happy thought flee his head. His stomach danced in anticipation of the awkwardness to come, and the corner of his mouth twitched spastically. This was the last place on earth Fillig wanted to be.

"Hey Larrle," he said in greeting to the troll in the Welcome Hut. He still snickered at the lame attempt to make grunt workers excited about coming to a grueling job. *Welcome Hut, my ass,* he thought. *More like hut at the gates of hell.* He half expected Cerberus to come begging for a scratch behind the ears. Instead he found Larrle.

"Fillig, that you? What are you doing here? If I had a way out, I'da never looked back."

"Yeah, well, it turns out the job market's tough out there. Can you page Onee? I'm hoping he has a position for me here."

Larrle erupted in laughter, his fat face split by a wide mouth and his eyes nearly disappearing into the folds of flesh surrounding them. "Really? You want to come back here? I heard you got some big-wig gig at TCB. Guess that was just a rumor, 'cause here you is come to grovel. I didn't peg you for the type!"

"Yeah, I was at TCB for a while, but now I need to come back. Please just do it?" Fillig swallowed the lump in his throat and attempted to control his shaking hands. He could feel the warmth of blood rushing to his cheeks, his obvious agitation only making Larrle laugh louder.

The round troll wiped the tears from his eyes with the back of his sleeves before picking up his hand-held radio and clicking it to the proper channel. Soon, Larrle's voice echoed through the entire quarry.

"Mr. Onee, Fillig Schist is here to kiss your ass. I repeat, Fillig is here on his knees." He began laughing again before taking his fat finger off the button.

Fillig resisted the urge to snarl and instead put on his most pleasant face. "Funny."

Granu would never forgive him if he screwed this up.

He waited forty-five minutes before he felt the vibrations of the approaching sniggle. Hulking creatures which dwarfed all other sun-avoiders, sniggles frequently found jobs in the manual labor sector. Onee was large, even for his species, and his grey skin chafed and bled with each step, more than typical sniggle hide. Many companies attempted to create ointments and creams for the condition, but despite claims to the contrary, none did the trick. The beasts were accustomed to broken skin and raw appendages. The smell was revolting.

"Fillig. What can I do for you?" Onee's mouth was small, and his yellow eyes took in the sights with slightly blurry results, making him occasionally crash into walls. His blue quarry uniform stretched across a broad, round torso, the hardhat fitting too tightly, pushing rolls of forehead flesh forward beneath his hairline.

"Mr. Onee. Good to see you." He cleared his throat as he launched into his prepared spiel. "As you know, I spent six good years here at the quarry, and though you thought I was overqualified for my last post, I was hoping you would reconsider. I love the quarry, and I don't plan to push for advancement anytime soon." Fillig fought the bile that coated his tongue. Though he didn't come out and say it, the line about advancement was a direct reference to the Blight to put any concerns to rest. The quarry was completely unprotected from the billys. In retrospect, Fillig should have seen this coming, but he'd fool-ishly fallen for the promises of his sniggle boss.

"Your post has been filled."

Fillig's heart sank at hearing the news he already knew. He wasn't expecting a warm reception, but he thought Onee might jump at the chance to put him in some equivalent position; he'd been a good worker. But the sniggle's tone was anything but welcoming. If he couldn't get hired on in some capacity, he didn't know how he would get to the sunsuits.

"Oh, well, is there anything available?" The saliva drained from Fillig's mouth. "I'm desperate." The last word hung in the air for a moment like a blood-sucking pixie staring down a cornered kitten just before the deadly strike. Fillig heard a stifled chuckle from Larrle but didn't look in his direction.

"Sniggle groomer."

Fillig's eyes popped, and for a moment, he forgot the direness of the situation. "But you said I was overqualified for foreman! That's like, five steps down at least! Sniggle groomers are drop-outs or kids looking for extra spending cash."

"It's all I got, take it or leave it. Now, if you're done wasting my time, I gots to get back to work."

"No, no. I'll take it."

Onee's tiny mouth opened in a rare grin, his brown teeth peeking out from between cracked lips. The motion caused his skin to tear at the corners, and two droplets of blood trailed down, turning him into a mustached giant. "Alright then. We'ves gots three who need washin' and two more's need antibiotics in their nethers."

Fillig sighed. Now he had to position for a day shift or confess to having another gig. It shouldn't be too hard since he now knew what Onee thought of him. "Can't I start now?"

"And have a night shift?" The sniggle's booming laughter made the small stones on the ground dance. Larrle was nearly doubled over inside the hut. "Report in the morning. Gidd will train you."

"Train me? To clean sniggles? I think I already know how to do that."

"Fine, then, go it on your own. Grab a suit from the preparation hut on the way out. Or do you already know how to survive in sunlight too?" The sniggle erupted in laughter echoed by Larrle as he tossed a badge to Fillig.

Fillig sighed. "Fine, I'll be back in the morning. Thanks Mr. Onee." Fillig thought he might shatter his back teeth from clenching so hard.

Sniggle grooming by daylight hours was the highest of insults, but if he could snag the suits now, he might just be able to get out of having to report back for the vile job. Fillig headed to the Prep Hut, and he swore to make Granu pay for putting him through this.

The quarry was nearly entirely tented to keep the dangerous rays from affecting the daytime workers should their coverings fail. The Prep Hut, a lean-to structure at the canyon's edge, connected to the northernmost caverns of New Metta via a gate with key-card access. The location provided internal access to the space where workers could cover up before accessing the outdoor parts of the quarry, a huge, blasted crater in the rock north of the city. When he arrived, his hopes were dashed. One full suit was laid out on the bench, likely set out for him after Larrle notified the custodian over the radio about a new daytime employee; the rest remained locked up until morning when those who normally kept night hours had to report for meetings and such.

He had to show up at dawn prepared to work. At the end of his shift, he would find the opportunity to smuggle the other three suits out. He just needed to make it through an entire day of massaging and cleaning broken, oozing, hulking sniggles. Fillig nearly retched at the thought; he could think of nothing more disgusting.

He tossed the suit over his shoulder and headed home, striding by Larrle at the Welcome Hut without a word, to change before reporting to TCB. It was going to be a long night and day.

20

SURVEILLANCE

K radduk, thankful the camera was hidden so well within the writing utensil, stuffed his face with the nightly midnight snack offering, narwhal stew. Glad for the rare taco reprieve, he sucked the tender meat off the base of the horn with a slurp, then used the tip to pick tendon from between his teeth. The action kept his nerves in check. On the outside, he was cool as a waternut, but inside he was a mess, exhausted from his morning tour duty shifts and worried that at any moment, he may say the wrong thing to the wrong person. He prayed to the Underlord that the troll across from him was as oblivious as he seemed. A pen was such an innocuous instrument, he reminded himself, that even if it were detected, it would raise few concerns. Zet would assume its presence was accidental. Hopefully.

He dipped his spoon back into the bowl but came up with nothing. It was empty, leaving him with nothing to do but listen to Zet talk. The cafeteria was bustling at the busy midnight hour, and his companion was deeply entrenched in a story about the many characters he encountered taking tolls topside. All toll collectors were trolls because that's who the humans expected to encounter when they crossed the bridge. Any other creature might give the humans cause to question their own perceived false memories. But they had fables about grumpy trolls demanding payment in exchange for passage. Zet was average-sized, not grumpy in the slightest when out of character, and a bit short on intelligence, but overall, he was a nice guy. Kradduk almost felt guilty for using him.

The troll's collection bag sat on the floor near his left foot, the toe of Kradduk's boot pressed against it under the table. It was a heavy, burlap material, tied with twine to keep it closed. With all TCB's protocols, Kradduk thought they'd be more controlling over the deposits, but Zet explained to him earlier in their friendship that he was personally responsible for the safe delivery of each night's haul. Every penny would be counted by the machine used to collect it, and if the deposit didn't match to the cent, Zet would be forced to cover the difference or surrender his post. In the latter case, more drastic punishments may be applied depending on the severity of the negligence and the amount of the discrepancy.

"Why did you agree to that?" asked Kradduk one day.

"It's either agree or lose my chance to work for TCB. It's been my dream since I was a kid, you know."

"Hm. It seems like a steep price to pay to sit in a booth and collect tolls all night."

Zet looked affronted. "Hey, didn't you ever have a dream? Something you'd give up everything else for the chance to do?"

Kradduk thought back to his time with his mom in the tiny apartment they'd occupied before coming into money. She'd worked all kinds of jobs at all kinds of hours under all kinds of bosses to ensure he was taken care of, and the only dream he'd ever had was to make enough money so that she didn't have to worry another night of her life. When she seized her piece of the New Metta high society by the throat, Kradduk's mother made his dream obsolete. Since then, he'd done very little, other than see to his own fleeting whims and desires. He sometimes wondered if there was more to life, a thought that occurred to him now more frequently than ever before. For some reason, he found himself more occupied with philosophical ideas when he spent time with Granu.

He shook his head to clear it. One thing was sure, Kradduk didn't want to cause Zet to lose his dream job. Underlord knew, the poor sap didn't deserve that. Kradduk didn't plan to take anything from Zet's deposit, just to add something to it. The simple troll should be in the clear so long as Bridge Protection didn't discover that the pen was really a camera. Kradduk realized he was holding an empty spoon midway between his mouth and the bowl. He dropped it with a clatter, wondering how long he'd been frozen that way. Thankfully, Zet was still talking.

"And she just went on and on about the merits of good relations between trolls and humans, as if she weren't completely terrified, her boyfriend shaking in his shoes the entire time. I think she might have been trying to get me into bed! Isn't that disgusting? It's amazing what goes on in the heads of such simple creatures. I considered taking her as a pet, but I think that's a violation of the hunting ban, isn't it? I mean, is it? I wasn't going to kill her."

"Yeah, I think so. I knew a human-rights activist once, a roommate of my best friend, and he had a family of them, but I think he got them from the Grimsby mammal exchange."

"Ah, yes. Perhaps I'll look into that instead. Nabbing a customer would probably get me fired."

Kradduk nodded. "I'm sure that would be frowned upon, ban or not. What amazes me is how the creatures pay a troll to cross a bridge, interact with you like that, then convince themselves the memory was flawed somehow."

"I know, right? I wondered about that before, about how they like to pretend we don't exist. How do you think they do that?"

"My theory is that it's the pack animal instinct that overtakes them. Like, believing in us would make them feel the need to do something about it, and that's too dangerous for their tiny minds to fathom. Instead, they embrace mass delusions. It makes them feel safe."

Zet stared blankly at Kradduk. The conversation was a bit too deep for such a simple troll. Kradduk sighed as Zet launched into another story about a tasty-looking toddler hanging out the window of a station wagon.

Kradduk ran a finger along the inside of his empty bowl and licked it as he waited for Zet's usual post-lunch run to the restroom. The troll made a habit of leaving his deposit with Kradduk for the few minutes it took him, because, in his own words, he didn't want to pee on the goods. Kradduk couldn't figure out how Zet had made it to a position of responsibility in the company. How had nobody targeted him to lift one of his deposits? It would be so easy. It was a good thing Kradduk wasn't in this for the money. They'd only been dining together for three weeks, so what Zet did with his deposits beforehand, Kradduk hadn't a clue. Perhaps he'd find a way to suggest that Zet make his deposit before lunch in the future to save the guy some trouble ahead.

Like clockwork, Zet got to his feet soon after finishing his own stew, made his excuse, and headed to the restroom. Kradduk waited until he was out of sight, took a furtive glance to ensure Big Pig, stationed at his usual cafeteria lookout spot next to the grub window, wasn't paying him any mind, then pretended to tie a shoe lace. With a quick motion, he clipped the little pen to the bag, camera side out. When Zet returned, Kradduk was sitting upright, sipping sludge soda from his straw.

"Alright man, I've got to get to the deposit hatch and make a final count. It was good to see you again. Same time tomorrow?"

Kradduk nodded, nearly choking on his soda. Final count? He thought Zet simply tossed the bag in the hatch. If he were to open the bag, he was sure to see the pen clipped to it. In the best case scenario, he would remove the pen; in the worst, he would send it to Bridge Protection for inspection. This was bad. Kradduk took a deep breath and reminded himself who he was. This was where he shined, thinking on his feet. He could manage the situation.

"Yo, Zet, I've been thinking. I have some pull here, and you're such a diligent worker, I bet I can get you a promotion. If collecting tolls for TCB was your dream, managing the toll collectors must be something you've considered."

"Really? Oh, Underlord, that would be amazing! Can you really do that? Kradduk, you don't know what this means to me!"

"Hey, now, don't get emotional on me." Kradduk smiled. "Why don't you come up to my office, and we can chat about it."

"Now? Oh! But I've really got to make the deposit. I need to be back in my booth topside in twenty. Can we do it tomorrow at lunch?"

"Hmm, I don't know. I mean, if this isn't something you really want, I don't want to waste my efforts. It would look bad on me, you know."

He hated to manipulate Zet, but he needed to eat up the rest of midnight snack break so he wouldn't have time to make a final count. If he could stall him for fifteen minutes, the troll would be forced to make his drop without taking the time to count the cash.

Zet's face got tight, his lips pursed. He glanced down at the bag in his hand then at Kradduk's stern expression before deflating. Kradduk had him.

"Ok, can we make it quick, though? I really need to get down to the deposit hatch."

"Sure. This way."

Kradduk led the way up the stairs, stopping to chat with Cinda, a chubby swog, along the way, as Zet puffed and stared at his watch. When Kradduk made eye contact, Zet thrust his arm in his pocket and forced an awkward smile. Five minutes passed before they arrived at Kradduk's office, and poor Zet was fidgeting, his fat fingers entwining around each other before separating, turning, and entwining again.

Kradduk took his time sitting down, rifling through some papers and adjusting his chair before he began.

"So, where do you see yourself in five years? Not taking tolls, I'd wager."

Zet swallowed hard. Likely, he hadn't been expecting a full interview.

"Um, I'd like to be on the management track, overseeing the toll-takers and whatnot just like you said. In five years I hope to be doing that."

"Ok, well, that's what we're aiming for here, but I'm thinking it won't take five years. So, you plan to be a company man for life?"

"Yes. I want to make a career at TCB and bring my son on too. When he's old enough, of course."

"Zet, because we're friends, I'm going to let you in on something. Advancement here is tricky. If you're too ambitious, the higher-ups start thinking you're gunning for their jobs, and they get rid of you. You have to play it with the right amount of gumption and complacency so they know you can get the job done but don't see you as a threat."

Zet nodded, his face somber.

"I think you do that well, but you need to keep it in mind, especially during interviews. So, let's move on. Your background is in accounting, is that correct?"

Kradduk wrote down each entire question and answer, verbatim, on a pad of paper, forming each letter meticulously before moving on to the next question. By the time he made it through five interview questions, Zet was sweating.

"Kradduk, I really appreciate this, but I'm going to be late for my shift. I don't think that will help my case for promotion. Please don't think this isn't important, though. It's everything I want. But my supervisor is a stickler for schedule, you understand?"

Kradduk thought the troll may cry, so he gave him a reassuring smile. He'd taken seventeen of Zet's twenty minutes. There was no way the troll would have time to do a final count. He'd be lucky if he had time to get to the hatch, toss the bag in, then get back to his booth in the time he had left.

"Oh, of course. I didn't mean to take so much time. I just want to be thorough when I give my recommendation. I'll have a talk with HR, and I bet you'll be toll supervisor in no time. Tomorrow for lunch?"

"Of course, um yeah, tomorrow. Hey, Kradduk, what about the billys?"

"Oh, don't spend time worrying about them. They're sure to attempt some kind of intervention should you get the promotion, but TCB has precautions in place."

Zet nodded, bid a hasty goodbye, and didn't take the time to wait for Kradduk to stand before bolting out the door and down the hallway. Kradduk listened to the thundering steps tear down the hall. His part of this puzzle complete, he shut down his computer. He wanted to get to the tavern and watch the footage with Granu before having to be back for the morning tours. Goron's was a fifteen-minute walk away, so his cohorts were reviewing it for the second or third time when he arrived.

He found her sitting in the booth with Len staring at his open laptop.

"Did you know that the Big Taco uses biometric scans?" asked Len excitedly. "What I wouldn't give to spend a day with your tech department!"

"Don't you work nights?" asked Kradduk.

"Yeah, but I called in sick to give me time to get the program to pull manager data up and running. I have more sick days than I know what to do with. It's the only upside to Ichtam."

Granu smiled at Kradduk, her green eyes sparkling. "So, I take it you didn't have too much trouble getting the camera in place? This is good stuff."

Kradduk smiled back and motioned for Len to move so he could squeeze next to Granu to view the footage. Len scowled but obliged. The screen showed a dark passage and Kradduk had a hard time deciphering the image as the deposit traveled on a conveyor belt through the walls of the offices of TCB.

"Ha! So Fillig was right. It travels through the walls," said Kradduk. "I knew I had the location of the taco stand right."

"All this in order to hide it?" said Granu. "You'd think it would be more efficient to simply hire extra guards."

"Nah. There are enough professional criminals in New Metta that someone would find a way to take out the guards. Much better to outsmart the criminal element. That's why we have the advantage here. We have the brain power to think through this um, concert, instead of attempting to strong-arm our way in, and that's exactly what's needed," said Kradduk.

Len nodded. "Intelligence is far underrated in New Metta, I've always said."

"So, what am I looking at?" asked Kradduk, squinting at the screen.

"According to my reverse calculations from the taco stand, we're right about here," answered Len, jabbing a pen at the blueprint on the table. "We've passed two biometric scans. They're obviously scanning to ensure no molents are passing through. And Fillig thought they wouldn't fit! Shows what he knows."

"I wonder if that group knew about the scans. That's why they didn't try to go in this way," Mused Granu.

"Nah." Kradduk shook his head. "I don't think most underlings do this much recon before attempting to break in. They thought they figured out the location of the vault and went for it. I doubt they knew about the drop protocol."

Granu nodded. Most of the attempts were half-assed at best, but, it would make sense that the Big Taco would have measures in place to ensure no underling could access the taco stand if they were to think of it.

"That's probably why they keep the location of the drop box hidden in Bridge Protection too," she said, half to herself.

"Wow, you three are getting cozy." Dreatte's voice was light and mocking.

That grawback sure does know how to sneak up on a troll, thought Kradduk. Though, she likely was just going about her table rounds, and they were too engrossed to notice.

Granu chuckled awkwardly. "We're watching a trailer for Guts and Glory."

Kradduk grinned from his spot pressed between Granu and Len.

"Whatever." Dreatte set down a flagon for him with a thud. "Oh, you better watch that paper of yours, it'll get ruined when the puddle spreads."

Len stared, Kradduk smiled, and Granu's eyes bulged. The blueprint was precariously close to the puddle forming on the table from the dripping above. She snatched up the paper and folded it up. Dreatte moved on to another table.

"That was close," said Kradduk without a hint of the adrenaline that flooded his body.

"Too close. We need to be more careful," agreed Granu. "I don't think Dreatte would turn us in, but who knows who else is lurking. Oh, look, this is when the deposit finally reaches its destination!"

On the screen, Kradduk could make out a room filled with shelves. Many of the shelves contained boxes, presumably filled with cash. The closer ones were filled with bulging bags. The bag holding the camera had dropped off the end of the conveyor belt, and a mechanical arm hoisted it up to an empty spot on a nearby shelf. Robotics. That explained why nobody saw anyone going in or out of the treasury. Another robotic arm was emptying bags from one shelf into boxes that were then hoisted onto the other shelves. It would take months to fill the space, then the money was likely moved to the bank at a strategic time, when nobody would be near the exit. Kradduk wondered if they took it out from Bridge Protection offices or from the topside.

"If the room were full, we could watch to find out how they make the transfer," said Granu as if reading his mind. "That would probably be the optimal time to make the hit, but we'd have to wait until the room filled up again to move, and there's no telling how long that takes."

"Right now, it looks like there's enough cash on those shelves to hurt Figg bad," said Kradduk.

Granu smiled. "And set us up for life."

"How do we know they won't make a transfer before the room is full?" asked Len. "If we make our move right after the transfer, the room will be nearly empty."

"We can't be sure, but it only makes sense that they'd wait until it was full and make fewer trips throughout the year. That's how I would do it," said Granu.

Kradduk nodded. "The Big Taco is cautious. They won't risk exposure by making more trips than necessary, and there's sure to be cost associated with the security needed for the moves. They aren't going to spend a dime more than they have to. I think

Granu's right. As long as we hit it before the room is full, we're golden."

Len snapped the computer shut.

"Well, at least now we know what we're dealing with," he said.

"Yep. Loads and loads of cash," said Granu, her face lit up like the celebration of Underling Independence. "Lyssa was right. We need to figure out how to carry more."

Just then, a gorgeous, stacked troll sauntered by. Kradduk dove from the booth, shoving Granu in the process, ran a hand through his hair, and disappeared after her.

21

SOMETHING ROTTEN

Fillig tried to think of anything but the task at hand as he used the long nail of his forefinger to pick bits of rock and rubble from the cracks in a sniggle's thick, gray hide. He was dizzy from holding his breath against the onslaught of stench. It was the smell of flesh-rot contaminating the very air around him. His quarry-provided sniggle cleaning sunsuit came equipped with a barf bag stitched into the neck area, and the training videos he'd watched when he first arrived instructed him to be discrete when using it. At first he thought it a silly precaution, but as the day wore on, he realized that his stomach would not hold his morning meal for long. Whenever he removed a piece of rock, the oozing began. It wasn't so much the sight that unsettled him, it was breathing in decay and feeling knots of maggots wriggling between his fingers as he worked.

Fillig's heaving earned a harsh look from the sniggle he was cleaning, but since he was new to the job, he escaped without a reprimand. The scalding shower he planned for later wasn't nearly enough to handle this, and he'd yet to work on the ones with infections raging in their open wounds. He was expected to debride dead tissue, scrub the wounds clean, and apply antibiotic ointment, all while the creatures groaned and jumped at his every touch. His stomach lurched threateningly once more as the sniggle he was currently grooming let out a moan that sounded closer to sexual pleasure than pain. Never in his life had he been so degraded. He packed up his quarry-assigned medical bag, bid the sniggle good day, emptied his barf bag, and went on to his next assignment, a female with a staph infection and maggots writhing in the crevice of her neck.

"You missed this one," she grunted when he thought he was finished. She held her arm up to reveal a green pus crater beneath it. Fillig swallowed the bile rising in his throat. Thankfully, he didn't have much actual food remaining in his gut. He focused on the money. When this was all over, he'd be richer than the Underlord. He would never have to work another day in his life at TCB or the quarry. It was that thought that dragged him through the eight-hour shift that felt more like twenty.

"Alright, ma'am, I'm ready to exfoliate your back. If you could lie down on your stomach like so."

"Oh! This is a new service! How lovely!"

The beast named Broand was the first sniggle he'd encountered all day with the security clearance he needed for the next part of his plan, flopped to the ground with a thud that made Fillig worry about an avalanche, seeming to pay no mind to the uneven, rocky slab, and splayed out in all her naked glory. That sight alone would have been enough to make Fillig heave, had he not already spent the day up to his elbows in sniggle slime. He took out a coarse wire brush, passing her pile of clothes on the way back to her side. There it was, her ID badge, attached by a retractable cord to her coverings not two feet away.

They were in the cavern which served as the medical hut, but the nurses were all going about their business in other areas. Fillig tiptoed silently to within arm's reach of the pile of clothes. He looked back at the sniggle. She was still on her stomach with her head facing the cavern wall. With a deep breath, Fillig darted out his hand and snatched up the ID badge, snapping the retractable cord as he pocketed it. When he was finished with it, he would drop it on the ground in an area of the quarry that sniggles frequented. Everyone would think Broand was careless and got it caught on a rock, a usual occurrence for the lumbering creatures. It's why most quarry workers wore lanyards and only a few were given access beyond the front gate. He couldn't bring himself to call his luck good, all things considered.

"What is taking so long?" groaned Broand, turning her massive head to search for him. She had to push up on one arm to do so, exposing a massive breast to Fillig's view.

"Oh, excuse me," she mumbled. Though her cheeks flushed, she didn't move to cover herself, and her eyes lingered on Fillig. He swallowed another gag.

"Just getting the ointment prepared," he lied as he snapped his gaze away and closed the distance between them. Fillig fumbled with a tube and squeezed some ointment onto her back, causing Broand to lower herself back onto the slab with a groan. By the time he finished scrubbing her down with the wire brush, she was nearly asleep.

In all, he'd worked on five sniggles, most of them covered in sweat, scabs, and pus. He had one more to go before it was time to call it a day. Sure Broand would discover her missing badge before he was able to make use of it, Fillig rushed through cleaning his final sniggle, a bullish male with dried blood caked between his toes.

He forced himself to wait until the shift change was over before entering the locker cave, which was located in the cavern directly adjacent to the Prep Hut, his true target. He took a long, hot shower to give the locker room time to empty of the rest of the day workers and to wash away the sniggle stench that clung to him. When the cavern was clear, he dressed and made his way down the rows of lockers and showers, through the cave opening and out into the hut. His heart pounded in his chest, and blood rushed to his face. He had to do this quickly, before the custodian came to lock things up for the night.

The gear cage, located in the center of the hut, was wide open, providing access to any underlings that came and went during the day hours. He only had a few minutes before the need for coverings disappeared with the sun. Fillig surveyed the hut to ensure he was alone before rushing to the cage and snatching three suits from pegs, stuffing them into the large duffel bag he brought for the mission. He struggled to get the bulk entirely concealed in the bag. Cursing under his breath, he tugged on the zipper as it got caught every few inches.

Then he heard the rattle of the custodian's keys.

"You there! What are you doing?" The zimble's hooves echoed on the stone floor, bouncing off the wood, plank walls, and reverberating through the room.

Fillig used his foot to shove the duffel bag out of the cage. When the custodian approached, he was arranging one of the hanging suits, giving the impression that he was returning it after an outing in the sun.

"Sorry. My shift ran long, and I didn't get back in time to put this up."

"If you have a day shift, won't you need it tomorrow?"

"I was filling in for a friend. My normal shifts are at night." Fillig felt the shakiness in his voice, and he prayed the custodian couldn't hear it.

"Ok then, hurry up. I need to get home," said the zimble, snorting in the reverse-sneeze way that his species frequently did. "Sir?"

The zimble's tone was gruff. Fillig's heart felt like it was in his throat. He was caught, he just knew it. "Yes?"

"That had better be clean."

"Oh, it is. Have a good day," he said, hoisting the bag over his shoulder as if it were the most natural thing in the world. He attempted to walk quickly without looking like he was in a hurry. When he got to the lockers, the panic set in. He tore through the locker room where he slipped on a puddle and nose-dived into a bench before righting himself, tasting blood from his tongue. He must have bit it on the way down. Before long, he was at the underground gate leading to the New Metta caverns. He used the stolen ID badge to let himself out into the connecting underground passageway, abandoning his plan to ditch it where it could be found.

Fillig didn't stop running until he reached Goron's. Passersby stared, unaccustomed to seeing a troll move so quickly, and one or two shouted at him to slow down and watch where he was going. Fillig didn't care. He'd never stolen a thing in his life and adrenaline coursed through his veins, pushing him onward. He could barely breathe by the time he pushed through the heavy internal door of the bar. Granu was off to his right, sitting in their booth.

"By the time you make it through your period of unemployment, you're going to be a raging alcoholic," he said between ragged breaths, spattering blue blood across the table's surface. Granu startled at the sound of his voice. She'd been staring at her laptop again, obviously waiting for something.

"Fil. Did you get them?" she asked, nonplussed by the blood.

He waved the badge in Granu's face. "Yeah, I got them. I'm so glad I never have to set foot in that hell hole again!"

"Um, Fillig—" she started.

Fillig groaned. "Don't say it. Please don't say it."

"If you don't go back the theft will be reported, and you'll be the likely suspect. You have to report for your regular shift and pretend like nothing happened. Besides, the plan was getting the ID badge back to area its owner frequents so they don't suspect you. Did you forget that part?"

Fillig's heart and face both fell. "No! I did what I was supposed to. I got the suits. I can't! What if they suspect me anyways?"

"Then you should have been more careful. Who did you swipe it from? Tell me you didn't use your own!"

"Of course I didn't use my own. I'm not an idiot."

"Well, you're kind of acting like one now."

"I took it from a sniggle I was cleaning." Fillig was almost pouting, but he didn't care.

"So, tell me this, does she frequently take her clothes off at work? If the suits come up missing, and she's the one documented leaving at that time, don't you think she'll tell them that you had access to her badge? That it's missing?"

Fillig sighed. She was right, of course. He knew all this going in, but the thought of going back was soul-crushing.

"I can't spend another day cleaning those disgusting sniggles! Do you even know what I had to do today? What sniggle grooming entails?"

159

"No, and I honestly don't care. You will go back. You will do what you were hired by the quarry to do. And, you will act as innocent and oblivious as possible. Hopefully your long history with the quarry will keep you off Bridge Protection's radar."

Fillig was full-on pouting now. "Fine. I'll go back for one more day. I'll plant the ID badge, but then I'm out."

"No. You're not. You will continue working for the quarry until the heat dies down from the stolen suits. What the heaven happened to your face, anyways?"

"Granu, you're telling me to work two jobs, one well-paying and the other an insult to my existence, for an indefinite period of time?" Fillig wasn't sure if he should bite Granu or cry. The former option wouldn't solve his predicament, and the latter would lose her respect, so he just stood and stared.

"Not indefinitely. After a week or so, you can quit." Granu scrunched up her face and chewed on her bottom lip for a moment. "On second thought, you should stay until after the concert. It's only 13 days. I'm sure you can handle that."

Fillig was dumbstruck. He stared at Granu for a full minute before turning and striding out the door without telling her why he was bleeding. He'd thought about staying to help her with whatever she was working on, but he'd never hated her more in his life. What happened to his sweet, timid friend? He barely recognized this dictator.

He needed to get a few hours of sleep before going to his shift at TCB anyways, especially if he was going to continue to work days at the quarry. Granu should have been grateful at the very least, but no, she'd ordered him around like he was her servant. She didn't even care how much he suffered. Still, deep down, he knew that she wasn't wrong. They had to avoid attention at all costs, and the sunsuits being stolen would have the quarry on high alert. Thankfully, the quarry didn't have TCB's level of security. So, he made his way to his apartment, slammed the door behind him, and went to bed.

22

THE KNOCKOUT

The blonde's name was Heigle, and she was amazing. As quick-witted as she was beautiful, she had Kradduk wrapped around her little finger within minutes. Underling Connect really did understand compatibility, it seemed, not that Kradduk would ever admit to using it. To all onlookers, it seemed as if Kradduk had randomly approached the beautiful troll. Dinner conversation was witty and light, and his date was intelligent and more hilarious than anyone Kradduk ever met with the possible exception of Granu. He spent so much of the meal laughing, his cheeks were sore. Kradduk had no idea how he managed to convince her to come to his place so quickly. They bantered all the way to his penthouse, and when they got inside, he found himself enjoying the conversation so much, he didn't push for anything more to happen. It was the strangest sensation, to enjoy a female's company so thoroughly. Other than with Granu, he'd never felt a connection this intense. Heigle was everything he looked for in a mate. Perhaps it was time to consider settling down.

Kradduk found himself opening up to her about things he didn't even know he was hiding from the world. She asked about his life, and instead of inventing a story designed to impress her, he answered honestly. She asked about family, and he answered honestly about that too. His dad left before he hit wontog, and his mom struggled to make ends meet. Kradduk was listless, a playboy who at one time lived to see his mom taken care of. But when she had achieved a certain status on her own, he was left with no focus. He had talent and tenacity but very little drive. He did well at TCB with his natural intelligence and gift with words and reading people.

Heigle seemed to savor his every word with her perfectly plump mouth. She asked questions, smiled at all the right moments, and when he spoke of his family, she reached out and held his hand. Her dark eyes were filled with sympathy when he talked of sadness, of mirth when he talked about happy times, and of hunger when he flirted. However, the conversation took an interesting turn when he mentioned TCB. Heigle seemed very interested in his work there, even more interested that she'd been in the rest of his life. She'd heard rumors of another attempt to rob the place, and she wanted to know what he knew about it. Her excitement was off-putting, and Kradduk dodged questions that were too close for comfort. Still, he didn't find it easy to deceive her, and her huge, black eyes seemed somehow sad when he changed topics. He felt like he'd let her down. As the day neared noon, Kradduk leaned in for a kiss, but Heigle turned her cheek and stood abruptly.

"It was nice speaking with you, Kradduk. I'll be in touch," was all she said before she left hastily. Kradduk stood dumbfounded as he stared at the door she closed behind her. He really thought he had something special with Heigle but then, what was that cold exit about? A cheek and a formal goodbye after soul-baring conversation lasting well into the day. He scratched his head and tried to ignore the sinking feeling in his gut. He would never understand females, that was for sure.

That night, when Kradduk reported for work, he was surprised to see Heigle standing in his boss's office, holding a file.

"Kradduk," she said formally. She was dressed in a navy pantsuit with spiked, red heels, and she wore a powerful shade of red lipstick. Oh, this was bad. This was very bad.

"I heard you met our new head of security, Ms. Heigle Limestone," said Dammon, who was not only VP but also Kradduk's direct supervisor and long-time mentor. Unlike Bartock Figg and the rest of the Figg family, Kradduk considered Dammon a decent guy as far as swogs went. "She had a bit to say about you. This is your one and only chance to come clean. You've been a valuable employee and friend for some time now, Kradduk, and I want to know everything about your associations with a computer hacker named Len Peat."

Heigle stood beside Dammon's desk, her back to the wall and one brow arched as she watched Kradduk. He nearly shivered, pinned by her icy gaze.

Frantically, he played out the conversations from the previous day in his head. She had asked about security, he'd hedged. She had asked about his access, he'd covered. She had asked about his friends, he had talked about his relationship with Granu. She had asked about his personal finances, he'd answered truthfully that he was well-off. He hadn't given anything away, he was sure. Was he sure? Despite his openness with Heigle, he wasn't as stupid as Fillig, thank the Underlord, and he hadn't given any indication of the nature of his relationship with Len or the heist, had he? He didn't remember talking about Len at all. It felt like there was a porcupine circus in his stomach.

"Hacker? The only Len I know is a troll who had a one-night stand with my best friend," said Kradduk. Smooth as bug butter. He couldn't bring himself to look at the troll he'd spent much of the day with, but he could feel her eyes boring into him, evaluating his words.

"How close are you?" asked Dammon.

"We've had a few drinks and shot the shit, but that's it. He's not exactly my kind of troll. He's the nerdy, awkward sort, if you know what I mean. I don't know what Granu was thinking. She could do so much better."

"Don't play coy, Kradduk," said Heigle, earning a sharp look from Dammon.

"With all due respect, I can handle my employees, Ms. Limestone. Can you please leave us? I'll send Kradduk down for a statement when I'm finished with him."

The air vibrated with the rage rolling off Heigle, but she turned and left without a word.

After the door slammed, Dammon turned back to Kradduk. "Kradduk, what do you know about Len's work with computers?"

"I know nothing about computer hacking, if he truly is into that. You know that. You know me, Dammon. I've saved TCB more times that I can count. Why would I work with someone like that? I know his name and face, and that's it."

The smaller creature sighed. "I'm so glad you told me. I'm sorry for the pretense of your meeting with Heigle yesterday. As you know, we sometimes make unsavory choices in the name of maintaining security here at TCB. She's has been following you for some time, and when she saw you with the hacker, I feared the worst. Forgive me."

Dammon's shoulders relaxed, and he continued. "Len has somehow managed to break into a small corner of our security system. We have safeguards in place, and we tracked the IP address all the way back to his place of employment, Ichtam Enterprises. He is the only one there with the skill to achieve such a feat, according to the head of HR. A carpoid. Can you believe that?"

"Wow, I've never met one. Dammon, I had no idea he was capable of something like that," said Kradduk.

"I'm glad to hear that. We are bringing him in for questioning. Lucky for us, it was only a small breach, not capable of accessing much sensitive information. At least, that's what I'm told."

Dammon stood and walked Kradduk to the door. "I hate to do this to you, Kradduk, but it's just a formality. I need you to go to Heigle's office to give an official statement. It shouldn't take long. Do you know where she is? We've got her set up in Jub's old office. We let him go after the molents dug in last month."

Thankfully, those molents had gone for the decoy treasury and were apprehended without further incident. Still, it didn't reflect well on TCB to be infiltrated, especially when all other attempts were little more than hordes of underlings charging Bridge Protection with knives and pikes. A large blaster could take down most attackers without any true threat to Bridge Protection or TCB on the whole. The frame was built of solid steel.

Kradduk nodded and shook Dammon's hand before walking out the door. His heart was beating faster than it had any right, and he was sure the other troll would hear it. Heigle was a plant. Figures that the best date he'd ever had would be with a female who was working him. He felt like a real cud-chewer. Was this what it was like to be one of the ladies he lied to in order to get into bed? He felt used and dirty.

Kradduk had to find a way to warn Granu, but right now, he was more concerned with keeping his own head.

When he reached her office, Heigle was waiting for him, tapping her red manicured nails on a desk. When did she have time to get them done? He swore they weren't so threateningly sharp yesterday. All signs of the vulnerable, funny, amazing troll from the previous night were gone. In her place was a calculating monster, intent on feasting on his every weakness. Lucky for Kradduk, he had very few weaknesses. He hung back in the doorway, racking his brain for a plan.

"And I thought we had such a great time last night," said Kradduk, playing it cool.

"Of course you did. You're a dirty cud-chewer, oblivious to the thoughts or comforts of the women you profess to enjoy so much."

Kradduk smiled to cover the wince. "So they tell me. I was told to give you a statement about my relationship with Len, so here it is. He's a troll that my best friend banged. Now, he hangs around her like a lost puppy waiting to be skewered. That's it. Am I free to go? I find your company uncomfortable, all things considered."

"Imagine, you uncomfortable. I've been watching you long enough to know you. I've seen the way you work, the way you think, and you'll not be playing me."

Kradduk felt like he got punched in the gut. He thought this troll really understood him, but she had him cast the same way the rest of New Metta did, as the shallow, blasé playboy. Well, if that's what she thought of him, that's who she'd get.

"So, we're done then?"

She remained seated. "No, you may not go. Sit down. I have some questions."

"I'm sure you do."

"The hacker was scribbling in a notebook last night. What about?"

"Was he? I didn't notice."

"You know he was."

"Well, I was more interested in checking you out, if you recall." Kradduk made direct eye contact. Heigle broke it nearly instantly. Ah, so she wasn't nearly as self-assured as she seemed. Kradduk filed the knowledge away. "I do remember something about designing a program to increase sales potential at Ichtam. That's where he works, as you know."

"Yes, I'm aware."

"That's what he said. He got a promotion and wanted to make a good impression. He told Granu that if he designed said program, it was sure to get him in good with his new boss. Then they ran through ideas until they decided to target CEOs and other top officials at major corporations rather than marketing departments. You know what? Maybe that's what this is all about! Did the breach in security have anything to do with that? With a high-level official?"

Maybe he could spin this.

"I'll be asking the questions here," Heigle blurted before taking a deep breath. She straightened out her already wrinkle-free jacket. "That's interesting. You do know that it was the camera in Dammon's office that was hijacked, don't you?"

"Really? What could he possibly want with spying on Dammon? It had to be the first iteration at his marketing strategy. Dammon would be a good swog to approach if you're trying to sell the kinds of services Ichtam offers. And you know those computer types. They're not always the most socially aware. Perhaps he didn't realize how the intrusion would come across. He doesn't strike me as the daring type, but maybe if he didn't understand the risk." Kradduk was grasping at straws, but if he could find a way to plant a plausible explanation, he may be able to save Len's neck.

"You're one to talk about socially unaware. You thought I was into you."

"Way to keep it professional, Ms. Limestone. Or is it Mrs.? Did some poor sap draw the short stick?"

She flushed. That was it. Keeping her off-balance was his best shot at selling his story. At this moment, he was thankful for his experience working the ladies.

"It's Ms., and let's stay on track here. We're talking about Len."

"I thought we were talking about yesterday."

"We're talking about the breach in Dammon's security camera. You know, the VP of Operations. One of the only employees here with information about the whereabouts of TCB's treasury?"

Kradduk took a shot. "With all due respect, everyone knows where the treasury is. First floor, east wing."

Heigle chuckled, confirming that she knew the one he referenced was a decoy. She should, as the head of security, but TCB made some questionable calls.

"Can we please get back on track?" she said.

"Hey, you're the one who keeps bringing up our date. I must have left an impression on you."

"It was work. Get over yourself."

"Whatever you say. Have you spoken to this troll you're painting as a criminal mastermind? He's not exactly a smooth talker. If he's up to something, he'll spill it as soon as he sees that pretty smile of yours. From what I can tell, he's a sucker for a strong woman."

Heigle smiled. "Ah, flattery. I was beginning to think you weren't going to try your regular tricks. I still won't sleep with you Kradduk, if that's what you're going for here."

"Nor I you, you shrew. Though, I hear that the bitchier women are hellcats in the sack." Kradduk winked and made a *chlink* sound out the side of his mouth.

The phony smile melted from Heigle's face. "Get out. Now."

"I thought you had questions for me?"

"Get out now, before I cook you for supper."

"Oh, if you could manage that, honey, I doubt you'd be stalking me like I'm a lost, juicy-legged toddler." Kradduk didn't think Heigle was buying his story, but alternating between compliments and insults seemed to rattle her to the point of distraction. If she was letting him leave, she didn't have enough on him to prove anything. He planned to keep it that way.

"I assure you, my interest in you is purely professional. Even that much makes my skin

crawl. Now, get out of my office before I have Bridge Protection escort you," she hissed.

"I thought you were going to cook me?"

"NOW."

"Alright, alright, catch ya later honey buns." Kradduk blew a kiss in her direction as he left her office. He thought her head may explode, and the idea made him chuckle.

Even when she seethed hatred, that troll was intoxicating to be around. Kradduk shook his head as he walked down the hall, turning around to flash her a classic Kradduk smoldering grin through the glass wall. She returned an icy stare. Too bad he'd been the one to do most of the talking yesterday. It would be nice to have some insight into the way her mind worked, but for now, he had to go with what he did know. She craved control and respect. He could work with it.

Now, if he could just get a message out without arousing suspicion. Len was probably already as roasted as a unicorn rump, but he had to reach Granu before TCB put it all together. They'd been best friends for years, so a phone call wasn't entirely suspicious. His only shot was to call and hope against all that she understood the things he couldn't say directly.

The phone rang three times before she picked up. "Hey Granni," he greeted, using a pet name he hadn't spoken in years. Granu hated it, and it was sure to tip her off to something being amiss.

"What's wrong?" she immediately asked. Good. If anyone could pick up on his code, it was Granu.

"So, you know the project your boy Len was working on for work, the one where he wanted to target high ranking executives at major companies for promo deals? It seems he targeted my boss, and now,

get this, they think he's planning to rob the place or something."
Kradduk laughed as the sound of stilettos running on tile echoed
down the hall. Heigle was coming. Fast. That confirmed his suspicions
that his phone was tapped.

"What—oh, Kradduk."

"Hang up immediately!" Heigle demanded, charging toward him
with teeth bared. A bit of red smudged her upper canine, and a strand
of blonde hair was loose from her too-tight ponytail. Kradduk could
only imagine what she'd be like if she let herself lose control. He
chewed his bottom lip.

"Granni, I gotta run. It seems my date from last night wants more
of my attention. I had no idea she was so needy."

"NOW!" yelled Heigle. Kradduk hung up his phone, but Granu was
already gone.

"Was that a message?" demanded the troll, her expression savage.

"Um, no. What kind of message could I possibly send, and why
would I do that?"

"You warned her!"

"Of what? She's not even into Len. She couldn't care less if something bad happened to him. Honestly, it would likely make her happy
if someone could get him away from her. He keeps leaving cats and
babies on her doorstep. She's bound to eat him sooner or later."

"Why would you call her?"

"I thought it was hilarious that anyone would think Len was planning anything on the scale you're talking about. I know you're trained
to be paranoid, but come on. Granu's my best friend. I thought she
would think it funny too. And she did!"

"I have your phone bugged. I know what you said."

"So?"

"I know you warned her."

"How? If you have it bugged, you know all I did was talk to her
about how unbelievable it is that Len would be planning to take on
TCB. I mean, the boy spends all day in chat rooms and playing games
online with other recluses. Pull his history from his laptop. I guarantee I'm right. He likely lives in his parents' basement. I didn't warn

Granu because there's nothing to warn her about. As far as Len goes, I don't care what happens to him any more than Gran does."

"His parents' basement, huh? Is that what you're going with?"

"What do you mean? I have no idea where the guy lives."

"You mean to tell me that Granu is your best friend, you've visited her home a million times, and you had no idea that Len lives in the apartment next door?"

"Ah! That would explain her hooking up with him! I wondered what got into her head, but proximity can be key when enough alcohol is involved. That reminds me, where do you live?"

Heigle's eyes narrowed. "You know I heard everything you told her." She was back-tracking. He had her on the run. He just needed to keep his head straight and avoid any more mistakes.

"Damn, girl. I knew you liked me, but that's going a bit far."

Her red lip rose, and a low growl escaped. She turned on her heels and strode out of sight, to Dammon's office, no doubt. Twenty minutes later, Heigle was knocking on Kradduk's office door, still exuding contempt. Dammon must have shut her down again.

His phone call cost Kradduk the rest of his night as Heigle trailed his every move, making up excuses to grill him further and waiting for him to slip up somehow, but he never did. He used the opportunity to toy with her in every way possible. In all, he had a great time, baiting then switching tactics. Near the end of the night, he thought she might believe his position on the Len situation, but when news came that Len had fallen off the grid, she got suspicious again.

Kradduk couldn't believe his luck. He thought they arrested Len before telling him about the situation, but apparently not. Dammon must put more faith in him than he thought. Kradduk almost felt bad, but when it came down to it, Dammon was just a casualty of war. Bartock Figg was the true target, and anyone who got in the way was an acceptable loss. That phone call may have saved the measly troll's life.

Heigle resumed her stalking, firing questions when she thought he was at his most relaxed, but he kept with his story and did his best to remain unreadable. At one point, he asked her if she had any real work to do, and when she didn't answer, he offered to help her update her resume.

Whenever she took control of the conversation, he shifted it, and she gave him the rise he sought time and again. He thought she must tire of the game, but if she did, she showed no signs. It was highly entertaining. At the end of his shift, he insisted on speaking with Dammon to find out if he was being legally detained. If not, he was heading home alone, he declared, unless Heigle had other plans for him. She was welcome to join him, after all.

23

THE PRICE OF GENIUS

When Kradduk got off the elevator and stepped into the hall, he nearly tripped over Len, waiting with his back to Kradduk's green door and his knees pulled to his chest.

"What the heaven are you doing here? Everybody is looking for you! You think they don't have someone watching my place? Are you insane? I thought you were supposed to be some kind of genius!"

Len was paler than usual with dark circles under his puffy eyes. His head shifted back and forth, and he jumped with every sound the building made. Unlike other complexes in New Metta, Kradduk's apartment didn't occupy natural caves. Rather, it was carved directly into the rock, with floors constructed of marble and walls likewise framed out. That made for a smooth interior through which irrigation channels and pipes ran to keep water from dripping into the living spaces. It was the pipes that made the sounds, making Len flinch with every groan and drip.

"I didn't know where else to go. I got here minutes after Granu's call, so maybe they didn't see me come."

"The doorman let you up? That means at least one creature knows you're here. Don't move from this spot."

Kradduk took the elevator back to the lobby, leaving pitiful Len to jump and shake on his own. Finkin was behind the counter, smirking.

"Mr. Kradduk. I didn't see you come in," he said, his green head feathers puffed as was customary in the service industry. Only Dreatte at the tavern seemed to ignore the custom, but nobody dared make a point of it to her. Not if they wished to keep all their fingers.

"I came in the back. I need to ask you a question."

Finkin's gaze shifted subtly to a corner of the room where a camera was mounted. Kradduk understood. They were being watched. TCB's reach covered all of New Metta and much of the surrounding area as well, and even the prestigious apartment complex was at the mercy of their prying eyes. Kradduk would have to change tactics.

"Did a package come for me today? I'm expecting a delivery from Zumbu's."

"No, sir, it did not, but the morning post has yet to arrive."

"Ah, well, can you buzz me when it comes? It's a collectible, and I won't have it sitting in the lobby for anyone to steal. Here, for your troubles." Kradduk slipped Finkin a tip. To the camera, it would look like a pittance, but beneath the single was three hundred bucks. The astute grawback would know about the search for Len Peat—hacker extraordinaire—by now. He would expect payment for his discretion.

"No trouble at all, though nothing could be stolen from my lobby. Not on my watch. I do thank you for your concern and generosity, sir." Finkin pocketed the cash.

Kradduk got back on the elevator, thinking how lucky he was to live in a building where the staff knew when to be discrete. Otherwise, he'd have been set out in the sun by the authorities with no questions asked. He made a mental note to tip Finkin better in the future.

Len was crouching in the corner just outside the door to Kradduk's apartment when he returned. He stood when the elevator arrived, his bloodshot eyes darting around like he was a prey species instead of king of the food chain. Kradduk shook his head, unlocked the door, and shoved the shaky troll through, none too gently.

"We have to get you out of here. It won't be long before they find some reason to get a warrant to search my place. You can't be here."

Len nodded silently while Kradduk flipped on the TV. He turned it to the news, hoping that nothing connected to the heist showed up.

Len's shaking stopped abruptly. "Is that a Megatriatic screen with Concrete surround sound and a Biff subwoofer? Amazing. Can I hook my laptop up to it?"

"Shut up. I'm watching to see if you made the news."

"Oh. Sorry." The little troll curled up in a chair in the corner of the room as Kradduk tried to think of a plan. He could call Granu, but calling with a bugged phone was out of the question. He was sure he signed a release to allow TCB to do that during on-boarding, but there were so many forms, he really had no clue. It's not like they didn't basically own him anyways. He'd never win a case against them. He might as well go against Rat Life Universe, the theme park giant who retained half the lawyers in New Metta to enforce copyrights on their merchandise. There, the ticker at the bottom of the screen gave a detailed description of Len along with a hefty reward offering. Shit.

A knock on the door nearly sent Len through the ceiling. Kradduk motioned for him to get in the bedroom, and Len scurried away. It was only Finkin.

"Your package arrived," he announced, using a dolly to place a large box just inside the door. It was empty save for some leftover packing peanuts, and it was large enough to hold a chair or a small troll, as the case may be. Finkin gave a wink, and Kradduk tossed him the remaining cash in his wallet.

"Finkin, I could kiss you," he muttered.

"The tip is affection enough, Mr. Kradduk. If you plan on moving your collectible to the storage unit, however, I advise you wait until sun-up. Anyone looking to steal it should be changing shifts about then. Good-day." With that, the grawback was gone. The storage unit! Of course! It was right next to the parking deck. They could use Len's phone to contact Granu and he could leave at sun-up. Trolls really did underestimate grawbacks, but that would work in Kradduk's favor tonight.

When Len emerged from the bedroom, he somehow looked even more strained. He listened as Kradduk explained the plan, nodding along before settling silently back into the corner chair. Kradduk changed the channel, choosing an epic fantasy movie about intelligent humans eliminating global warming while traversing the world. Hopefully, this would calm the troll down. The last thing they needed was for the genius of the group to suffer a mental break. Now, Kradduk just had to find a way to contact Granu. At least there was one patch of darkness in this blazing unicorn shit-show of a night: the billys wouldn't be jeopardizing the mission with antics at Ichtam. If they could get Len to safety, he'd have to stay off the radar indefinitely.

24

THE ROUTINE

Len had gone to Kradduk's when Granu specifically told him that the information came from TCB. What an idiot. What excuse Kradduk must have given the heiress molent in the apartment above his to use her phone, Granu couldn't imagine, but her gut told her to answer the unknown number calling her cell toward the end of the night. Sure enough, it was a breathless and none too pleased Kradduk.

"Gran, the dumb-ass taco collectible is here. I need someone to pick it up by the storage units at sun-up or the concert is off," was all he said before hanging up without waiting on an answer. Great. Granu shook her head, the phone still pressed to her ear. *You knew what you were taking on when you agreed to lead this heist,* she reminded herself silently.

Kradduk's. After the bizarre conversation with Kradduk earlier in the evening, Granu had immediately instructed Len to go to ground. What possessed him to head to the one place TCB was sure to have under surveillance? She cursed under her breath. All she could do was hope that Len had arrived before Bridge Protection was able to get in position. For a computer genius, that boy had no common sense. Granu figured if TCB had cops watching Kradduk, they may have them on her too, so she stuck to her routine, spending the morning hours at Goron's, heading home to sleep through the afternoon, then going to the coffee shop for some evening quiet before her cohorts were free. The coffee shop during normal work hours proved far more private for her planning and thinking, and they accepted credit cards. She made a quick call from her back table to Fillig.

"Granu. I'm at work." So Fillig was still pouting.

"I know. I wouldn't bother you unless it was important."

"I think I've given up enough of my time already, if you know what I mean." The way Fillig avoided conversation, Granu could tell he was paranoid about saying too much.

"Fillig, they can't have tapped your personal phone. Kradduk's is provided by TCB and is definitely compromised, but yours is still covered under the Underling Privacy Clause. Relax."

"Perhaps you're right, but speaking of personal matters while on the job isn't exactly smiled upon, especially when there are other creatures around trying to work."

Granu could kick herself. Just because Fillig's phone was secure didn't mean his surroundings were. TCB security was more than just some bugged lines and dirty cops. Some cautious leader she was turning out to be.

"Right, ok, I'll be fast then. You need to send Lyssa to Kradduk's place just before the end of her shift. There's something she needs to pick up from the storage unit at day-break. No sooner, no later. Got it?"

"Fine. I'll take care of it. Have a great day Gran." Fillig sounded overly cheerful when, just moments before, he was tense and tight-lipped. If his words didn't tip eavesdroppers off, his tone surely would. Fillig was far too sincere a troll to pull off direct deception of any magnitude, a trait Granu was painfully aware of the moment she signed on for this. She made a mental note to avoid calling him during night hours unless it was absolutely imperative. In this case, it was. They had to get Len away from Kradduk's place, and Kradduk had made it clear in his clipped message to get it done at daybreak. He hadn't left room for negotiation.

Shifts changed at daybreak, and the night crew would be ready to go after spending hours watching nothing happen. At the same time, the day shift would be groggy, working in opposition to their natural rhythms. It was the perfect time to strike. Granu was surprised at Kradduk's shrewdness. When he had a goal, that troll was unstoppable.

She'd chosen Lyssa because Fillig sending his underling on a last-minute errand near the end of her shift was plausible and was unlikely to arouse suspicion. Also, Bridge Protection wouldn't waste personnel following her through her shift at work and wouldn't be prepared for her to leave the facility before the end of her shift. She could get to Kradduk's and pick Len up before they had a chance to realize she had gone. That is, if they had even connected her to Kradduk, which was unlikely with so many degrees of separation between them. Lyssa was Len's best shot of getting out of there alive.

A troll with a dyed blue mohawk and three nose piercings, brought Granu her check.

"No rush," he muttered before moving back up the narrow room, but Granu knew he didn't like her camping out at the table ordering nothing but an earthworm grainy brainy brew, which she sipped for hours every day while staring at her laptop and making phone calls. Granu set her credit card on the table and prayed to the Underlord it wasn't maxed out.

Lyssa couldn't take Len to Goron's, and Granu had no idea where she would stash him. Granu suspected that Lyssa was smarter than she let on; she would figure something out. All Granu could to do now was wait. She shoved her card back in her purse, called the serving troll back over, and ordered another brew.

"Whatever," replied the surly troll.

Kradduk and Fillig were both under strict orders to proceed as normal under any circumstances, or in Fillig's case, as normal as he could while working a second job scrubbing sniggles. What would Bridge Protection think of his daytime gig if they were following him? As long as they didn't get wind of the missing sunsuits, it didn't matter.

After sipping on her drink for another hour, Granu paid her tab and headed into the maze of caverns toward Goron's to wait for Kradduk. He rarely worked longer than a few hours in the middle of the night, so he'd be free any time now. It must be nice to pull a hefty paycheck for such little time. Granu wondered how she could get a gig like that. *Get a rich parent*, she thought.

"Excuse me, ma'am. Do you have any spare change? I'm out of work, and my children are starving."

"Huh?" Granu looked around until she spotted the source of the voice, a ratty grawback approaching on a Segway through the crowd. Granu was walking right by Tarmond, the upscale chain department store where groups of beggars made a living off unsuspecting wealthy underlings. Every morning, a bus brought them in, and they dispersed, each with their own story of misfortune designed to guilt people out of their cash.

"I'm out of work too. I don't have anything," replied Granu.

The grawback's feathers were tattered with clumps missing, and makeup powder dulled her colors, making her appear more haggard. She stood upon a Segway which she maneuvered through the crowd to locate her marks. At Granu's dismissal, she shifted into reverse, the Segway beeping as she slowly moved backward into the crowd, giant yellow grawback eyes locked on Granu's face the entire time. The moment seemed to drag on to the relentless sound of beeping, but finally, the beggar was gone. Granu shook her head and continued on. It really was a shame that creatures like that preyed on the goodwill of others while those who really needed help fell through the cracks.

The thoroughfare was crowded at this time of night with under-lings on their way to or from work or play, and Granu found herself moving through the crowds defensively, making slow progress toward the bar's neon green sign as water dripped on her from the stalactites above.

"Hey Gran, how's it going?" Kradduk emerged beside her, the crowd parting to let him through. He flashed a smile, but it was shaky. Kradduk was never less than one hundred percent self-assured, so Granu squinted at him as if attempting to read his error codes. He made direct, focused eye contact. Usually, his head was swiveling as he surveyed the crowds for females to target, but this time, the only place he looked other than directly at Granu was in the direction of a molent who was following closely behind him along the busy passageway between the coffee house and the bar. The molent stood out because he didn't walk with the same vigor at the other commuters; he strolled casually, keeping pace with Kradduk, his blue button-up shirt and cargo khakis giving him the look of a laid-back traveler. He wasn't fooling anyone. Kradduk had his hands thrust in his expensive suit pockets, and he didn't make a single insulting joke.

Show time.

"Kradduk!" Her voice sounded overly friendly.

Get it together Gran, she thought.

She swallowed a lump in her throat, steadied her voice, and continued. "So, I was thinking of what you said about that poor sap Len, and I'm sure you're right. He doesn't have the balls to plan anything against TCB. Underlord, he barely has the balls to talk to me, and he saw me naked!"

Granu stole a glance at the molent. He was closing in.

Kradduk let out a breath, likely relieved that Granu had picked up on his cues. "I know, right?" he replied, missing the opening to rag on Granu as he kept to the script and reached out a hulking arm to grasp the large brass door handle of Goron's. "It's amazing how someone so smart can have no clue how his actions come across."

"Yeah. Well, I hope they go easy on him. I'm sure they've apprehended him by now. I don't think he'll last long during questioning. I hope they don't toss him into the canyon, though. He was a nice troll, even if he wasn't the best mate."

"They're more likely to carve him up and take his picture for the Chronicle with an apple stuffed in his mouth. That's usually the punishment for attempted robbery."

"But he didn't attempt anything!" said Granu. "I feel guilty for giving him the idea to target executives for his sales software."

Kradduk nodded. "You couldn't have known he'd hijack the camera of Dammon Rupp. So stupid. So sad."

They stopped short on their path to their usual table, finding a group of swogs sitting in their booth. The molent spy nearly walked into the Granu's backside. She growled low in her throat.

"Excuse me," muttered the molent, moving past her.

"Come on, Gran, they don't know it's our place. Let's go to the bar."

She followed Kradduk's lead. The molent headed them off to scale the stool adjacent to the only unoccupied pair. He ordered something from Kell, a red drink with a tiny umbrella. Granu sighed. Kradduk reached out to squeeze her shoulder, a reassuring gesture. It looked like they'd need to keep up the charade for a while longer.

"Yep, well it is what it is. Hey, did you watch 'Going Grawback' last night? Great episode. I see why Krud would fall for Cassi. She's got a good head on her shoulders," said Kradduk, drawing her back to the script. Granu was so glad that it was Kradduk and not Fillig alone with her. The other troll would have already confessed every indiscretion to the molent, down to time he chomped his schoolmate's leg in kindergarten.

"I'm not much for that reality trash. Wait, what? What have you done with Kradduk? Since when do you notice a woman's brains?" Granu was genuinely surprised by Kradduk's take on the show. While the topics were scripted, she thought it would seem more natural if they weren't simply memorizing lines, and pop culture topics should be generally safe to freestyle.

"Well, she's a grawback. Not really my cup of blood, but she is smart. She's managed his career well, that's for sure, with the move from court to screen. It's no wonder he fell for her."

They continued discussing the merits of the popular television show until Fillig arrived and picked up on the need to fall back on the scripted topics when Granu made an excuse to order a taco and over-enunciated the word. He did better than Granu had expected, considering his inability to lie, though at this point, it was easier since she and Kradduk had set the tone. Granu gave herself a silent pat on the back for having the hush protocol scripted just in case they found themselves in this very situation.

Nobody mentioned Len or TCB, so the conversations were very

close to the mundane things they spent hours chatting about before they ever conceived this suicidal plan. Granu found herself laughing. It was nice to take a break from the grueling throttle of leadership and kick back with her buddies for once. If this is what she had to look forward to after the hit, only without the burden of worry over income, it would all be worth it.

Eventually, the swogs occupying their booth paid up and left, and the threesome were able to snag a bit of privacy in their usual corner. One round in, and the molent was nowhere to be seen. They continued to avoid discussing the plan, however, in case the tavern was bugged. TCB didn't screw around, and Granu was determined to keep one step ahead of them. Since they'd been followed here, the tavern was now off-limits for discussing business.

2 5

THE CALM

J ust after sun-up, Granu's phone vibrated in her pocket, signaling a much anticipated text from Lyssa. Fillig's love interest was proving useful after all, having successfully retrieved Len and, after ensuring TCB didn't have a tail on her, taken him to her place on the south side. Granu signaled Kradduk, who sat next to her, with a flick of her ear—the agreed upon sign for "all's well"—and they both relaxed a little knowing the current crisis was contained. Fillig had left hours before to nap before heading to the quarry. He would be relieved about Len's escape and excited to hear Lyssa's message—Len wanted to push up the heist date now that the breach had been discovered. Apparently, he was convinced that TCB would have his access point closed down quickly even though his program hid the extent of the breach. Since TCB thought the breach was limited to a single camera, they may take a week or so to update their software, removing only the affected camera in the meantime, but they weren't a company to let a weakness in security exist for long.

Fillig stopped in for a quick shift-change drink. When Granu said they might go to the concert sooner than expected, his lips puckered and his eyes widened, conflicting emotions on full display. His casing job wasn't nearly complete, but now it seemed like they'd have to go in without all the information or not at all, but that also meant a sooner end to his sniggle cleaning days.

Granu shook her head at him, indicating that she wouldn't say more here. Without the freedom to speak openly and with no need to continue wasting the time of the TCB spies, the trio paid up. Granu slipped a prepaid phone she'd picked up from a kiosk outside the coffee shop into Kradduk's jacket pocket when she hugged him good-bye. Once the heat died down in a day or two, they would start meeting at Fillig's instead of the tavern. But for now, they kept to their routines just as Granu instructed.

Lyssa agreed to keep Len holed up at her place until heist day. It was the only way to keep him off TCB's radar. Risking him would risk the entire operation. Over the next few days, the trolls communicated in notes passed at the tavern which they destroyed immediately after reading by soaking them in the table water, and Lyssa kept her distance. At this point, it was best to limit in-person interactions between her and the rest of the crew since she was harboring a fugitive. That fugitive was imperative to the success of the mission. She received information from Fillig at work or from Granu through texts to her private cell. Fillig even went so far as to mope for a day about his supposed break-up, in case TCB got wind of their relationship.

"Why does this always happen to me?" he asked Granu, his voice holding a note of desperation far too believable to be put on. He must be channeling his disappointment about having to stay away from Lyssa. Granu made all the appropriate, appeasing comments, even threatening to rip his throat out if he didn't quit whining. To any outsider, it would sound like a completely natural bar conversation.

At Kradduk's suggestion, Granu kept her phone on her at all times so TCB wouldn't have the opportunity to have a spy snatch it up. Tampering with her phone would be illegal, of course, but TCB would not be deterred by pesky laws. Kradduk knew that more than anyone.

On the second day of the hush period, Lyssa sent word that Squeath had finally opened up to her about a structural weakness, but it wasn't near the vault, so it was a dead end. Still, Granu jotted it down on her blueprints. After three days free from any obvious tails, Granu felt it was safe for them to meet at Fillig's.

Fillig's apartment was nearly as spacious as Kradduk's, and he lived closest to TCB. They could see the east end of the target from his tiny window when he moved the blocking boulder aside.

"Heigle must really have it bad for me," said Kradduk. "She's done nothing but follow me around every night until about 3 a.m."

"Of course she's following you. She knows you're up to something," said Fillig.

"So she claims, but I think she just likes me. A zimble herd made an attempt today, so she'll have to let up now or somebody else will beat us to the vault while she's distracted. Someone is always planning a hit, which is great for us since it keeps Heigle and Big Pig constantly on the lookout for new suspects. Staying focused on an escaped computer hacker would distract her from more immediate threats. She's smart enough to know that."

"Thank the Underlord for that," said Granu. "I was hoping someone would take the heat off us before we had to make our move."

"I really think she likes me."

"You would," said Granu, rolling her eyes.

"We have a connection."

"You have a connection to anything with a hole in it," said Granu. "Now, can we get back to work?"

Kradduk feigned offense, clutching his heart with his fat hand as he gasped.

"We've been over this a million times. It's solid," said Fillig, ignoring the jab. He was sitting on the couch next to Lyssa, his hand caressing her knee. Every few minutes, he would stare at her for a moment longer than necessary. It was making Granu uncomfortable, so she could only imagine how Lyssa must feel.

If she felt anything one way or the other, the troll made no show of it. "I've convinced Squeath that there's a defect in this wall here, but he wants me to focus on the area he knows is a problem. Tonight, I will try and get him to agree to let Fillig address the fake defect near the vault," she said.

"We may have to push back the date again if not. I don't think we're ready," said Granu.

"Len says we can't. He's run a million simulations, and everything seems solid, but he's afraid to run another real test to see if the hole he found is still there. He insists they won't leave it for long, and if it's already patched, we're screwed."

"Underlord, you're beginning to sound like him," said Fillig. "I'm sick of you being holed up with Len. I want you all to myself." He nibbled her fingers, and Granu gagged.

"You think I want to spend any more time with that snoring, butternut-stealing troll of a troll?" asked Lyssa, pulling her hand away.

"I thought Len was a carnitarian," said Granu.

"So did I, but he sure seems to help himself to my pantry every time I get it stocked," replied Lyssa.

"Heigle can get into my pantry, anytime," said Kradduk.

"Oh, for Underlord's sake, can we focus here? Lyssa's right. We need to go in clean if we're going to do this," said Granu. "On the other hand, if they left the breach for a week, then why not two?"

"Sure, you all would be fine with putting it off. You're not cleaning pus out of bleeding sniggle cracks daily while your girlfriend shacks up with another guy," said Fillig.

"I miss you too, Filli bear," said Lyssa with a soft smile that didn't touch her eyes. "I'll ask Len, but I know he'll say a week is already too long. He's ready to move now, and when I told him it wouldn't be until Friday, I thought his head was going to explode all over my goat-tuffed rug."

"I know you're all just waiting on me to green light this. My better judgment aside, I think we're as ready as we're going to be," said Granu. "I feel in my gut that it's Friday or never, so let's make it work. The longer we talk about it, the more likely TCB is to discover us, and that's far worse than unknown variables."

"You mean the Big Taco," said Fillig.

"Um, Fil, we're in your house. I think we can drop the code now."

"But then we might slip out in public. Better that we keep up the habit."

Granu shrugged, refraining from mentioning that he didn't correct Lyssa.

"Who are you and what have you done with my Granu?" asked Kradduk. Granu knew what she was going to have for dinner two weeks ahead of time, so acting without having all variables secured was entirely out of character.

Granu shrugged. "You were all thinking it. I'm the only hold-out at this point. So let's do it. Let's get this over with so we can resume some kind of normal life."

There was solemn nodding all around.

"Okay, now that we've had a meeting to accomplish nothing whatsoever, I need to be getting home," said Lyssa. "Unless we need to question, discuss, then confirm any other details we've already decided on?"

Granu scowled. How could Lyssa switch from sweet to caustic and back again so quickly? Lyssa laughed. "I'm just kidding. But, really, I don't like leaving Len at my place all day long. I'm pretty sure he's clogging my internet history with porn sites."

Granu shuddered. Fillig reached out and clung to Lyssa's hand as he sighed dramatically.

"I can't wait until this is over so that we can be together again." He leaned in and kissed Lyssa passionately before she pushed him back gently with both hands on his chest.

Kradduk snorted. "Get it together. It hasn't even been a week! You're giving trolls everywhere a bad name," he said, curling his lip in disgust as he smacked Fillig's arm.

"You're one to talk. 'Heigle can get into my pantry whenever she wants. Heigle is so hot. Heigle said the funniest thing today.'"

Kradduk shrugged at Fillig's imitation.

"Fil's always been a sap for the ladies. You know that. Besides, he does have a point," said Granu, shutting the door behind Lyssa and clicking the deadbolt into place.

"Where do you get this stuff? What ladies?" Fillig was affronted. "It's not like I'm Kradduk here. His door is always swinging open and closed. He could have anyone he wanted, but all he does is play games with them. It's not fair. I just want to settle down with a nice female and procreate. Is that too much to ask?"

"No, of course not," said Granu, rubbing Fillig's shoulders. "I think it's nice. Lyssa seems really into you."

"She's not. I can tell. She just likes the danger of this game we're playing. I'm fooling myself. I thought she loved me, but I guarantee you that once this is all over, she will go find someone else. Someone more daring, more exciting. Someone like Kradduk." Fillig stood up from the chair to go pour himself some Giddle.

"Don't sell yourself short," said Granu. "You're a great catch."

"Then why haven't you ever been interested in me?" asked Fillig.

Kradduk's eyes widened, and Granu paused, her glass partway to her mouth.

"It's just not like that. You know it. You've never been into me either. I'm too small, I have creepy eyes, and I'm a touch anal retentive. You can do better than me," she sputtered.

"A touch?" Fillig laughed.

"Your eyes are beautiful," blurted Kradduk. His own mouth dropped for a moment, as if he'd startled even himself before he snapped it shut.

Granu stared unblinking at Kradduk. He found her attractive? What? She'd never considered that either of her best friends could have feelings for her, but here they were, acting as if she were the centerfold of PlayDate. She felt like she was suddenly warped into some parallel universe.

"Let's get back to work," said Kradduk, snatching a paper from the table and retreating to a tweed chair in the corner of the room.

Granu was confused. Did Fillig have feelings for her? He seemed hurt that she'd never considered him as a potential mate. Did Kradduk have feelings for anyone? He certainly never gave her the impression he was ever looking for a real relationship, let alone one with her. All his mooning over Heigle was surprising in its own right, but now he was acting like, well, like Fillig.

"I guess you never really know anyone," she muttered to herself as she made her way down the bustling street back to her apartment.

26

THE TEACHER

Hello Noss, how are you? It's been far too long!"

Granu pressed the phone to her ear while sitting in what she was beginning to call her second office, the dark corner of the coffee shop. She hadn't left Central New Metta High on the best of terms after her near-death experience at the Rockborn home. She and the administrator weren't friends, but she had to find a way to orchestrate this field trip. If the molent on the other end of the conversation detected Granu's forced friendliness, she didn't let on.

"Oh, I'm doing alright. I actually just started working for TCB as their outreach coordinator," said Granu. "Yes, the GRUNT program falls under my control." That was it. Noss's tone changed from suspicious to plain jubilant as she chatted Granu up.

The only way Granu would be allowed to bring fifteen juvies into TCB would be through the GRUNT (Gifted Reserve of Upcoming New Talent) program, aimed at students who were the brightest in their classes. The objective was to get high performing students on TCB's radar early. The program boasted a placement rate of 95% at TCB in various entry-level positions. Parents would eat one another over the chance to get their precious offspring in, so pretending to oversee the program would be a sure way to gain access to the student transcripts Len needed to create forgeries for the juvies Granu had selected for the distraction.

"Oh, you know our program? Great! I'm contacting you to organize a tour for Friday. Trolls only for this particular class. Yes, I'll send over the paperwork, and you pick the students, only TCB quality, of course. This visit will happen outside normal school hours, in the early morning. Yes, I know parents won't want their teens up so late, but they can make an exception for the GRUNT program tour, can't they? It's the only time we offer since it's when our night teams are finishing up. That's what I thought. Ok, I'm sending over the forms now, you fill them out, provide recommendation letters and transcripts—just as a formality mind you—and I'll take care of everything else. Great. Good to talk to you too. Bye, now."

Well, that was easier than expected. Granu had worried that the late notice would be an obstacle, but she didn't want to provide too much of a window for parents to ask questions. The clout of TCB would be enough to ease any concerns over the rushed planning, and Noss would bend over backward to get the forms returned by the end of the day.

Once she had the transcripts, Granu would have Len alter the names so she could get her own, handpicked juvies to take the places of the outstanding students. If she posed as both the school representative to TCB and as the TCB rep to the school, she could make this work. Maybe.

Kradduk made his way to the back of the long room just as Granu was hanging up.

"Hey. You're sure all we need is the official GRUNT request forms and the transcripts to get the field trip scheduled?" she asked.

"Wow, no time for chit-chat, eh?"

"Not really."

"Yes, I'm sure. I spoke with Egleton, the outreach coordinator, and he owes me a favor. I told him my cousin wanted a tour and could only get in through the program, and he's going to fast-track approval for the trip. It's as good as done as soon as you get me the forms. There's nothing to worry about, Gran."

Egleton. That was the real coordinator's name. Hopefully, Noss wouldn't look him up before sending the papers over. As if on cue, her phone dinged with an email notification. Noss had already returned the forms.

"Got 'em!" she said.

"The forms? Already? Didn't you just send the requests over this evening?"

Granu grinned. "Like ten minutes ago. You underestimate the desperation of a parent with a mediocre student. Welp, gotta run."

"Hey, I just got here! You're not going to sit with me while I snag a cup of grainy brainy brew?" Kradduk was just pulling out the chair opposite Granu.

"No. I need to get these to Len so we can get them back before anyone asks the wrong sort of questions. But thanks for picking up my tab."

Kradduk sighed. "No problem. Catch ya later, I guess."

Granu was already halfway across the room when Kradduk's butt hit the chair. She didn't look back.

Travelling by back passages, Granu made her way to Lyssa's place. After a quick glance to ensure she wasn't followed, she rapped on the door three times, then pulled it open and slipped inside. The apartment was dark and quiet.

"Len, are you here? It's me."

Shuffling, groaning, and thumping answered her as Len tumbled out of a closet.

"Granu! What are you doing here? You nearly gave me a conniption!"

Granu waited while he righted himself, then followed him into the living room. She'd told Lyssa she would be coming by in person to get the forgeries handled since she didn't want to be communicating with Len over the internet, but the other troll must have forgotten to let Len in on the plan. He certainly didn't appear ready for company in his slippers and tighty-whities with his hair in disarray.

"I've got the forms. I need the forgeries like yesterday," she said.

Len snatched her laptop from her with a scowl and retreated to his corner chair without bothering to dress. Granu stood awkwardly for a moment, then took a seat on the couch to wait for what seemed like hours but was likely only forty-five minutes.

"Here," barked Len thrusting the computer back at her.

The forgeries were impeccable. Granu nearly felt bad for the deception since the students and parents alike would be thrilled at this sham of an opportunity. Each of her mediocre, wontog-ready juvies was now a shining example of the next leader in New Metta, at least on paper. Granu emailed the doctored forms to Kradduk so he could get the trip approved and was about to leave when Len stopped her by clearing his throat.

"What do you plan to do with the real outstanding students?" he asked.

"Oh, I figured I'd just give leave them in some wrong meeting location," she answered.

"Granu, Granu, Granu. You are adorable. These kids are the *crème de la crème* of Central New Metta High, and they're not going to just accept this blow. They will figure us out long before Bridge Protection does and report us to the police. You don't think there's a single troll in the group that couldn't pull up and tamper with their own transcripts? No, you need something more convincing."

Granu gaped. "Really? You think the juvies will figure us out?"

"The juvies who qualify for GRUNT? Absolutely. Didn't you major in education? Don't you have the first clue what they're capable of?"

Granu stammered. She was top of her class, and here she was, having her smarts questioned by this little cud-chewer. Her eyes tinged pink for a second before she realized that the cud-chewer was right. These weren't normal underling students. She'd have to dispose of the trolls in a more permanent way.

"So, we should kill them? You realize that means premeditation. That falls under 3rd degree deviousness."

"You really are an all-or-nothing kind of troll, aren't you? I'm not suggesting we kill them. We should just change the date of the field trip at the last minute, or at least tell the school we are. Push it back a week due to some fabricated issue on TCB's end. By the time the juvies realize the trip isn't happening, your wontog teens will have torn the bridge apart board by board."

"Oh, I guess that does make more sense." Granu blushed. Sometimes the simplest answers were the best.

"I thought you were supposed to be some criminal mastermind, Granu. Don't you read any comics at all? Villains always manipulate circumstances to come out on top."

Granu stared deadpan at Len, but he had already returned to his computer.

She decided to let it go. All their tensions were running high with the heist looming, and if she ate him, this would all be for naught. "I'll leave you to it then. For now, I need to go introduce myself to some unwary parents."

Len grunted something in return.

27

THE DOUBLE-CROSS

L yssa took a quick survey of the busy passageway, carefully peering into the well-lit horizontal cracks in the rock emanating from the main passage to ensure she was alone, before entering the cave that contained the entrance to her apartment. Water ran from the ceiling, down a wall, and fell off a stalactite into a pool in the crevice just outside her place. Her red, wooden door appeared purple next to the blue fluorescent light shining off the puddle. She pushed it open and called out the code word as it banged shut behind her.

"Fizzbig! Are you here, Len? It's just me."

"My darling!" Len emerged from around the corner, a goofy grin plastered on his pasty face. "I am elated to see you. You've been gone so long, I feared my tiny heart would wither, deprived of your life-giving beauty."

Lyssa laughed. Only a few days had passed since she'd seen Len for the virile mate he could be, and she still wasn't quite used to his fawning. Coming from Fillig, it seemed desperate and pathetic, but from Len, it was poetry the likes of which she'd never heard in underling society. Only her books gave her such beauty in the form of words. A floor-to-ceiling built-in bookcase on the left side of the living room held all her tomes, each faded with use. Three were out of place, removed by Len so he could use their verses to charm her.

It shouldn't surprise her. He spent most of his time coming up with new ways to show his appreciation for her rather than falling back on the tired traditions of fried babes and weeds. Just today, he'd hacked her personal laptop so that when she powered on, a gorgeous mountain scene rendered in blood met her eyes, and a message of love scrolled by, a promise of the future they were planning together as superheroes conquering the world.

"When you leave my sight, it's as if the moon has taken away its light." He gave a little bow as he took her hand and brought it to his lips.

"Been working on that one all day, haven't you? I don't know when you have time for the heist when you're so preoccupied up with me." She stooped to kiss the shorter troll, entangling her fingers into his dark, wiry hair. Many would find him repulsive, but Lyssa knew that a troll was much more than the body that contained him. Len was a rebel, a dangerous force of intelligence and daring, and nothing turned her on more than a troll who craved the light even when it threatened to end him. He was the perfect combination of romance and destruction.

"All I have is time, my love, and I plan to spend all day wrapped up in you." He nipped her bottom lip.

"Sounds divine. Shall I cook us up some supper?"

"I already have a leg roast in the slow cooker. It should be done in ten. Come, sit with me and tell me about your night."

Lyssa took her place next to Len on the overstuffed sofa facing the television. Wires hung from the TV, but otherwise, Len had put everything back in its place. She knew he spent most of his time trapped in her apartment sitting in the blue plaid chair, inches from the screen as he ran his laptop through her system. She didn't mind so long as he cleaned up after himself. She wouldn't have her place looking like some messy bachelor pad.

"My day was great. I convinced Squeath to put me on the eastern defect, so I'll have reason to be elsewhere when everything goes down."

Len smiled and draped an arm over her shoulders. "Good. Is everything still on schedule?"

"Absolutely. Friday marks the beginning of the rest of our lives." She leaned into Len with her head resting on his shoulder, and he lightly brushed his lips against her forehead.

Lyssa's apartment was smaller than Fillig's but in a better locale with access to shops, and the upgrades didn't end at the cream-colored unicorn hide couch with reclining seats or the built-in bookcases. Maise granite, prized for its iridescence, lined the counters and floors, and carefully etched trenches in the ceiling and walls directed the dripping water to the edges of the room and into a drain, creating a soft waterfall sound and ridding the space of the dampness plaguing most New Metta homes. All of her lighting was recessed into crevasses in the stone, giving the space a warm, luminous feel to contrast the chill of cavern life. The thought of leaving it all behind put a rock in the pit of Lyssa's stomach, but it couldn't be helped. The future held far more for her now. The amount of money they planned to steal would make returning home impossible. Eventually, the authorities would come knocking.

"How are things on your end?" she asked. "Are you ready?"

"Yes. Everything is in place, and Granu is clueless," said Len, flipping on the television with the remote. "She came by here today."

"Let's not underestimate her, Len. The only reason she isn't on to us is because she's too focused on TCB and not looking within. She's smart, that one, so we'll have to be careful." Beyond her extensive book learning, Lyssa's true specialty was reading people. Kradduk and Fillig would both be blindsided by the betrayal, but Granu was a risk. If she caught wind that something was amiss, she could botch the entire scheme.

"She's not smarter than I am." It was a statement, but Len looked to Lyssa for reassurance.

"Nobody is smarter than you are."

He grinned. "It really couldn't have worked out better, me hiding out here. You're much better at keeping up fronts than I am. I'm not around her enough to give us away."

Len reclined his seat, kicking his legs up as he retrieved a glass of milk from a little red side table and slurped it down.

"You're the only troll I've ever met who drinks goat milk. You'd think the origins would turn you off," said Lyssa with a shudder.

"Hogwash. It tastes great, it's good for the mind, and if the goats have a problem with it, they can take it up with me."

Lyssa shrugged. It still seemed unnatural to her, but there was a movement of trolls consuming various portions of goat. Ingesting your enemy was the path to enlightenment, according to that quack in the commercials peddling the products. Billy powder, billy milk, billy meat—it was all a way to boost brain development. Lyssa never bought into dietary crazes, and she seemed to do just fine on her own.

"Whatever you say. I'll stick with grog, water, and Kid Piss, thank you very much."

"You don't need any kind of enhancement, my love."

"Yeah, well, we'll all need a little help to get through this week. You're right though, you are very transparent. It's best we keep you away from the others. I still can't believe that no one ever recognizes you for the superhero you are. Your disguise is impeccable, Mr. Peat."

Len's chest puffed out and the arm under Lyssa's head tightened. He turned from the TV to kiss the top of her head. "That's why I love you. You see me, my putrid petal. Oh, that reminds me, I have something to show you."

He pulled his computer from the side table onto his lap. "Look at this. I want to throw off the disguise when this is over. I want the world to see me the way you do, to recognize my greatness."

Lyssa cringed internally. Len was brilliant, true, but his way of interacting with others was somewhat off-putting. She held her breath as she pressed in to see the computer screen. It flashed from the normal desktop image of a moon high over a blood red mountain to a bright green screen with a metallic silver border. Len's face appeared, covered in silver paint with a blue "F" painted over his features. The top of the letter bisected his forehead, and the second line went straight across his nose, making it seem like he was peeking out in the empty space between. His eyes were encircled with thick, smudged, black eyeliner.

He spoke in a booming voice that must have been augmented with reverberation. "I am Leniscious the Fierce, the mastermind behind this heist. Quake in fear of me. I've robbed the most protected place in New Metta, and now, the world shall fall at my feet. I've scoured your security system and embedded myself in the heart of it. You shall never be rid of Leniscious the Fierce! Nobody can rival my brilliance, my daring! Nobody can stop me!"

It ended with him clucking in a maniacal way that Lyssa was sure was meant to be menacing laughter. She burst out laughing.

"What's so funny?" asked Len, his lip quivering.

"Oh! I'm sorry, love," she gasped, wiping at her eyes. "You're serious? Oh, well, Len, I mean, come on."

Len shoved her away from him as he scrambled to his feet, jostling the table and sending the milk careening toward the cast-off computer.

"My laptop!" screamed Len, snatching it off the couch and using his shirt to soak up the drops before they permeated too far into the keyboard. He cast a dirty look at Lyssa as if she caused the accident. Lyssa was pressing her hand over her mouth to try and control her laughter, tears spilling over her cheeks.

"Len, sweetie, I didn't mean anything. I just think it could use some tweaking," she said through tight lips, forming each word with care.

"Then why are you laughing? What's so damn funny?"

"You have to admit, it's a little over the top. The makeup," The laughter bubbled out again. "The voice."

"All superheroes are over the top! How else does the world know their value?" Len's face was bright red.

"Yes, of course, I know." She changed the subject as much to control herself as to redirect Len. "How do you plan to broadcast this, anyway?"

"I'm going to post it on the head of security's machine after I delete all her files. Heigle. The one Kradduk goes on about. It's brazen and effective, and they won't have any clue how I did it. I'll schedule it to broadcast over their entire system. Every computer, phone, and tablet connected to TCB will show my face at once. We'll be long gone by then, of course. I refuse to let Granu get credit for what I did. As if she could pull this off without me."

"I get that, I guess, but why would want to reveal yourself to the masses? I mean, if we get away with this, we will double-cross The Five and we'll have pulled one over on the most guarded place imaginable. Isn't that enough?" Lyssa stood and put an arm around Len's waist. He let her.

"First off, they're not my friends. That disgusting excuse for a female troll Granu only remembered my name because she needed me for this job, and the rest sicken me. Second off, I've spent my life being underestimated, unappreciated, and undervalued. I will have the world know me, know that I'm a superhero." Len deflated, and his voice took on a vulnerable quality that made Lyssa's stomach rumble. "Like you do?"

Lyssa thought the troll might cry. She knew she'd probably lose control and eat him if he did, so she decided to reassure him once more so it didn't come to that.

"I think this makes you a supervillain, not a hero, Len, and that's why I love you. I've seen greatness in you from the start. If you need to do this to prove something to the world, that's fine, but never think you need to prove anything to me."

"Lyssa, you're amazing, and you're right." A gleam came into his eye, and he stood up straighter. "I am the greatest supervillain of all time."

"Yes, you are. But can we work on the name?"

Before he could get upset again, sirens ripped through the cavern. Lyssa stared at Len for a moment, her mind reeling to make sense of the chaos. Had they been found out? She darted to the door, flung it open, and stuck her head out. The passage lights were all blinking, and over the siren, a recorded voice boomed, "New Metta is facing a threat. Seek shelter immediately. I repeat, seek shelter immediately."

A molent scurried up the passage, her chest heaving.

"Hey, what's going on?" yelled Lyssa, but the creature didn't stop to answer. The sirens were nearly deafening, so Lyssa didn't hear the beating of hooves until the unicorn was nearly on top of her. The animal's eyes rolled around in its head, and a laser rainbow shot from its horn, reflecting off the stone and bouncing down the passage. Lyssa slammed the door just in time to hear it splinter as the rainbow struck it.

"What is happening?" yelled Len in order to be heard over the sirens and the voice as the message played again.

"I have no idea, but it has nothing to do with us," replied Lyssa, slamming the deadbolt into place. "There was a unicorn in the caverns."

"A unicorn? How did it get down here?"

"How would I know?"

"All this for one dumb beast? I know they can do some damage when frightened, but this seems like overkill for one unicorn."

Len flipped to the news as Lyssa barricaded the door with a bureau. According to the emergency alert ribbon running at the top of the screen, the billy goats had struck again, this time hijacking the unicorn farm and setting the beasts free in the streets of New Metta. It was their boldest move yet, targeting the entire city rather than one troll, and the supposed catalyst was the manure initiative by the students of Vinkle U. So far, there were many reported injuries, but remarkably, no fatalities. The animals had caused immeasurable damage, however. During an interview, the dean of the university stated that the animals were released on campus prior to escaping the university, that the excrement had been trampled and the collection sites blasted with rainbows, and that any destructive student plans were destroyed. He was careful to emphasize that the manure initiative was not sponsored by any faculty.

"How do the billys always know so much?" asked Len.

"MeMaw says that they have psychic powers, each goat connecting with one troll, and that their religion preaches bungling all troll plans."

Len looked at her like she just sprouted a tail. "Religion? Psychic links? No. They must have access to some amazing technology. Perhaps, if all goes well with TCB, we should rob them next."

"If they had a mind to, I think they could probably rob TCB themselves. Underlord, they could probably destroy New Metta entirely." Lyssa was back on the couch, settling into her favorite spot. According to the report, it would be hours before the unicorns would be contained.

"Yeah, but they don't. It's the strangest thing. All they want to do is be a plague to us. It's really a waste of potential. Maybe we could rally them and get them to accomplish something more meaningful. They could be our fierce little minions." Len was digging through a bag of Naughty O's looking for the treasure inside.

"Where did you get those? Oh, never mind." Lyssa was getting used to the troll cleaning out her pantry nightly. "At least the commotion wasn't about us. You don't think the billys know about our heist, do you?"

"Only if your MeMaw is right, and I don't believe in psychics. I'm the only one of The Five working online, and my intelligence is far superior to any spyware the billys might employ. I'm more worried about another unicorn stampede. I swear, those animals are stupider than humans."

28

BEST LAID PLANS

G ranu, Fillig, and Kradduk were discussing the unicorn debacle when Lyssa approached the corner booth. It was the buzz of the city. Apparently, the sirens had given everyone the scare of a lifetime, convincing each they'd been discovered. As if Bridge Protection would make such a show, setting off the city's emergency alarms while SWAT teams approached a band of criminals on the brink of hitting them all where it would hurt most, the wallet. No, the entire crew would be dead before they even knew they'd been discovered. When the sirens blasted, Fillig screamed like a human toddler, Granu jumped to her feet nearly overturning a table, and Kradduk nearly shat himself in front of a stunning brunette, or at least that's what they each claimed.

To reach the table, Lyssa had to maneuver around a couple molents playing Critterhole. She didn't turn her head despite the oddness of the scene. The smallest of New Metta's underlings usually avoided the game, fearful that a drunk troll or swog would mistake one of them for a rat and fling them at the deadly spike by mistake. These young males must have something to prove. A fair-sized crowd pressed in around them, yelling encouragement and laughing as one of the molents struggled to heave a thrashing squirrel into the air. Lyssa had to shove her way through.

"We are cleared for the concert, trolls," she said, making each of the nerve-shot trolls jump before they all burst into nervous laughter. Granu shot her a warning glare, and when Lyssa shrugged, nodded her head toward the gathered group with a twist of her mouth.

"What? They're all occupied with whatever that is." She seemed to take in the scene for the first time, sneering in response. "They aren't listening to me."

"I'm listening to you," slurred a troll who was lingering at the back of the gathering. He licked his lips and pressed his body against hers. "I'll take you to any concert you want, baby."

"Oh, snog off." She shoved him off her.

"Bitch."

Fillig rose to defend her honor, but Lyssa waved a hand dismissively. The drunk was already back to goading the molents.

"As I said, we are good to go. So says our technological genius." Lyssa held her arms out waiting for a response.

"Really? You beautiful bearer of good news," replied Fillig, leaning in to kiss her on the cheek before scooting to the inside of the booth. She absently wiped the back of a hand across her face as she took the vacant seat next to him, opposite Kradduk.

She dropped her voice to a loud whisper. "I got Squeath to allow you to work on the fabricated defect in the hall near the treasury starting tomorrow, Fil, but he wants me to lead my own team in working on the true defect. It was the only way I could swing it without looking suspicious."

Granu's head swiveled around to scan the faces of the nearest creatures. When she seemed satisfied that nobody was paying them any mind, she said, "Wait, that means that you'll be out of position when we strike. Absolutely not. We're all going in together. And what are you even doing here? You're not supposed to be seen with us, remember?"

Lyssa looked around with comically wide eyes, mimicking Granu's paranoid maneuver. Granu didn't know if the gesture was to appease her or to mock her, but nobody was paying any attention to the table of trolls sitting in the corner. Meanwhile the molent, loudly proclaiming he had the situation under control, was now being chewed up by the squirrel, his blood splattering over the onlookers as he thrashed. Lyssa winced in a show of sympathy.

"But the true defect could be catastrophic to the structure of the western corner if someone should mess up, say, at precisely the moment the security systems go down. Taco Protection would assume the outage was due to the damage. It may buy us some time and draw out any remaining patrols not dealing with your wontog-crazed juvies."

Lyssa seemed to stress the code words, her voice mocking. There was no doubt about it, Lyssa was openly taking digs at Granu. Wasn't she the one who supported implementing a code in the first place? Granu rolled her eyes. At this point, she had more to worry about than a little mouthing off. She didn't like the idea of the team being any more scattered than the plan already called for. It increased the chances of someone getting caught and being caught meant certain death.

However, adding to the chaos at a pivotal moment could work in their favor, even if it did mean one less troll to carry the cash. The element of surprise was integral to the success of the plan, and rocking the bridge while juvies rampaged would certainly be surprising if not fatal. Granu shuddered as she realized she appreciated Lyssa's foresight. The difference between success and becoming dinner could be a matter of mere seconds. Granu took a deep breath, swallowing her pride.

"Alright. It's a good idea."

"Of course it is," chimed Fillig.

"So, now that we know what the inside of the taco stand looks like, does anyone have any ideas for ways to carry more cash? With this one out, we'll need them." Granu knew the duffel bags would hold a lot, but nowhere near the amount in the boxes on those metal shelves.

Kradduk spoke up. "What about those suitcases with wheels? You know, the kind the airlines let you take as carry-on. We would have the bags strapped to us, and if we rolled those instead of just carrying a bag, we could toss an extra bag on top of it and carry another. They should be easy enough to toss down the exit hatch into Protection Central, too."

"Kradduk, that's a great idea!" said Granu. Working at TCB gave Kradduk more real-world experience than the rest of the crew had combined. Of all of them, he was the only one who'd ever been on a plane. Granu thought putting that much trust in human engineering was foolish at best, but here he was, using his observations to fix their problem.

"Do you know where we can get three?" she asked.

"Yeah. The Big Taco has loads, and they're not valuable enough to guard. I'll get them."

Fillig was chewing the inside of his cheek. "Granu, are you sure the Bridge Protection offices will be empty? What about Big Pig?"

Granu nodded. "Big Pig will be the first one out the door when my juvies turn, and with Lyssa's secondary distraction, Little Pig will be the only one left to respond. It should be empty."

"And if it's not?" he replied.

"Well, that's what we have blasters for, isn't it? Fil, you're not going to human out on me are you? I need you to keep your head in the game. Once we clear Bridge Protection, we'll be mere steps from the western tower. Then we go up. Got it?"

Fillig looked from Granu to Lyssa, then steeled his features with a deep breath. "Yeah."

"Great." Perhaps having Fillig obsessed with a female was just the thing she needed to keep him from losing his nerve. "Oh, Kradduk," she said, turning to face the hulking troll sitting beside her, "one more thing. You will be picking up the rest of our supplies from *your guy* tonight before you go into work."

"What? He made the deal with you, he'll be expecting you," replied Kradduk.

"Well, he'll just have to be disappointed, then, won't he? Oh, and I told him you'd show him a little something, too."

"Oh, man! Come on, Gran! I just bailed us out, and this is how you thank me?"

Granu gave her best impression of the classic Kradduk wink and took a long swig of grog. Kradduk's face twisted into an unfamiliar expression of either horror or amusement, Granu couldn't tell which.

"Alright, ladies and gents, I need to get some rest before reporting for my shift in hell," said Fillig, smacking a stack of cash down on the table to cover his portion of the tab before taking leave. "So, Lyssa, want to come to my place for a bit? I've got a rack of ribs and a bottle of Giddle we can split."

"That doesn't sound like rest," said Granu.

"It better not be," said Kradduk with a grin.

"Is that your way of seducing me?" Lyssa batted her eyelashes, making Granu groan.

"Um, well, I mean, if you want, I guess, but I really do have ribs and Giddle."

"Relax, Romeo. Yeah, I could use some grub. Let's go."

"See you later Gran," said Fillig. By the smile painted across his goofy face, you'd think he'd completely forgotten that Lyssa wasn't really into him. What a fool. Kradduk followed suit, paying the rest of the tab on his way out.

With everyone gone, Granu pulled out her notebook, deeming it less likely to draw attention than her laptop, and resumed obsessively pondering every variable of the plan, sketching building schematics from memory and jotting notes about where to dump the excess bags if they needed to make a run for it. The only weak link was her—well, her distraction, anyway.

She was good at identifying the cues of wontog, but even the top psychologists couldn't pin it down to the minute. Perhaps she should have thought of a different distraction. What happened if none of her juvies transitioned at the right moment? She sighed. She was just being paranoid. She'd gathered as many juvies as possible to maximize her odds, and she was sure that at least one or two would snap when she sprayed her "perfume," which was a mixture of male troll blood and female troll urine. The combination should bring out their most primal urges, triggering the change if they were anywhere close. That was another of Len's contributions. He really was bright. She made a mental note to treat him better when this was all over. Besides, now Lyssa would be creating a secondary distraction, so in the worst-case scenario there should be a loud structural blow to the bridge to draw Bridge Protection away from the vault. As much as Lyssa bothered her, Granu had to admit that the troll added value to her little crew of miscreants.

So, as long as Len took down the computers and Fillig blew a hole in the wall, there was little that could go wrong.

"Hey, Gran, where's the rest of the crew this morning?" asked a chipper Kell. The bartender was standing next to her table, looking at her like she just walked in out of the sunlight.

She snapped her notebook shut. "Oh, hey Kell. When did you get here?"

"It's pretty early. Dreatte clocked out a while ago. I figured you looked busy, so I left you alone. You know where the bar is. So, where's the gang?"

"Fil is working two jobs in addition to waiting hand and foot on a female troll that seems to barely tolerate his existence, and Kradduk's likely shacked up with some floozy. I'm just here for a quick nightcap."

"The sun's been up for two hours, Granu. I don't think this qualifies as a nightcap."

Granu wrinkled her nose at the molent. "Just bring me my grog, smartass."

"As you wish."

29

PREPARATIONS

W hat are you doing with those?" The sharp voice held notes of accusation, but so did everything that came out of Heigle's mouth.

Kradduk dragged the three carry-on luggage bags tied together behind him through the white tiled hall. The wheels rolling over lines of grout made a train-like chugging sound that reverberated off the empty walls. The space called for pictures or some other accoutrement to compensate for the lack of windows, but there was nothing adorning the clinical white walls as far as the eye could see. TCB cared about the comfort of their workers less than they did about upholding the law. Heigle, in stark contrast, seemed scrupulous to a fault. Kradduk wondered how long she'd last here.

"Borrowing them. I'm taking an in-town vacation." Kradduk knew that the head of security was likely to catch him, so he hadn't bothered to sneak. He'd merely walked to the executive level closet containing travel gear, helped himself, and sauntered down the hall like he owned the place. Heigle's sudden appearance caused him no concern. He would need to shake her before he stashed them, however. He could explain taking TCB property for personal use but stashing it near the treasury for ease of access come heist day was an entirely different matter.

"They belong to TCB. You have no right to borrow them unless it's for a business trip. What do you mean by an in-town vacation, anyhow?"

"I mean that I've got a suite at the Golden Tower for the weekend, and I have a romantic getaway planned. Dammon doesn't care if I borrow TCB supplies, or at least he never did before. Is your employment here so superfluous that you're on inventory duty now?"

Heigle's face flushed to match the polyester suit that clung to her curves with perfection. "I'm to report any and all suspicious activity."

"Oh, ok. And borrowing three suitcases is awfully suspicious. Who knows what I might be up to. Transporting valuable pencils from the stock room, no doubt. Or pudding cups. No, tacos! Go ahead, report me."

"If it's a romantic getaway, why do you have three?" Heigle's chin rose victoriously and a smile played at the corner of her mouth. She thought she had him.

"Romance means different things to different trolls." Kradduk winked, and Heigle's face grew three shades darker. She looked like an incredibly attractive, blonde tomato. Kradduk laughed as the smugness on her face melted into anger. He could spend a lifetime torturing this female and love every second.

"You sicken me."

"Yet you've followed me around every night since we met. Are you having regrets about how our evening together ended?"

A frustrated squeal peeled out of the bombsell's throat, and Kradduk laughed again. She turned on her heels and charged down the hallway, out of view. Kradduk was sure she wouldn't report the theft, but even if she did, his swog boss would side with him. While TCB guarded its treasure fiercely, the swogs in charge encouraged a fraternal atmosphere that didn't include keeping company supplies on lockdown, particularly if they could be used to get some ass.

Kradduk had secured the remaining supplies the night before. Eight pulse-resistant duffel bags, three standard Wickles bags, cross-body straps, and everything else they would need to load the cash. Granu could only fit two duffel bags on her back due to her short torso, but Fillig and Kradduk could each get three, making up for Lyssa missing out on the exit. Add those to the bags and suitcases they planned to carry, and they'd make off with a nice haul—perhaps not cleaning out the entire vault, but enough to set them up for life. It was all stuffed into the three suitcases he'd just snuck by Heigle. If those bags were opened, he'd have difficulty coming up with a plausible explanation. He hoped Heigle hadn't noticed him sweating.

Kradduk produced a disposable phone from his pocket, one of the prepaids supplied by Granu, and sent a text. A moment later, the device chimed, a text notification from Len. It was go time. Len tripped a reset code in the security system for this quadrant, and it took exactly thirty seconds to reboot. Kradduk had to get to the closet, stuff the suitcases filled with empty duffel bags inside, and get out of the hall before the camera was back online. Thirty seconds, flat. After that, the camera would come back on, and the closet would lock. Crossing his fingers, hoping that nobody came into the hall during that time, Kradduk darted in, thundered down the hall, and skidded to a stop at the closet, catching the door knob to halt his momentum. He flung open the door, stuffed the bags in, slammed it shut, and ran back the way he came. Launching his body through the door, clear of the affected camera, he nearly collided with Heigle, who must have been lurking. She squealed in alarm at his sudden appearance.

"Watch where you're going! What in heaven are you up to now?"

"Why are you always here every time I turn around?" It was Kradduk's turn to be frustrated, and it wasn't lost on Heigle. She smiled, a dazzling sight that spread to illuminate her eyes. Kradduk's anger subsided.

"I am where I'm needed. Always."

"Well, you're not needed here. I'm through playing your games." He pushed by her and headed to his office to put in a couple hours of work. The troll narrowed her eyes at him but let him go without further badgering.

During the next hour and a half, Heigle passed his glass wall no fewer than ten times. *She must be spinning her wheels to find out what I'm up to*, he thought, but he was confident that she wouldn't find anything. The only possible evidence against him was locked in a custodian's closet that could only be opened by a custodian—until Len took down the security system again, that is. The thought of the damning evidence stuffed in the closet gave Kradduk a thrill.

The last time he saw the head of TCB security walk by, her eyes locked on his, he counted to one hundred after she disappeared then shut down his computer, picked up his briefcase, and left. This was his last full night working for TCB. The thought put a smile on his face, and he whistled all the way to Goron's.

30

STONE RESOLVE

The next night ended before Granu had time to register it beginning. Kradduk had a new horror story to add to Granu's unfortunate experience at Shorty's—something to do with watching mole rat porn while Shorty and his troll were in the corner doing heaven knows what—but Granu didn't feel bad for him in the slightest. He'd knowingly sent her to that cud-chewer, and he deserved every moment of humiliation he suffered. Besides, he ended up with extra PODs and a set of ankle holsters for their pulse blasters. From the sound of it, he didn't have to show anything to get them either. The way she saw it, he got off easy.

Keeping away from Shorty was only part of the reason Granu had sent Kradduk, in truth. It also kept her from having to spend any one-on-one time with Lyssa. Granu wondered, briefly, if the red-head had played her, getting herself out of the most dangerous part of the heist to watch from the sidelines while still pulling in the cash. Either way, the facts were the same. They could use an extra diversion, and Lyssa had been able to get Fillig in position with the rest of the demo team. She'd done her part, and if she wanted out of the danger, Granu wouldn't hold it against her.

"Hey, Gran, look at this," said Fillig, emerging from his room. He pulled a ski mask over his face.

"What the hell? You look like you're about to rob the sleaze-e-mart. Take that off!"

"But it's added protection! I thought you were all about caution?"

"Fillig, we're going to have sunsuits. And you look ridiculous."

"I thought I looked like a badass." Great. Now Fillig was going to mope again. Granu didn't have the patience to pander to him today.

"No. It's stupid."

Fillig snorted but must have picked up on Granu's mood and dropped the conversation. Her throbbing temples rattled her brain. The pain was so great, Granu thought her head may explode if she didn't rest, so she snuggled down into Fillig's old corduroy couch, leaving him to his pouting. In ten short hours, she would enter TCB with a group of adolescent trolls intent on seeing the inner workings of the most successful company in New Metta, all of whom were completely unaware of the danger posed to themselves. It hadn't been hard to get their folks to sign the release forms. It was every parent's dream to see his or her little wart get hired at TCB, and none of them had bothered to check on Granu's phony credentials. For their part, the juvies were just glad to be out of school for the day. She did feel a tad guilty leading a pack of young ones into the center of a dangerous heist, but they had to grow up one way or another, and wontog was likely to kill off a few of them regardless. She might as well make use of it.

Fillig muttered a begrudging "good day" after rifling through the kitchen for a bedtime snack and slamming his bedroom door.

"Get some sleep," she responded to the back side of the door, rolling over to face the couch cushions, her eyes trailing up and down the faded green ribbing.

Memories of the attack she'd suffered at the hands of her charges flooded her mind, causing her to toss and turn as she chased sleep. Wontog, the change a troll made when their mating hormones surged into effect, was vile, violent, and uncontrollable. Some teens oozed green or yellow goo from their pores, some bled from their eyes, and nearly all endured fits of rage, shredding any living creature within smelling range. They beat on doors, scaled windows, crashed through walls, thrashed, kicked, scratched, spat. You name it, it happened during wontog. The look in Tigg's eyes, the raw hunger as he had charged her—that image would be with Granu until the day she died. In the moment, she'd fallen back on protocol, ducking his advance and fending him off as she scrambled to her purse where she kept her restraints. That's when Beda bit. She'd never seen it coming, but she'd felt the searing pain of teeth sinking into her side, and as Beda shook her head back and forth, her jaws clamped down, Tigg attacked again. If it weren't for Gilda, the groundskeeper checking in for her shift, the Rockborn teens would have devoured her.

That's how Granu became so adept at smelling out wontog. When you lived through something so horrible it haunted your dreams at night, you became damned good at recognizing the warning signs. She would never be taken by surprise again. She was sure she smelled that familiar stench clinging to the juvies she'd chosen, yet she was putting herself in their paths anyway. Considering she'd avoided all schools and areas where juvies congregated since the attack, this was insanity. There would be fatalities, she was sure of it, but she intended on ensuring that her crew was not counted among them. Even the parents of her charges didn't know how close wontog was or they wouldn't agree to let them leave home, instead keeping them contained in specially equipped teen bedrooms deep in their caverns. Granu thought that if she ever reproduced, her offspring would spend the time from 12 to 18 years old on lockdown, at least until the change occurred. That was how it was in the old days, before the Troll Discrimination Acts. Now, locking teens up was as illegal as discriminating based on the Blight.

Once this was all over, Granu wouldn't have to worry about wontog until she had kids of her own. She could live in the mountains or maybe by the beach, where hunting bans and Discrimination Acts didn't exist. Perhaps Fillig and Kradduk would stay with her, or maybe Kradduk would keep true to his word and travel Fairbax in search of willing females for his exploits. Either way, they'd be free.

Perhaps if Fillig's couch weren't so damned soft, she could get some sleep. She tossed and turned throughout the early hours of the day before giving up and moving to the floor. It was no luxurious coarse granite, having been worn down by feet over the years, but it was better than the sofa. Fillig snored steadily in the other room, and when Granu finally got comfortable on the floor, she could only focus on the hog-like sound reverberating through the caverns of his home.

The sun was blocked by a blocking boulder painted green and white to match the old couch, but Granu knew it raged outside, just waiting for some poor sap to stumble out into it only to have every molecule of water in his body evaporate spontaneously, leaving him a solid rock in the image of his former self. This was the time when she should be deep in sleep, but she couldn't calm her mind. With nothing left to plan, she felt helpless, committed to a course of action that would bring about the end of everything she knew.

She went to Fillig's cupboard to find something to munch on. Her rummaging unearthed a stale pack of cigarettes tucked into the back of Fillig's junk drawer. To heaven with it. Her nerves needed it. She lit one and grabbed a bag of petrified pixies from the pantry. She loaded them up with hot sauce and turned the television on, lowering the volume so she wouldn't disturb Fillig in the next room, and wasted the rest of the day watching a marathon of *Living Above*, a reality show about a society of underlings creating a town in the mountains. Granu snorted each time the sun fried someone. They earned it with their hubris as far as she was concerned. No intelligent underling trusted some shoddy roof.

"Did you get a wink of sleep?" asked Fillig, emerging hours later from his room with a stretch and a wide yawn. "What is that smell?"

He wore a powder green robe which fell open every time he moved.

"Fil, man, put the boulders away," griped Granu, shielding her eyes and pointedly ignoring his question.

"Oh, sorry." He tied the robe tightly around his middle.

"No, I couldn't sleep. Your damned couch is soft enough for a human to cuddle."

"Yeah, I can't afford the kind of furniture Kradduk can. That won't be the case tomorrow if we pull this off. Then I'll sleep like a baby on Maise granite with a pillow of cold cash, and so will you. Grainy brainy brew?"

Granu grunted as Fillig filled a cup for her. Coffee was one of the few human concoctions the underworld embraced, as its effects were amplified in trolls, which was helpful considering how deeply they slept. The chunks of small mammal brain soaked up and enhanced the bitterness. Granu could use the boost after her sleepless night, and Fillig needed it to fully wake.

"That's a pretty big if. I called Len. He's ready and standing by. He's going to tap into the system first so that he can see when we are in position through TCB's monitors, and as soon as the juvies start acting up, he'll notify Lyssa and tank the system. We'll be out of contact for exactly 15 minutes. You will need to bust the wall open as soon as you hear me and Kradduk running up the hall. We may have a pack of wontog-possessed teenagers chasing us, so don't dawdle. We get in and out through the floor hatch in under 10. Got it?"

"Yes, Gran, I got it. I got it yesterday at Goron's, the day before at midnight snack, and last night before bed. I got it during daylight hours when I was trying to sleep, and you kept chanting it under the door. You need to relax and trust us. You know, maybe you should lay off the coffee."

Granu sneered at him as she refilled her mug, then she shrugged. "I know, I'm sorry. Do you have your sunsuit ready?"

"Of course. Do you think I'm going to open a door to the day completely unprotected? Really, Gran. But are you sure I have to wear the sniggle-cleaning suit? It still smells like vomit."

"It's that or leave Lyssa without one. I know she won't be chased, but she's still supposed to meet us at the van. Though I might prefer Lyssa as a statue."

"I'll put it on under my clothes so all I need to do is snag the head-piece. Do I just carry that in to work?"

"Kradduk packed the head pieces in the suitcases. That way, there's less bulk to smuggle in tonight." She wrinkled her nose as a thought occurred to her. "You'd better grab the right one. If I end up with your barf bag, I'll rip your arms off and beat you with them."

Fillig nodded. "Lyssa has hers already, right?"

"Yes. As soon as she detonates her PODs, she'll get out. She should beat us to the meeting point. How did you get out of work yesterday and tonight?"

"I told them I had the flop. Nobody wants to risk exposure to that! I told the quarry that too. I still don't understand why I had to keep working there. You said I could quit after I got the coverings, then you said I could quit when the heat died down, but here I am, still picking dirt out of festering wounds. The next thing you're going to tell me is I have to go back when this is all over. Nobody cares about the suits anymore."

"Our coverings say "New Metta Quarry" in three different spots. As soon as TCB gets emptied by trolls wearing quarry suits, they will care again, I promise you."

"That's why I should be far away from there!"

"And you can be, as soon as we're successful. If we fail, you'll need to keep your head down and go about business as usual. That means going back."

Fillig gasped then began to sputter. "What? You don't think they'd suspect the guy who's been daylighting grunt work while he has a sweet gig at TCB—the target of our little heist, might I remind you?"

"No. We'll come up with a story that leaves you needing cash. Make it look like TCB doesn't pay enough. Everyone knows they're crooks. It won't be a surprise to hear they treat their employees like crap."

A knock on the door announced the arrival of Len and Lyssa. Fillig leapt to his feet and checked his robe before answering the door. Len was looking more vibrant than Granu remembered. He even cracked a smile as he greeted her.

"Are you ready for this? You'd better have the van there when we pull out or we're all done for," said Granu, looking him up and down appraisingly.

217

"Good evening to you too, Granu. Lovely to see you." Len gave an exaggerated bow.

Granu resisted the urge to growl.

"Leniscious the Fierce is ready for anything," he added.

"He's ready, don't you worry," chimed Lyssa before anyone could comment on Len's self-given nickname. Granu bit down on her tongue.

"Ok, then. Grab some grub and get in place. I guess it's time. See you on the other side." She gave the biggest, most confident smile she could muster, determined to appear calm and collected, then left to pick up her horde of hormonal teens.

31

THE BIG TACO

Granu led her group of juvies to the cavern beneath the south-eastern tower of TCB. An enormous elevator that could hoist thirty trolls or five sniggles at a time waited, doors open, as they piled in, weighing the apparatus down despite the high capacity. In close quarters with teens who could enter wontog at any moment, Granu's skin itched, her heart raced. The elevator groaned as it carried them up through layers of earth and stone.

The teens chattered nervously, most only casually acquainted from their classes at Central Metta High. Their parents were overjoyed the teens were accepted into GRUNT, and they didn't question Granu when she delivered their invitations complete with instructions on where to meet, despite the students' mediocre academic records. Perhaps each set of parents thought their offspring the only under-achiever of the bunch, but most likely, they were just hoping nobody noticed that little junior wasn't TCB material. With any luck, none of the parents would find out about the delayed field trip notice. With no cause to contact the school, they'd remain oblivious until it was all over, and the teens who were actually accepted would have no idea they'd been replaced.

Fourteen juveniles showed. Granu lost one to wontog just hours before it was time to leave, which was expected. Surprised more hadn't already turned, she was proud to have gauged them so well even if it did mean she may have imagined symptoms in a few. A quick survey of her teens told her otherwise. Three were beginning to sweat already, a symptom frequently dismissed as normal troll cooling, but the crisp air was chilly today, and Granu knew better. The rotten smell of wontog made the air thick. She didn't have much time. She prayed to the Underlord that none of the juvies lost control in the confined space of the elevator or she wouldn't live long enough to pull off the heist.

Granu's breath rushed from her lungs as they reached the first floor and the doors opened. She was alive. For now. She took a deep breath of fresh air and faced the gauntlet of consumerism, giddy with relief as she scanned the gift shop and lobby beyond. From what Fillig had told her, the other side of the bridge was a mirror to this one: two elevators, two entrances, one huge gift shop connecting them. Nodding to the friendly cashier, Granu led her pack through the store and up the gleaming marble steps leading to the reception desk.

There were three stories to TCB, though nobody could tell by looking at the exterior. Two office levels were hidden beneath the topside with security checks and the gift shops located on the bottom floor. The group emerged into a small space, all white, glass, and chrome, where a swog in a red polyester suit sat at an elevated desk. At first Granu thought it odd that a swog would be on receptionist duty considering everything Kradduk and Fillig told her about speciesism at TCB, but then she realized that the receptionist doubled as security personnel. Now, that made sense.

Whatever the case, the swog greeted them with a smile and signed them in, comparing each troll with the picture on the transcripts loaded into the computer system. Granu said a silent thank you to Len when everything seemed to check out. The receptionist gave Granu a stack of ID badges to distribute. Her lips turned downward as deep ridges formed on her wide, pink forehead when she surveyed the waiting juvies.

"Is he alright?" she asked, waving her hooved hand toward Kadu, one of the males near the rear of the group, who looked around disoriented, his head swiveling from side to side as his body slightly rocked back and forth. His chest was heaving, a sheen of sweat making his wide face glisten in the fluorescent lights. His pupils were dilated, his breathing ragged, his arms wrapped around himself. Shit. Granu opened her mouth, but the swog didn't wait for an answer before picking up the phone.

"We have a 503 in the lobby. I repeat, a 503 in the lobby."

"What's a 503?" asked Granu when the receptionist smacked the phone down.

"Wontog."

A collective gasp emerged from the teens as they stepped away from Kadu, leaving a circle inside which he stood, looking panicked.

"But don't worry, we have a containment facility in the Bridge Protection office. He will be safe and so will all of you. I'm glad I spotted it before he turned. TCB takes pride in our high level of training for on-the-job emergencies like this."

Of course they do, thought Granu.

"It will be alright, everyone. You'll be alright, young troll." The swog nodded reassuringly at the rest of the group, all of whom were gaping at Kadu. His eyes were beginning to turn red and yellow mucus beaded on his cheeks. Granu put on her best shocked face and thanked the receptionist as she ushered the rest of her group through the security door. She left poor Kadu to wait for the containment staff before the nosy swog had time to notice signs in the others.

A cold claw of fear wrapped around her heart. There was no turning back now. A Bridge Protection patrol led by a grawback holding a restraint jacket rushed past them, out the doors. Boots on the tile and muffled shouts told Granu they'd confronted Kadu, but the sounds quickly faded as order returned.

The rest of the juvenile trolls were excitedly chattering about how close they'd come to witnessing a wontog. One shared a story of his older sister eating a neighbor's pet pixie farm while another hyperventilated.

"Calm down, everyone. Kadu will be fine. In fact, he's lucky he was at such a well-prepared facility when he turned," said Granu, hoping an authoritative voice would hush them before they drew the attention of anyone who would think to run a check on the rest of the group. Instead, it seemed to excite them more.

When Kradduk showed up to direct the group, he had to clear his throat three times, growing progressively louder, before they quieted down enough for him to speak. He wore a more loose-fitting suit than usual, likely to hide the bulky sunsuit beneath. Granu felt sexy in her added layers, like she'd put on an extra fifty pounds, but she knew it was artificial.

"Hello, and welcome to TCB. I'm Kradduk, one of the operations managers. I'm pleased to welcome you, but unfortunately, I will be unable to personally see to your visit. Rest assured that you are in good hands with the head of security, the charming and lovely Heigle Limestone." Kradduk gave Granu a quick look accompanied by a shrug before a rotund blonde in a power suit rounded the corner.

Granu thought she'd prepared for everything, but this was outside the realm of possibility. Heigle must have gotten wind that Kradduk was planning to escort Granu around the building and grown suspicious. Granu cussed under her breath. She should have thought of this. A huge blunder like underestimating the head of TCB security could get them all killed. If she had a way to call it all off without endangering everyone, she would, but Granu couldn't risk making any changes at this stage. It would endanger her entire crew. Besides, the wheels were already in motion. It would take an act of the Underlord to halt them now without the scheme being discovered. All she could do was hope like heaven Heigle wasn't prepared for wontog possessed teens the way the receptionist was.

"Hello kids. You can call me Ms. Limestone." She cast an irritated look in Kradduk's direction. "And I'm pleased to welcome you to TCB. Who here plans on pursuing a career with us in the future?" Nearly every troll raised a hand as Heigle continued her introduction.

She narrated a journey through all accessible areas of TCB's second floor. With the students, she was light, airy, and a bit funny if you weren't attempting to find a way out of her company. It was no wonder Kradduk fell for her. She was in the midst of a story about the materials used to build the facility—apparently salvaged from a nearby village after it was ransacked during the Human Taming Wars of 2020—when she stopped mid-sentence and spoke into her headset. Granu could hear her own heartbeat as adrenaline coursed through her system. She'd often envisioned her own death, but this was never the way it happened.

"What? I'll be right there." Heigle didn't bother to speak to Granu or give instructions before darting down the hallway, a blur of pinstriped navy wool and a cacophony of heels on tile. Granu waited for the sound to completely fade before taking a deep breath to steady her voice and addressing her teens. Maybe Kradduk had found a way to get Heigle away from them.

"Everybody, follow me. I've done some research on TCB myself, and since we've so suddenly lost our guide, I will continue our tour," she announced. This could work. Thirteen trolls stared at her, and four pairs of eyes were blazing red. A shudder shook her spine as she fought back a flashback of the Rockborn juvies. There was so much blood, and those red eyes, she could still see them piercing into her flesh. More than apprehension by Bridge Protection, she was terrified of this part. Wontog. Still, she thanked the Underlord that it was happening even as she quickened her step, swallowing the colossal lump in her throat. This was all a part of the plan, so long as she lived through it.

Granu halted abruptly. Her group was now gathered in the cafeteria, located on the first floor in the very center of the bridge. Creatures came and went with trays of food, and the din of chatter and activity would cover early signs of wontog. Here, they would cause the most chaos, and here, Granu was surrounded without any clear path to an exit. She pushed the thought away. If she turned back now, Kradduk and Fillig would be apprehended. They would be killed.

"Many say that the heart of any company is where the food is," she said when she was sure all of her teens were gathered around. Five red pairs of eyes stared at her hungrily, and another troll was beginning to shake. Damn, she was good at predicting wontog.

Don't let that be my last thought.

"Well, TCB employs a top chef to create the ultimate menu of tacos. Chef Gonzo. I'm sure you've all seen him on television going head-to-head with amateur cooks. Gather around and tell me what type of tacos you want, and I'll snag us some grub."

She had to move fast if she was going to make this distraction effective. If it happened in the halls, Bridge Protection would be able to contain it too quickly, and her crew would be vulnerable as they loaded the cash. It was now or never. Granu cast a wary look at Big Pig, who was scanning the room from his perch next to the food window. Rolls of pink flesh protruded from above his beltline, making him look like a cone of giblet jelly ice cream. He was far more dangerous, though.

Granu produced her perfume bottle, turned it outward, and sprayed it over her teens as they crowded in shouting their food preferences. Indignant protests erupted, but Granu pushed through the group and was running for the stairwell before they had time to process the events. Glancing over her shoulder, she saw three of her juvies set upon a stunned Big Pig, who had abandoned his stool to rush at them. He was no match. Vogel, the shy, sweet troll with big, brown eyes, sank her teeth into his flabby neck. Blood spattered the tables and panicked onlookers as she ripped him to shreds.

Granu ran as fast as her stubby legs could go, leaning forward to urge them on. The first time she'd faced wontog, her instincts had failed her; she wouldn't let that happen again. Her lungs protested with searing pain as she huffed and puffed, but on she pushed, desperate to reach the doors. Screams of teens losing their grip on reality and slipping into full-blown wontog preceded more screams, these from the unfortunate creatures closest to them. Dishes shattered on tile as lunches were dropped, adding to the chaotic sounds of surprise, fear, and death.

The ragged breath of someone following close behind her made Granu go stiff. For a moment, she was convinced it was Tigg chasing her down again. She ran through the swinging cafeteria doors, up a hallway, and to the corner building where a stairwell would take her to the third floor, not looking to see who trailed her. She was still regretting her last look back. When she reached the top, she stopped abruptly. Someone crashed into her, but there was no searing pain, no bite. It was Gigi, a chatty juvie from her tour. Six juvenile trolls had come with her in all, and they were staring in horror, some rocking back and forth, all panting.

"Ms. Scoria, what just happened? Did you see Bannir? And Vogel? I think Forster may be dead," Gigi babbled. Tears welled in her red eyes.

"Yes, they went into wontog."

"How did you know to run? You were already getting out before they started attacking each other," said Sunu, a sullen boy with shaggy hair and a scar across his cheek. "And what did you spray on us? It smells terrible."

Gigi continued. "We followed on instinct. I don't think anyone else came this way."

"I've been trained to spot it. I felt it, and I sprayed you with something to try and stop it. I did what came natural just as all of you knew to follow without being told. Now, we need to figure out how to get out of here before they kill everyone," said Granu.

"Then why did we go up the stairs? Instead of down? Wouldn't it have made more sense to get to ground?"

Damn juvie trolls and their infernal logic. "Because we need to stay out of Bridge Protection's way. Now come on." Her explanation didn't make sense. The stairs would have taken them down into the caverns, so Granu started walking before there were any more questions.

She quickly moved through the white halls from the southwestern quarter to the northwestern one. She followed the path she'd memorized from the blueprints to the hall attached to the treasury, where she found Fillig's team hard at work erecting a scaffold along the wall. Concrete dust filled the air from where they anchored it.

Fillig looked up to catch her eye, nodded once, then began speaking to his demolition team. Brows wrinkled, claws scratched heads, and mouths moved quickly as they talked, though Granu couldn't make out the words. A moment later, the crew cleared the hall, disappearing around the corner with Fillig bringing up the rear.

Just before he dipped out of sight, he turned and motioned to Granu to stay back before he pressed the tiny button on the device in his palm.

The deafening sound of four PODs detonating at once caused two more of her trolls to lose control. Gigi and Braun dove for the others, who fought them the way they were taught from birth. Heaven, these juvies were better at handling wontog than Granu had been. She had to get out of there.

Suddenly, all the lights went out. This was really happening. Granu fought for her breath, finding herself suddenly plunged into her worst nightmare: she was trapped in the dark with wontog-possessed trolls. Thankfully, softer back-up lighting kicked on—the emergency system.

She didn't have time to ponder the situation. She operated on pure instinct, running away from the teens and toward the vault. Kradduk burst from a nearby closet door as soon as he heard the blast, dragging the carry-on bags stuffed with supplies. He joined Granu as she ran into the smoke, both nearly colliding with Fillig hurtling through the air from the opposite direction. Fillig pulled his ski mask over his face as the three of them dove through the fresh hole in the wall into the room beyond.

"Really Fil? What the fuck?" said Granu, the sight of Fillig in his stupid mask jarring her brain into functioning again.

"Shut it and load up."

Kradduk unzipped the suitcases and tossed the head coverings and duffel bags to the others. They quickly ripped away their outer clothing so they could access the zippers on their sunsuits beneath and secured the head coverings, moving faster than they had during their many practice runs in Fillig's living room. When all zippers were zipped and buckles were buckled, they grabbed the bags and made for the shelves. Granu was the first to come to the stark realization that the room was empty. Shelves that once housed rows and rows of boxes of cash and jewels were bare from floor to ceiling. A string of profanity ripped out of Kradduk's mouth.

"It's a trap! Get out now!" screamed Granu as Bridge Protection patrols poured in through the hole. Kradduk yanked at the floor hatch, but it was soldered shut and didn't budge.

"Where is Lyssa's diversion?" she yelled, hysteria bubbling from deep within.

The ceiling hatch was the only viable exit, so long as it wasn't blocked as well. Kradduk unholstered his pulse blaster and shot at the incoming patrols, sending them flying backward through the hole as Granu ran for the steel ladder in the center of the room. She scaled it with Kradduk on her heels and Fillig not far behind, the metal groaning with the weight of three trolls as Little Pig tore through the opening, his face contorted into pure rage. More Bridge Protection patrols poured into the tiny space behind him. Granu threw her empty duffel bags down at the scrambling patrols fighting for space on the ladder, sending them tumbling back into the room only to be replaced by others. Her second bag hit Fillig square in the face, but he held tightly to the ladder and yelled something up at her. Fumbling with the latch, she finally got it free and flung open the hatch, climbed up the dark stairwell, and burst through the door on top of the bridge, allowing sunlight to stream through, turning the troll guards to stone in the room below. Their bodies crushed other guards as they toppled over.

Granu cringed at the sunlight pouring in from the openings along the side of the bridge, but her coverings were solid. Kradduk and Fillig scrambled through the door behind her. For a moment, everyone paused. Kradduk, Fillig, and Granu stood on top of the bridge empty-handed in broad daylight staring at each other in disbelief as the two grawback guards remaining below hesitated, shocked by the sudden death of their cohorts. Time ceased to exist. The grawbacks began to struggle to move the stone trolls out of the way.

Granu was the first to gather her wits. "RUN!" she screamed.

She took off, Kradduk and Fillig following. Granu fumbled with the holster at her ankle, freeing her pulse blaster just in time to shoot at the pair of swog guards in their path. The guards didn't have time to react. They stood with their porcine faces twisted in surprise and their eyes wide in the beat of a moment before they went careening backward. The trio of trolls tore by. Granu's peripheral vision was obstructed by the boxy hood of her sunsuit, which gave her a tunnel-like view of the expanse of bridge before her, and she had to turn her head to see her friends hauling ass just behind her. Her legs were shorter than the others', but she had far less mass to move with each step, and her agility helped her avoid the broken planks and other trip hazards that nearly toppled both Kradduk and Fillig every few steps.

"Go, now! The sun won't keep them from killing us," she screamed behind her without waiting for confirmation that Kradduk or Fillig heard her words as she hurtled her body in the direction of the meeting point. Len should be waiting with the van. She just had to get off the bridge. Granu zoned out as she pushed her body to its limit, adrenaline overwhelming the pain she knew she would suffer if she lived through this.

On top of the bridge, with bright sunlight flooding through the openings on both sides of the bridge, but covered head-to-toe in protective gear, the three trolls were slow moving targets for the highly trained Bridge Protection patrols. The bridge spanned miles, however, so only the closest guards noticed them at first; each pair was quickly dispatched in turn by pulse blasts from Kradduk or Granu. Since it was daytime, only swogs were on duty out in the open. The top of the bridge provided minimal cover since the sides were nearly completely open, and though grawbacks were known to perch under the shadowy peak, the crew didn't encounter any. The only trolls were secured in toll booths, and they weren't about to step into the sun to apprehend three insane criminals with a death wish.

Granu knew her luck wouldn't hold. Soon, every Bridge Protection Officer, swog and otherwise, would be aware of the situation. Just as the thought crossed her mind, two patrol guards started at the sudden appearance of the running trolls and recovered fast enough to give chase. They deftly avoided pulse blasts from Granu and Kradduk. Where was Fillig's blaster?

"Fillig, shoot them!" she yelled without turning around.

Without warning, Kradduk's enormous mass slammed into the back of Granu, sending them both hurtling forward twenty feet, well out of reach of the swog patrol, where they landed in a pile with grunts and cusses.

"What the heaven?" stammered Granu, clambering to her feet.

"Fillig just shot me in the ass."

"He what?" Granu looked back, and Fillig was bobbling his blaster as he ran toward them. The swogs were gone, having been shot out of the sky by Fillig by some miracle, but two more were giving chase. "Ooh, that's got to hurt."

"Tell me about it. It feels like I just had a really rough night with a sniggle."

Granu cringed at the thought as she helped Kradduk to his feet. They were running again before Fillig could catch up. Luckily, swogs were not very fast on foot. Unluckily, they were quite fast in flight. They rose into the air and swooped down at Granu, Fillig, and Kradduk.

"Shit," muttered Granu in what became her mantra for the day. She'd never seen a swog in flight and had no idea how those tiny wings could carry their round bodies at all, let alone with such speed and grace. Their skills were undeniable as they maneuvered through the air, avoiding shots and support beams as they zipped in and out of the open sides of the bridge, closing in.

Kradduk spun and landed a kick to the gut of the nearest officer, sending the creature zipping through the air in a spiral before it clipped a post of the bridge and plummeted into the canyon. The other snatched wildly at Fillig. Fillig wrestled with the swog before breaking free and falling back onto the bridge with a thud that nearly toppled Granu. She stopped in her tracks.

"Go!" Fillig screamed. The swog caught him again, but this time, instead of tackling him, the creature hoisted him into the air, pulling him out the side of the bridge and tearing at his coverings once they were both aloft. Fillig dangled, a wriggling body with flailing limbs. Granu did as he instructed. She tried to watch through the support posts as she ran, but the pair was a blur. There was a loud rip as the hood was torn from Fillig's suit, exposing his ski-mask covered head to the hot sun. A wretched sound ripped out of Granu's throat. Tears blurred her sight.

"Fuuuuuuuuu—" screamed Fillig as the color drained from his eyes and lips, the word never completed. For a moment, his body continued to run in the air, his arms grappling with the swog. In his last second of life, Fillig caught a hold of the swog's ankle and encircled it with a tight grip, his foot simultaneously finding a wooden support beam and giving a great shove. The pair shot away from the bridge into the open air. The swog struggled, but Fillig's entire body was now stone, and the weight was too much for his pathetic wings. They flapped wildly as squeals of terror woke Granu from her stupor. She sobbed or heaved, she didn't know which. Kradduk grabbed her arm, pulling her on as Fillig dragged the swog downward to certain death in the canyon below.

"Come on! He took the bastard with him! He wouldn't want you to die just because he did. Go. Now!"

With no one in pursuit, the pair ran onward, toward the west end of the bridge, toward an army of underlings armed with pikes and pulse blasters. No wonder they'd been able to run for so long. The entirety of Bridge Protection was gathered at the end of the bridge, waiting.

Granu strained to see the lamppost that marked the meeting place. There it was, just beyond fifty or so eager underlings frothing at the mouth. There. The street running between buildings that housed TCB workers. Their escape. Their freedom. But there was no van.

"Gran, just keep running!" yelled Kradduk.

She struggled to understand the situation. They'd been set up. Not just by Lyssa, but by Len too. Her knees tried to buckle beneath her weight, but Kradduk dragged her forward. She bit her bottom lip, a rush of blood pouring into her mouth, suppressed thoughts of Fillig, and pressed harder toward the waiting swarm. As they approached the front lines, Kradduk turned to her. He gave a nod, they clasped hands, and they leapt, their bodies soaring higher than any troll ought, clearing the pikes held by the first row of guards and landing on others with a crunch and screams of agony. She was pulled into a raging sea of underlings, writhing and crumpling beneath her. Hands and hooves grasped, but nobody caught hold. Spears took aim at her but were unable to make it through the crowd, and nobody dared use a pulse blaster in such tight quarters.

Granu's hand slipped free of Kradduk's as she flailed against bodies and arms in a desperate attempt to keep anyone from grabbing her. Time seemed to slow in the blur of bodies. She focused on her breathing as she kicked and punched. In and out, in and out, chest rising and falling as the world seemed to speed by her. She twirled and ducked. She jumped and thrust. Any moment, her coverings would be torn, and she'd turn into a statue like poor Fillig. But it didn't happen. So long as she kept moving, the swog hooves were unable to grasp her, the grawback claws were too hesitant, and the molent hands were too small.

A pale gray grawback swooped down from above, its talons sinking into Granu's shoulders. On instinct, she went dead-weight, collapsing into the masses, the only shade on offer. The grawback was wrenched free by the throng of bodies, but now she had holes in her coverings. Amazed that she hadn't been apprehended, Granu fought on, keeping low so the opening in her coverings wouldn't reach sunlight. If she was going to survive, she'd have to find cover. Unable to make out any individuals in the twisting mass, she kept fighting and pushing through the wall of creatures, holding onto one thought.

Stay alive.

32

THE MELEE

Granu ripped a shirt off a befuddled zimble and draped it over her shoulders as she torqued her body away from his wildly-kicking hooves and regained her footing. That's when she caught sight of the wontog teens and realized she wasn't the only one fighting. The thrashing of the crowd was more than just Bridge Protection attempting to apprehend two would-be robbers. It was a full-on brawl.

The juvies rampaged beneath the roof of the bridge, precariously close to the rays of sun filtering in from all sides, and they were slaughtering guards in all directions. That's why she hadn't been apprehended—the patrols were too busy keeping themselves alive to deal with her. As she wrestled against the bodies of guards, teens, and onlookers, Granu caught sight of Kadu, the juvie who'd turned at reception desk, wrenching the wing off a grawback.

Blood splattered onto Granu's coverings and a flurry of feathers showered over the crowd as Kadu stuffed the wing in his mouth with a sickening crunch. A swog came to the grawback's rescue, barreling into Kadu and sending him stumbling into the sun. Granu snapped her head forward to avoid witnessing the life leaving the body of the juvie who wouldn't even be here if not for her as he turned to stone.

Poor Kadu. He was supposed to be caged in a Bridge Protection cell. Granu clenched her jaw. If she was going to survive, she needed to focus on getting through the crowd, not figuring out how the juvies got topside. Hands grasped Granu's shoulders, and she turned with her arm cocked only to find herself staring into a visor slightly obscuring the wide eyes of Kradduk.

"We've got to get out of here!" he shouted, but she could barely hear his voice over the screams and fighting. He grabbed her by the elbow and dragged her through the flailing bodies, punching and kicking a path to the road. Remarkably, they emerged with sun coverings more or less intact, Granu's shoulders still covered by the stolen shirt. The sun was bright in her eyes, even through her visor, and she squinted.

Outside the brawl, the world was quiet, as if every bit of energy in the area were contained by some invisible dome a hundred feet in diameter. Granu looked back at the pile of swarming bodies. It resembled an ant mound, only with far more carnage. At one end, Bridge Protection was beginning to organize their ranks, having successfully contained two wontog-raging teens. The organization was spreading. Soon, they'd get the chaos handled and get back to hunting her and Kradduk.

She wasn't free of the mob for five seconds when a vehicle rounded the corner, nearly plowing straight into Granu. She dove backward as the baby blue Volkswagen SUV squealed to a halt a few hundred feet away.

"After all that, getting run over is not my idea of an acceptable death," she said.

"Nobody else is dying today," replied Kradduk.

"Over here!" A familiar voice Granu couldn't place. Following it seemed safer than any other plan she hadn't had time to consider, even if the disembodied voice did come from the direction of the rogue automobile. She ran and Kradduk followed. Dreatte, the graw-back barmaid from Goron's, was waving blue feathered limbs frantically from beneath a parasol next to the SUV, which was perched with two wheels on the curb.

"Granu, this way!" When Dreatte saw that she was successful in getting their attention, she folded her parasol and got into the passenger seat.

A guttural yell broke from the crowd as a swog guard dove out of the melee to hurl himself at them. With a screech, Granu ran toward the waiting SUV. Every muscle in her body screamed in protest, her legs threatening to give out from exhaustion, but somehow, Granu kept going. She could hear Kradduk's coarse breathing as he thundered along beside her. She stole a backward glance, a mistake. The swog had taken to the air and was rapidly gaining. Kradduk barreled toward the passenger side, so Granu dove into the backseat behind the driver of the idling vehicle. She slammed her door behind her.

A deafening thud shook the vehicle as the roof caved inward under the swog's weight. Kradduk's door wasn't closed when the SUV lurched forward with the revving of the engine, weighed down by the two trolls stuffed in the back and the creature on top. The little VW tore off down the road.

Somehow, the swog hung on. A hoof crashed through the driver's window, and the vehicle swerved left.

"The Clarksdale tunnel!" yelled Dreatte. "It's low."

The SUV seemed to drive itself directly to the tunnel as the hoof pummeled the air over and over again, never finding a body with which to connect. Dreatte was right. The human tunnel was not made for anything larger than a passenger van, and the swog was struck from the roof, his severed arm falling into the vehicle. A male voice yelled out in disgust.

Granu craned her neck to watch the swog's body smash into an electric pole before bouncing off the asphalt. Sparking wires fell from the sky across the road behind them and over the fallen swog.

"Now, that's a barbecue," said Kradduk with a wince.

"Hey guys! So, what brings you here?" said Dreatte, as if they happened to meet in the grocery store. She looked in the rearview mirror at the two trolls as she straightened a pair of oversized sunglasses blocking her face.

"Um, what the fuck just happened?" asked Granu.

"I believe we just saved your asses, if that mob back there is any indication."

"Beautiful and timely," said Kradduk. "We'd be statues if it weren't for you, you gorgeous grawback!"

"How did you know? How did you get here?" stammered Granu. She couldn't make any sense of this rescue, and she couldn't see the driver's seat directly in front of her. "Who's driving?"

"Kell."

So that's why she couldn't see the driver. He was smaller than anyone behind the wheel had any right to be, and far more blind if he was out in the daylight.

"Hey losers, trying to get yourselves killed?"

Granu caught a glimpse of the rearview mirror. Kell was wearing goggles of some kind and driving like the sky was falling, tearing through the streets of the small underling town at the edge of the canyon. Old Metta was really more of a village of businesses than a town, with only one stoplight and vacant buildings. Clarksdale was still a good fifty miles west, the tunnel named for the nearest city, not for its central location.

"What? How are you here? How are you not blind?" Granu stammered, shifting her body to try and get more comfortable in the SUV that wasn't designed to haul trolls. Kradduk's left leg was tangled with her legs, though she couldn't see his head due to the collapsed roof. Every time the SUV swerved to the left, her head struck the indentation. She was sure she'd have a bump by the time they reached wherever they were going.

"We thought you could use a standby just in case this little scheme of yours failed. I take it from that mess back there that it did."

"You knew what we were planning? All along? How?" Granu's mouth hung open as she frantically tried to put the pieces together.

"You idiots planned the whole thing at my tavern right in front of my face. Dreatte's too. It doesn't take keen observational skills to figure out what you were up to with all your papers, blueprints, and computers. Why would you plan a hit like this in a public place in daylight, anyhow? Haven't you watched a heist flick, like ever?"

Granu had been so worried about TCB spies that she completely forgot about everyone else in New Metta. Right now, she was thanking the Underlord for her oversight, but who else might have overheard their scheming? Things could be so much worse. If he wasn't right and in the process of saving her life, Granu would have growled at Kell.

"The plan was good. It should have worked," she muttered. "What do you suppose happened to Len?"

"He screwed us, Granu," said Kradduk, echoing Granu's own fears. He was still breathing heavily, filling the enclosed space with the fragrant smell of sardines with each exhale. How did he always seem to have his sex appeal turned up to eleven? Granu shook her head at the thought as he continued. "He sold us out."

"The money, it's gone."

"They must have pulled it off sooner somehow, him and Lyssa. They must have schemed up a way to double-cross us during all the time they spent together. Poor Fillig. He thought he was in love," said Kradduk.

"Poor Fillig," agreed Dreatte. "I got here just in time to see him fall, and the speed he fell—well, it was something. He had to be stone. Poor guy. I'm not sure he would have fit, though, so there's that."

"We would have had to strap him to the roof," said Kradduk.

"Him? You're the one taking up all the space. It would have been your ass tied to the roof," said Granu.

"You know you like being close to me."

"Really, Kradduk? After everything, after losing Fillig, that's what you've got to say?" They lost Fillig. Saying it aloud made it real.

"He knew the risks, Granu, as much as the rest of us." Kradduk's somber tone belied the shallowness of his words. "Besides, we all grieve in our own ways."

The route to Clarksdale was long, and Granu's body throbbed. She couldn't imagine how Kradduk was feeling, having been shot, but they were alive, and that was something. Nearly a half hour passed before she gathered her thoughts.

"I've replayed every moment in my mind," she said, "and what I still don't understand is how the juvies got topside. Kadu was locked up before we even made it inside." Granu knew she should just thank her lucky fleas to be alive, but all of her plans were destroyed. The last month of her life was washed down the toilet, and Fillig was dead. She desperately wanted to understand.

"That was my doing," said Dreatte. "I have a cousin who works for TCB security, and I made sure she created chaos on the topside. She hasn't checked in yet, but she must have found a way to do what I asked. I have to admit, though, that's not at all what I had in mind."

"Why would she do that? She risked her job! Heaven, she risked her life!"

"She hates the TCB swogs. Do you know how little respect we grawbacks get there? We're nothing but conquests to the higher staff. I wouldn't put up with it myself, mind you, those filthy swogs and trolls always trying to get her alone. I'd take out their eyes. Still, it put her in a good position to help. She's so overlooked, they wouldn't suspect her of a thing. Still won't, even after all this."

Granu's face scrunched. "So she did it just to get a jab in at TCB? And you. I still don't understand, Dreatte, why would you and Kell risk yourselves to come here just in case we failed? And how did you know exactly where to be exactly when we needed you? I just don't get it."

The grawback shrugged. "You're our best customers."

33

THE GETAWAY

Len drove the blacked-out van down the highway, obeying all the rules of the road. It was illegal for an underling to be on the roads during the day without registering the trip with the feds ahead of time, so he didn't want to risk being pulled over by one of their highway patrols, especially within 50 miles of New Metta. Though, at this point, did he really care if he brought trouble to that city? He'd pulled off the heist of the century, a crime punishable by death. They couldn't kill him twice.

He now had everything he ever dreamed of: money, the hottest female in Fairbax at his side, and the notoriety of a supervillain, having double-crossed The Five and left his crew for dead. Granu deserved it for the way she'd cast him aside. Like she was some catch. She'd learned her lesson, he'd wager. He took a moment to wonder about whether she'd survived. Not likely considering the trap they'd laid, but he liked the idea of her living to realize how stupid she'd been to let him go. Len chuckled. Life couldn't get any sweeter.

Classical music flooded the van. Len didn't care much for the aggressive stuff that was popular in New Metta, preferring the strings and pianos played on the human station NPR, if only they'd stop their infernal talking. Currently, he was being serenaded by Berlioz's *Opus*

Number 24 as Lyssa snored loudly in the back, cushioned by the bags of cash. They were heading to Mount Clipps, a popular vacation destination for underlings that made a terrible hideout thanks to the reality television show *College Crematorium* that was filmed on the streets. What felons on the lam would take refuge in a place where cameras recorded every street? It was the least expected move they could make. All they had to do was snag some disguises and lie low for a while before planning their next move. There would be a next move, of course. Len had a taste of the life he'd always craved, and he wasn't about to give it up to retire with his cash from one little heist.

Besides, Lyssa fell for Len when she found out about his dreams to become something more, something amazing, and he planned to surpass his putrid petal's expectations. There was no limit for him now. With the cash they were sitting on, they'd never need to work a day again, so he decided to dedicate his life and resources to being the best supervillain of all time. He was like Zaamble, the arch nemesis of Giddeon Gamut, an overlooked and underappreciated wretch who decided to turn his life around one fateful day to take over Cramp City. Len would get the recognition he deserved, he was sure of it. He was the genius mastermind behind the theft of the vault contents of TCB, a day that would live in infamy. His only regret was that he couldn't stay and hear the buzz or bask in the fear and adoration of his countless fans. Nothing else would be spoken of all week in New Metta, but Lyssa was right, they couldn't risk discovery, especially with the little message he had set to broadcast as soon as the systems were restored. He'd scheduled the blackout to keep Granu from knowing he was long gone and to lead her further into the trap. He couldn't have her survive to turn him in.

Eventually, his reverie was broken by his gurgling stomach.

"Lyssa," he called, lowering the volume on the radio.

He got grumbles in response, so he made the executive decision to stop near Winsel, an underling town a few hours from New Metta, for a snack. He pulled into an underground parking garage and found a spot among those reserved for trolls on the deeper levels. By this time, Lyssa was stirring.

"Are we there?" she grumbled, climbing to the front in a tangle of limbs. She was beautiful with her red locks in wild disarray and her breath smelling of onions and sleep. Purely radiant.

"Nowhere near, my love, but I need to eat, and I thought you could use some nourishment as well. With the head start we got, we are in no rush."

Lyssa grunted in agreement, and they exited the garage into a tunnel leading to an abandoned subway system. Many underling cities were added onto existing underground structures left by humans, and this little town was nearly completely contained by the subway lines.

Len and Lyssa had abandoned their cell phones and computers before leaving town, knowing they could be traced. They could buy new, better supplies when they were clear of detection, but for now, Len was desperate to hear word of the heist. He wasn't used to being off the grid. He hoped for a frenzy, for his name plastered in the papers, his face on the televisions as every family in New Metta tuned in to witness the miracle of TCB, the safest institution in New Metta, being brought to its knees. Nobody would feel safe ever again. He stopped at a bookshop and found the evening's newspaper already on the shelves. He paid a molent and carried the paper under his arm to a well-lit cavern not far from the parking garage. The place was illuminated with neon signs and fluorescent lights. The tables were constructed from old classic cars, and the floor was covered in black and white tiles. Gaudy was what it was. Len spread the paper across the red '69 Cadillac hood once they were seated. There it was, the front-page headline.

TROLL TRIO ATTEMPTS TO ROB TCB AMIDST UNTOLD CARNAGE: ONE DEAD, TWO ON THE RUN

A picture of Granu and Kradduk spanned the entire page, unrecognizable due to their standard-issue quarry sunsuits, diving feet-first into a waiting posse of guards at the end of the Bridge. Their hands were linked, and they were at least ten feet off the ground. Trio? Trio? There was not even a mention of the security system failure or the fact that nobody saw where the cash went, or that it went anywhere at all. Did they think that Granu and Kradduk made it vanish before making a suicidal dash along the bridge? No. TCB was covering up their failure. They were supposed to be impenetrable, after all, and one successful hit would make them more of a target than they were already. Still, it burned that Len wasn't getting any coverage at all.

"Len, we got away clean," said Lyssa, concern painted all over her face.

Len hadn't realized she was watching him seethe.

"I guess so, but a little credit wouldn't hurt," he replied. "It's ludicrous to think that three trolls could have pulled this off and the money would just disappear. It says that one died, and two others are still at large. That means they escaped. How in heaven did they get past this?" Len jabbed the picture with his stubby finger, right where the mob was gathered at the end of the bridge. "Granu is free. How do you suppose she pulled that off? She's not as smart as everyone says, you know."

"I'm sure Kradduk had something up his sleeve. He's a sweet-talker, that one. And he's not exactly stupid."

"He's not exactly intelligent, either. I can't believe she got away."

"Hey, it could have been Granu who died. It's hard to tell from that blurry photo." She squinted down at the picture.

"No. It had to be Fillig. One of these trolls is huge and the other is far too small to even be a troll. It must be Granu. Disgusting, really, how little she is for a female."

"There's no need for that. At one point, you thought her beautiful. Besides, you're not exactly huge yourself," said Lyssa. "In fact, I'm fairly certain you're smaller than she is."

Lyssa's moral compass was a marvel, logical in its own right, but very, very askew. It's what Len loved most about her.

"Yeah, but I've got charisma." Len grinned goofy and wide at the troll sitting across from him.

She giggled. "And money."

"Yeah, there is that."

"The article didn't mention your video. I bet they're keeping that quiet for now too. Once they put the pieces together, they'll likely link me to the crime. They'll think we're the two who got away."

"You're right, of course. My name will be on the cover of this paper sooner or later. Even the brightest of stars takes time before its light strikes the earth."

"Yes. You'll get your recognition. You already have your reward, and you have me."

"You always know how to darken my day, my putrid petal." Len leaned over the table and kissed his lady. She was right, he would get the credit he deserved in time. His name would be known throughout Fairbax, and Lyssa was at his side. He didn't need anything more just yet.

Len and Lyssa shared a frog slime sundae after their meal, taking their time to savor the sludge. They still had a long drive ahead, and there were no signs that Winsel was on alert for fugitives yet, probably because the heist was actually pulled hours before Bridge Protection believed. When they were finished, Len paid in cash for the meal, the molent server sneering at his measly tip, and they left without any incident. Lyssa took her turn behind the wheel as Len slept soundly on his bags of cash.

34

THE CLEANER

TCB was abuzz when Kradduk reported for work. The sun blazed, but he went in early in order to keep up appearances. Under different circumstances, he would have reported as soon as he got wind of the hit on TCB, so he waited a few hours after the failed heist, took a shower, put on a suit, and headed back to the scene of the crime through one of the internal access points as if he were rushing in for damage control.

The fires caused by the PODs in the northwestern quarter had been extinguished, but the structural damage was beyond anything TCB's demo department was capable of repairing. They were trained in construction only in the context of demolition, after all. Debris filled the halls—broken glass from shattered walls, cement dust and explosive residue, broken pieces of furniture, papers and files, all marring the pristine marble floors and white walls. The cafeteria was a bloodbath, littered with bodies and broken tacos.

Workers bustled around in organized chaos, each group carrying out some task or other. Kradduk started toward Dammon's office when he came face to face with Heigle, whose eyes were ablaze.

"I can't believe you'd show your face after pulling a stunt like this." She wasted no time.

Normally impeccably put-together, Heigle was a mess, her hair in disarray and makeup smeared around her eyes. Of all the destruction around him, that frightened Kradduk the most. He needed to get Dammon alone as soon as possible if he was going to manipulate his way out of this one, but he couldn't say anything she could use against him. He twisted his mouth into a smirk.

"Rough day?"

"Oh, don't play coy with me. I know you did this, and as soon as I have the proof, you'll be out in the sun. I'll use your statue to hang my laundry." She spoke through clenched teeth.

Kradduk had no doubt that would be his fate if he didn't get a handle on the situation quickly. He looked into her eyes and flashed his most charming smile. Poor Heigle didn't know who she was up against.

"Sweetheart, if I just emptied the TCB vault, I would be living it up in the hills of Friddum, not wasting my time here with a miserable wretch like you. Feel free to waste your time searching for your nonexistent proof. I have actual work to do."

Kradduk strode away, down the hall, and directly to Dammon's office. Heigle followed from a distance like a sun-blind molent desperate to make it home.

The swog was pacing in circles, his suit disheveled and papers littered across his desk. Kradduk left Heigle loitering in the hall as he closed the office door behind him.

"What can I do to help?" he asked, jolting Dammon from his thoughts.

"Oh, Kradduk. I'm so glad you're here. Please, come in and shut the door."

Kradduk glanced at the closed door. He opened it slightly and then closed it with a thud, causing Heigle to start then glare before pressing her face against the glass wall. The office was soundproof, like every space in TCB, so she must be trying to read lips. Kradduk walked deliberately to stand by Dammon's desk in order to disguise his injury and avoid the pain of sitting.

Dammon took his seat behind his desk and began to rifle through the stacks of files and papers. He pulled out a red envelope, opened it, and laid out the contents. Pages and pages of reports all typed with immaculate formatting and consistent fonts. Kradduk caught sight of his name in multiple places.

"Heigle has it in her mind that you did this. All of this. Oh, now don't think to speak to that. I know you don't have the know-how to pull off something this big, and if you did, you wouldn't be sitting in my office right now. The thing is, her electronic documents were destroyed with the computer infiltration. All I'm left with to find the true thief is this stack of reports she gave me, and they're all about you. Len is a sneaky bastard, as it turns out. But all he took was her files. And she's been hounding you since she started here. You know what I think?"

"I couldn't possibly."

"I think she's trying to set you up. I think she's been working with that Fillig character and Len. Oh, and that Lyssa floozy too. That one had us all fooled, let me tell you, with her big eyes and, um, figure. Squeath nearly told her how to rob the place himself, from what I hear, not that he's the brightest, but don't quote me on that." He shot a paranoid glance to the glass wall. Heigle's head ducked out of sight, but Dammon didn't comment on it. "And we know how devious females stick together. Heigle says Fillig was one of your best friends and that she'd seen you along with some female troll, Granite or something?"

Dammon slid a photo of a stone statue across the desk to Kradduk. Fillig. Kradduk winced.

"Granu."

"Ah, yes, Granu. Seen you with your heads together over a table at a tavern on many occasions, that's what she said. But I know the story is bullshit."

Through the cloud of panic, Kradduk saw his moment in perfect clarity. Even as the words left his mouth, he felt sorry for Heigle. He knew that it was her or him at this point, and it sure wasn't going to be him. He cleared his throat and drew his brows together for added sincerity.

"Dammon, let me stop you for a moment." He approached the swog to place a hand on Dammon's arm. "I need to be perfectly honest with you. She's right. Fillig was one of my best friends, and Granu is too. I've been going over it in my mind since I heard Fillig's name in connection to all this, and the only thing I can figure is that's how they met. Through Granu. But, I need you to know she had nothing to do with any of this and neither did I."

"You did know Fillig Schist?" Dammon's body froze, his eyes locked on Kradduk's.

"Yes. That's what I'm telling you. I've never hidden anything from you. I never thought Len capable of this, and if I didn't see the picture myself, I wouldn't believe Fillig could be either. But Granu and I—we are as shocked as the rest of you."

Kradduk removed his hand from Dammon's arm and walked back around the desk.

"And, Dammon, if we were planning some kind of robbery, we certainly wouldn't do it at a tavern."

Dammon smiled weakly. "I know, I know. You're smarter than that. Kradduk, you are a true company man, and don't think I don't know it," he said. The swog's eyes were swollen as if he'd been crying, and dark rings encircled them. "You've been nothing but honest and patient ever since we brought on that female, and I think she's trying to use these connections against you, to shift focus off her. I won't stand for it."

"Thank you for your faith in me, Dammon. You've always been a mentor to me, and it means more than you could know. What can I do to help clean up this mess?" On the other side of the glass wall, he saw Heigle's shoulders slump when Dammon smiled in appreciation.

You'd better run! he thought.

"What you always do," replied Dammon. "The robbery will bring a lot of unwanted attention onto us. Keep the press and the authorities directed away from anything we don't want them to know. There's a press conference scheduled for ten. Get ahead of it."

"Yes, sir."

"Oh, and Kradduk?"

Kradduk paused on his way to the door.

"How did you know the robbery was successful? We haven't made any official statements, and only a handful of employees know about the missing cash."

Kradduk swallowed hard. Of course TCB wouldn't let the public know the criminals had gotten away with the cash. He formed his next sentences carefully. "The destruction is unmissable, Dammon. And it's already in the Chronicle that there was a hit, not that they have any details yet. It's my job to know things. It's what you hired me for. Well, that and keeping others from knowing things."

He'd already tipped his hand by letting on that he knew far more than anyone ought. Now, his only choice was to cling to his story and wait out the chaos. He prayed to the Underlord Dammon hadn't noticed his slip-up earlier when he'd indicated that Granu knew about the heist too. Thankfully, the poor swog was too worried about preserving his own neck to think clearly.

Dammon let him off the hook. He probably assumed that Kradduk had eyes and ears among other employees.

"Ah, yes." Dammon nodded. "I'd better call an employee meeting before the rumor mill really gets going and everyone sees that ridiculous confession."

"Confession?"

"Len Peat had it run on all the monitors. Dressed like he's in a bad comic and demanding respect. It's utterly preposterous that *that* fool could do all this," said Dammon.

"Wow. Yeah, we need to get out ahead of that too. It's only a matter of time before the wrong people start asking questions, making my job much more difficult," replied Kradduk. Every cell in his body was screaming at him to get out of there, but he had to get through this day if he and Granu were going to survive the week.

"Yes, it is. Kradduk? Can you please send Heigle in on your way out? I think I caught a glimpse of her in the hallway."

"Absolutely."

Kradduk didn't need to look far to find her. She was still lurking just outside Dammon's office, and she pinned him with a suspicious glare. He thought she'd be long gone once she saw that Dammon wasn't holding him responsible, but here she was still clinging to the hope that she'd beat him somehow. He almost felt sorry for the poor troll.

"Heigle. He wants to see you."

"What did you say to him?"

"Not much. He told me to send you in."

Heigle smoothed her hair with one hand, straightened her skirt with the other, and blew by Kradduk. When the door shut, Kradduk watched from behind the UV glass wall as Dammon motioned her to sit. When she did, the swog stood from his chair and walked to the window. Heigle must have foreseen his next move because she dove from her seat, making a dash for the door as the chair toppled to the ground behind her, but she was too late. Heigle's terrified eyes made contact with Kradduk's as Dammon opened the blinds, and the room was bathed in warm sunlight.

Kradduk closed his eyes. So, those windows weren't just for show —it was another of TCB's lies, one Kradduk suspected from day one. They were there for intimidation. Heigle would no longer be a problem. She was a truly splendid creature, and Kradduk had hoped to take care of her in his own, unique way. Now, all that remained was a statue in her likeness with a look of horror captured on her perfect face.

THE HOLE IN THE WALL
—PART III

S o they didn't connect us to any of it? Even after identifying Fillig?" asked Granu.

"Heigle did, but thanks to Len clearing her hard drive and Dammon's blind faith in me, we're in the clear. They're convinced the trolls from the Bridge were Lyssa and Len."

"Thank the Underlord. What happened to Heigle?"

"Let's just say she won't be pestering me anymore."

"Oh, Kradduk, I'm sorry. I know you liked her."

"Yeah. Well, there's nothing to be done about it now." He paused a moment before taking a swig of grog. "As much as I want to roast the little bastard, we have Len to thank for getting the authorities off our scent, too. He screwed us over, but he completely took us off Bridge Protection's radar."

Granu nodded. "If it weren't for his ridiculous confession, we wouldn't be able to even think about returning to a normal life."

"Is that what you want? A normal life?"

He sat at Goron's in his usual seat with his back to the wall. Granu was across from him, sipping from a flagon. Life went on as if nothing had changed, and in fact nothing had. The only notable change in her life was the empty space previously occupied by the troll she used to turn to when times got tough. Now, there was a piece of the world slightly askew, something just not right in her life. Poor Fillig. She couldn't imagine a day passing without missing him. She teared up at the thought but knowing his last act was to shoot Kradduk in the ass gave her a small measure of peace. Two weeks had flown by since their attempt at greatness, and, thanks to Fillig's sacrifice and Len's stupidity, nobody was looking for either of them.

Granu wiped at her eyes and nodded. "It must burn him up to not get credit for the hit of the century. You know that's the only reason he got involved, to prove something to the world."

Kradduk chuckled. "Well, it took them long enough to come out with his picture. Classic TCB. Even in the face of devastation, they're always trying to save face. I've been in constant contact with the PR department, and three have been fired just this week, all swogs."

"Would you admit to being cleaned out by Leniscious the Fierce? And that costume. You'd think Lyssa would have at least kept him from making a complete fool of himself."

When no new leads were discovered by Bridge Protection, Kradduk had convinced Dammon to release Len's confession, but they did it with very little fanfare a week after the incident. TCB was far more concerned with maintaining their image than with actually apprehending those responsible for the heist, especially when the New Metta Police Force was corresponding with the feds. This much money disappearing affected humans and underlings alike, and Kradduk was working full nights to keep the damage contained.

The day she saw Len's creepy little face in that makeup, Granu nearly keeled over from exhaustion after laughing herself into a fit. Even now, it gave her a good chuckle.

Dreatte brought a plate of barbecued fetus spines and another round. "Oh, you must be talking about Leniscious the Fierce again," she asked smirking.

"Yes, and the spandex. I mean, I knew he had a thing for super-heroes, but who would have thought he'd take it that far?"

Granu swiveled her laptop around, and flashed the picture that was circulating through New Metta at Kradduk and Dreatte. Len in blue and silver spandex complete with a cape and goggles strapped to the top of his head, his dark hair dyed white at the pointed ends, and silver and blue greasy paint smeared across his face in a large F. The caption below read "Wanted: $5,000 reward for information leading to capture."

"Hey, you should be thanking him," said Dreatte, but even she couldn't help but snicker.

"Oh, and I do," said Granu. "And Lyssa's disappearance makes her the other one they're searching for. She did work directly under Fillig, after all, and they have a positive ID on him."

"You keep forgetting that the little cud-chewer heisted our heist." Kradduk shook his head.

"Whatever. You were just telling me how you respect his troll-hood," said Granu.

"His balls, as in *cojones*. Not his trollhood. Geeze, Granu."

Dreatte walked away, shaking her head. Granu never did figure out exactly how she and Kell pulled off the rescue mission, but she was beyond grateful. She'd known better than to get involved in the scheme to begin with, and thanks to Dreatte, she was here to learn from it. Kradduk was just happy that someone got one over on Bartock Figg, even if there wasn't a big payout.

"We're damn lucky she cares for her customers," said Granu after Dreatte retreated to the kitchens.

"Hear hear. I need to tip her better," said Kradduk.

"You always say that, but I'd venture a bet that your tipping greatly influenced her decision to risk her life to save us."

Kradduk grinned. "Money makes the prey come 'round."

"Sad."

"Or maybe she just wants a piece of the Kradduk." His playful grin made it clear he was pushing Granu's buttons again. So, things were returning to normal ever so slowly.

"The Kradduk? Be careful. Before long, you'll be painting your face and laughing maniacally into a camera alone in your bedroom."

"I'm never alone in my bedroom."

Kradduk. Without Fillig to offer up condemnation for his boorishness, Granu felt guilty laughing. She would need to find another troll with a conscience to fill the void.

"Dreatte never did answer me about how she got the details about the heist, though. I mean, I know she and Kell overheard a lot, but I don't see how they got specific enough info to explain their sudden appearance at our meeting point."

Kradduk shrugged. "You know, Gran, I really don't care. I mean, they saved our asses, so all I feel when I think about it is appreciation."

"Yeah, I guess you're right."

They sat in silence for a time, grinding toddler bones in their teeth and tossing back grog. The tavern was relatively quiet, with a few small groups gathered at the tables and the bar. The usual cacophony of conversation was lower than usual, and the Critterhole platform was propped up against the wall.

"So, any new job prospects?" Kradduk asked.

"Nope."

"I can still get you a gig at the tar pits."

"Yeah. No thanks."

"Alright. Well, let me know when you need some more cash."

Granu scowled. "You know, I've been thinking about it. I won't keep letting you fund my life, so I'm going to give up my apartment and find something smaller for a while."

Kradduk bristled. "I told you, Gran, it's really no big deal. Besides, there's nowhere in all New Metta smaller than your place."

"It's a big deal to me, and I need to take some responsibility for my life. I think I'll go back to school, major in something more practical. Maybe Goron's or the coffee shop will take me on for a day shift to get through. Since I've already got my core covered, it shouldn't take more than a year or two to snag a business degree."

"You could move into my place. You know, save money while you get through school."

Granu shook her head. "Nah, that's just another way to leech off of you. Besides, you don't want me hanging around cramping your game."

"Alright, Gran, but promise me one thing. You'll let me help you before you end up on the streets, or worse." Kradduk's face grew serious, wrinkles forming around his usually laughing eyes. Were those worry lines? Granu hadn't seen this side of him. He might pretend like losing Fillig didn't affect him, but he was obviously worried about losing Granu too.

"Hey, I've been taking care of myself for years. Don't worry about me. I'll be fine. What about you, though? Here you are, working to cover up as much as you can for a company that you just tried to rob. Are you really going to keep bailing them out? How many incriminating activities do you hide for them every day? I mean, it can't be easy. And we were so close."

"Yeah, but it does give me the opportunity to keep the focus off of us—being in charge of the clean-up, I mean. And I get to witness the hits keep coming! TCB had to cut some very illegal operations, and that hit them right in the treasury, even if we didn't. I've been sanitizing operations ever since, and I'm not sure the company can keep on at current levels." He chugged the end of his grog. "Even better, Bartock Figg is absolutely ruined. Between allowing a dozen wontog-possessed teens devour his employees and losing everything in the treasury, more heads will roll, mark my words. And if it's not Figg's, well, I'll be biding my time, waiting for another opportunity to fuck him over."

"You got what you wanted from the heist," said Granu, "But it's still not enough? You want to hurt him further?"

"I don't think I'll need to. Everyone's so sure he's out, there's a big power play going on. The Figg family is trying to keep control, putting Edick front and center to try and get people to forget Bartock's failings, and Dirk Grost is running around telling everyone that he's going to Make The Bridge Great again." Kradduk laughed.

"Are either of these guys worth a shit?"

"Nah, but Grost would destroy TCB. He's openly speciesist, and his business sense is laughable. It might be fun to watch him tank the company."

Granu laughed. "That's so wrong."

"Nah, the people who deserve better will make it through. It's only the fat cats that'll go down."

"Doesn't that include you?"

"Gran, must I continue to remind you that I'm disgustingly rich? Do you even have a clue?"

Granu sighed. "No, you don't need to remind me. I just mean, how do you know it won't be your head that rolls?"

"Me? I had no hand in any of this. I was sentenced to tour duty against my will, and Heigle is the one who took control of the group of juvies. It's one of the reasons she was suspected of being involved. For all anyone knows, I'm an upstanding worker at TCB who, had I been allowed to go about my regular business, might have been able to prevent this terrible tragedy. Fifteen workers and four juvies lost their lives in the cafeteria, you know. I can spin this. I think I can even keep Dammon clear. And Granu I really can, um, take care of you. You don't have to worry so much about cash."

"Well, if anyone can survive, it's you," said Granu, pointedly ignoring Kradduk's repeated offer rather than shooting him down yet again. "Hey, Dreatte, you guys hiring?" she yelled across the room to where the barmaid was standing.

"Hey, Dreatte, you ever had a troll in ya?" asked Kradduk, licking his lips.

The grawback adjusted her apron as she made her way to the table. "As it happens, I've recently come into an inheritance. My auntie died and left me a sum large enough to get out of this joint. And Kell is taking an indefinite leave of absence for personal reasons, so yeah, this place will need some help. I'll get you an application if you really want to work in this hole."

"Considering the circumstances, I think I can make it work for a while, that is. I mean, I don't want to be a waitress my whole life, but it's an honest living."

"That it is," replied Dreatte, turning abruptly and walking away.

She returned a moment later with a paper application. Granu suppressed the disgust that the place still relied on pen and paper. Half of the underlings she knew didn't know how to write anymore since everything they did was digitized. Perhaps that was the test, knowing how to write on an application.

Dreatte gave Kradduk a good thwap with a dishrag to the back of the head as she left Granu to her scribbling.

"Was that my application? Am I hired?" He winked. The grawback rolled her eyes from across the room.

36

THE MIDNIGHT SNACK

Rain pelted the cabin in the woods as Len and Lyssa drove up the gravel drive in the middle of the night. Len sat forward in the van, squinting to see the path ahead as they were jostled about by the uneven, rocky road. He left Lyssa in the van to run through the pouring rain and open the lockbox with the combination given to him by the rental agency. Soaked, he entered and turned on the light as Lyssa made a dash for cover with a bag of cash stuffed under each arm.

The cabin was nice, if not as luxurious as the website described. It was smaller than the pictures, that was sure, but the furniture seemed comfortable, and the great room was lined with a huge window that probably offered up incredible views when the sky wasn't pitch black and full of clouds. Even better, the floor-to-ceiling blackout curtains were made to keep the sun out. Len walked over to ensure they would sufficiently block the morning rays, tacking them to the wall, as Lyssa began unzipping one of the bags.

"What the fuck is this?" she shrieked.

Len nearly jumped out of his skin. "What is what, my putrid petal?"

"This! What the fuck is this?" Lyssa's voice jumped at least an octave from her first exclamation. She inverted the bag onto the floor, emptying the contents onto the ground. Len hurdled the couch to inspect the pile of papers—it was decidedly not cash. He took in the bright ink on heavy cardstock bearing the image of a grinning swog and the words "TCB BUCKS" with horror. Coupons. An entire pile of TCB coupons, only redeemable at the gift shop of TCB. Lyssa threw the empty bag across the room and reached for the second, her movements quick with rage.

"How should I know? You were in charge of getting the cash loaded."

Lyssa unzipped the second bag and dumped more coupons onto the ground. She froze, her body stiff, jaw clenched, eyes boring into Len. "Get. The. Rest."

"Um, yes my love."

Len scurried out the door, returning soaked with load after load of bags, which Lyssa tore open one by one—they were all stuffed with useless coupons. When the last bag was empty, stacked on top of the others on the floor, Lyssa's chest was heaving. Thousands upon thousands of coupons filled the room.

"What happened to it?" gasped Len. "You loaded it up! You must know."

"Nothing! I emptied the boxes of cash into these bags, put them on the mail carts, and had the demo team wheel them straight down to the loading docks and into the van. How does money turn into this?" She picked up a handful of coupons and threw it in the air, blood flushing her face as the coupons rained down. She was far less attractive in her rage, and Len had a sudden urge to bite her. He wondered briefly if that's how most females felt around him. It would explain certain behaviors.

He waited until she was still again. "Well, logic dictates that something happened along the way. Was it out of your sight even for a moment? Calm down, let's figure this out." He couldn't stand emotional responses to situations that required a cool head. He never understood what good came of screaming and crying when most problems could be solved with simple thought and applied logic.

"What is that going to accomplish? Are you going to think this right? Are you going to think me a huge cavern in the mountains, an endless supply of tenderized children, and a Porsche? What about my Porsche?"

"Wow. It's a good thing I didn't see this side of you back in New Metta."

"What is that supposed to mean? You sniveling little prick. You cud-chewing bastard!" Lyssa turned on him and advanced.

"Putrid petal, calm down for a moment. Have faith in me, your supervillain. Maybe this didn't turn out right, but we need to figure out what happened so that we can learn for next time. You know I'm going to pull off another feat of brilliance."

"What did your supposed brilliance get us? Piles of worthless paper!" Lyssa spat her words, but, slowly, she seemed to deflate until she finally sunk to the ground, head in her hands, surrounded by coupons.

Len silently thanked the Underlord. He had no delusions that he could win in an altercation with the stronger female, and for a moment, he thought she might feast on him. She certainly didn't respond well to his casual observation about her current state. "Let's go grab a bottle of wine and go through everything that happened step-by-step."

Lyssa nodded silently, her empty eyes creeping him out. The brown, white, and red carpet was nearly invisible beneath the pile of TCB bucks, and the small cabin room held little else besides a king bed and an unlit fireplace. What first seemed like a quaint little space felt claustrophobic when stuffed with paper and an emotional troll. Some mountain paradise.

Len left. When he returned, Lyssa was in the same position on the ground, surrounded by brightly colored coupons with a print of the bridge on one side and a grinning swog on the other. He helped her to her feet and poured out a glass of 30-year-old Weasel Bloodwine.

"Do you really think you should have spent money on this?" she murmured.

"My love, please see in me what you did when we met. I am your supervillain, Leniscious the Fierce, double-crosser of The Five and conqueror of TCB, and I will take care of us. Every desire you have will be met. Now, please think about the vault. You loaded up the cash and then what?"

"After I tricked Squeath into letting me work on the defect in Bridge Protection Central, I loaded it up in boxes and had my demo team push it out on carts. They thought they were removing construction debris from the defect I kept covered with a tarp. I hid the real debris in my bag every day and made multiple trips to the dumpster. I worked so hard." She sucked in her bottom lip. Was he going to see the unflappable Lyssa cry?

The prospect made him snort. "None of that is relevant. Get on with it."

"It is to me," growled Lyssa.

"Alright, my darling. But were the boxes ever out of your sight, even for a moment?"

Lyssa paused for a moment to consider the question. Then, she gasped.

"Once. When security kept an eye on it while I pulled the van around, but the team was right there! They would have told me if anyone messed with it."

"Would they Lyssa? You're so naïve it's sickening. Everyone has a price. If someone paid them off, they'd turn a blind eye in a minute."

"How dare you talk to me like that?"

"I'm simply stating facts."

"Well don't, unless you want to be dinner."

"Honestly, Lyssa, your reactions confound me. I'm just going over the events, trying to figure out what happened. There's no need for such melodrama."

"Well, don't you blame me. This was your idea, you *genius*." She emphasized the last word as if sickened, and her lips pulled back to expose her canines.

Len realized his misstep must have been calling her naïve. He would never wrap his head around how sensitive some trolls could be, but he needed to get Lyssa calmed down before he pushed her to aggression. "My love, I only mean that you're too trusting. Too sweet. Any idea who might have been behind the switch? Obviously, the bags were switched."

Lyssa glared for a moment, chewing her lip. The pink receded from the whites of her eyes as she thought.

"Oh, Underlord! That damn grawback."

"What grawback?"

"She was the lead of a patrol, Sandy? Sell? Something like that. She was always snooping around during the week before the heist. Every time I turned around, she was there, watching. I thought I was being paranoid, but she saw me go to the dumpster, she saw me load the debris, she hovered near the construction site. I didn't see how any of that could tip her off to my plans, but it must have. It was her, I know it."

"Lyssa, someone was snooping around while we were planning to double-cross The Five, and you didn't think to say anything? Are you stupid? You must be!"

Len realized his mistake too late. He didn't have time to react or protect himself. The larger troll was a blur headed straight for his throat. He dove backward, falling over a chair, and Lyssa was on him. He did the only thing he could, being the smaller, weaker creature. He begged.

"Love, darling, putrid petal," he stammered. "Take a breath! Calm down! We're in this together, you and me. I'll make it right, I swear to you."

Something he said must have landed true because Lyssa stopped just short of a fatal blow.

"You will not test me again or I will rip out your heart and feast on it," she said between heaving breaths, the bulk of her body pinning Len in an unnatural position on the floor. Her dark eyes were dilated, the whites bright pink. He could feel the hot moisture of her breath on the tender skin of his neck.

"Yes, my love. I'm sorry I angered you. I shouldn't have pushed you so. I'm really just trying to get to the bottom of this."

"It is no more my fault than yours. You took the lead on this, and it's your responsibility to consider everything." Lyssa pushed her elbows into his flesh in order to right herself. Len struggled to keep from whimpering, knowing any sign of weakness would mean the end of his life. A small grunt escaped his lips, but, thankfully, she ignored it as she straightened out her blouse and pencil skirt as if she hadn't nearly devoured another living underling. Len also clambered to his feet, taking many steps back before pressing her for more information. A real genius didn't let opportunities to learn from his mistakes slip through his fingers, especially if he was planning to pull off a similar stunt in the future. But a real genius also knew to appease those who could end him. He must proceed more carefully.

"So, this grawback, she was around more than any other officers?"

Lyssa glared but answered the question. "Yes. She knew all my comings and goings, she knew about your breach in security. I thought she was my security detail because I wasn't threatening, that I was lucky to get her instead of Little Pig and his network of spies, but I was wrong." The last word hung in the air, daring Len to speak, but he didn't.

"Still," she continued, "I don't see how she would fit into the whole thing, her being just an officer and all." Lyssa's snarl melted, and she sat on the bed, looking utterly defeated.

Len rushed forward to throw his arms around her, but she shoved him off with a growl.

"Lyssa, my love, what are you so upset about? You're right. I'm the one who claimed this heist. What an idiot I must seem to everyone! To you. To Granu!"

"Her again? It's always been about her, hasn't it? You're no supervillain. You're nothing but a pathetic little troll pining after a female." She narrowed her gaze at Len, her lip curled in disgust.

He shivered, and his eyes darted to the door, but he didn't say a word. Her words cut him deeply, but now was not the time.

Lyssa stood and took a step toward him. "So you're going to make this all better? You're going to what? Pull some other heist? Rob some unsuspecting gold mine and shower me in jewels? Then you'll do everything you can to make sure Granu sees the greatness in you. Well, I can tell you one thing for sure, there is no greatness in you."

By the time she was finished speaking, Lyssa was inches from Len. Len tried to puff himself up, to appear less insignificant, more intimidating, but as much as he attempted to steel himself, he couldn't stop the warm flow of urine down his leg. Lyssa's nostrils flared. The whites of her eyes swirled with red, and she lunged.

Blue blood splattered against the rustic walls when Lyssa ripped Len's throat out. He raised his hands in a futile defensive motion, but he was too late. He slumped to the floor, the larger female clambering on top of him, devouring his corpse with a ferocity she'd kept tethered until this moment. She feasted on his flesh. She rolled in his entrails. She ripped at his tendons and crunched his bones between her powerful jaws. When she was finished, the cabin was covered in carnage, repainted in shades of Len.

Alone at last, Lyssa began to laugh. She laughed for so long and hard that anyone would think she'd lost her mind if they were to hear. Once she caught her breath, she waded through the blood-soaked coupons to retrieve Len's ridiculous supervillain costume from his suitcase. She turned it over in her hands, examining every inch as she ran her hands over the smooth spandex. Some supervillain he turned out to be. The laughter took her once more.

Len's lifeless eyes stared at her from the floor where he lay, the only witness to Lyssa's derangement, a mangled pile of troll refuse, and that made her laugh harder. She had more TCB bucks than New Metta was worth but couldn't even trade them for t-shirts or coffee mugs, and now they were all strewn throughout the room, soaked in blue blood. And here she was, holed up in a cabin with the remains of the one who was supposed to show her another side of life, an exciting side. She'd given up everything.

"You should have known better," muttered Lyssa to herself. For years, she'd relied on no one but herself. She'd had the right idea.

Lyssa took a final look around before collapsing onto the bed, her clothes soaked through with Len's blood, and slept, the comforting smell of death calming her nerves and lulling her into peaceful oblivion.

THE SERVER AND THE BARKEEP

Dreatte wiped away tears as she folded her apron and exited Goron's from the external door. Outside, a candy apple red Ferrari was parked at the top of the stairs beneath a rock outcropping designed to offer sun protection for those entering the parking lot. She was still sniffling when she climbed in next to Kell.

"Drea, you need to calm down. Life is good for us."

"Kell, I just feel bad."

"You shouldn't."

"I know, but I'm not a troll, I can't just pretend nobody lost their lives. Poor Fillig. That poor juvie. Poor Bridge Protection. Life means something to me, you know?"

Kell reached out an arm and gave Dreatte a squeeze around the shoulders. "Yeah, I know. You're not nearly as hard as you seem. I knew that from day one."

He peeled out of the parking lot onto a paved surface road. Kell drove faster than Dreatte found safe, but she didn't say another word. They'd spoken at length about their role in the heist, and there was nothing more to say. Kell was right.

Dreatte closed her eyes and took a deep breath. She earned this. The wind ruffled her feathers, sending some flying into the car behind them as the radio blasted the newest Giblets song, "Born to Lick the Carcass." She looked over at the tattooed molent. He was something else, a bad boy who oozed sex appeal. She'd been in love with him since the first time she'd heard him give a barfly a verbal smack-down. The physical one that followed sealed the deal. He caught her staring and smacked his lips together before turning his face back to the sun-soaked road.

The molent package was the newest technology in motor vehicles, a booster cage with hand controls replacing the foot pedals, heavy tinting on all the windows, and an emergency canopy that could close up all spaces at the flip of a wrist. Ironically, it was designed by TCB engineers. Combined with his driving goggles, he was safer than if he were underground. The upgrade didn't come cheap, but money wasn't an issue for the duo any longer.

As for Dreatte, the canopied windows let in the wind while protecting her from the sun during the day, and even if she did fade, her color would return with the next molt. She didn't need to worry about a thing on a night like this though. The moon hung low over-head and, this far from any human cities with their florescent lights and tall buildings, the stars shone brightly. She leaned forward to lower the volume.

"I'm glad things settled down so we could get out of there," she said after a while. "I couldn't stand seeing their faces every night, knowing what I know."

"Fillig was a fool, and there was nothing we could do for him," replied Kell, picking up on her remaining note of regret. "And that kid was just in the wrong place at the wrong time. They all were. He could have died during wontog anyway. There's no telling."

"Yeah." Dreatte's eyes filled with tears again.

"How many times have we been over this, baby? Where's that sharp-tongued badass I fell for?"

"I am who I am."

"And I love you for it, but Drea, we deserve this. But why do you keep torturing yourself?"

"Granu's been like a sister for the past few months."

"A sister who constantly underestimates you, treats you like an inferior creature, and would never hang out with you if you weren't bringing her round after round of grog." Kell was right, and Dreatte knew it.

"She really doesn't think she's a bigot, though. She thinks she's nice to grawbacks and molents. Maybe that's why it still feels wrong. She'll learn a few things waiting tables, I think, even if she does think it's beneath her."

"Look, Drea, they wouldn't have got the dough no matter what. It was sheer luck that we got a copy of their itinerary and that your cousin works security at TCB. Granu is a snobby bitch, Kradduk is a cad, and the two of them together set it up so that we could make our own dreams come true. And you know what? They owe us. They've been treating us like shit for years, and we saved their asses."

"You know it wasn't luck. You saw that hoofprint, and everyone knows what it means."

Kell laughed a rich, round sound. The copy of the Bridge blueprints, detailing the plan and exit strategy, conveniently tucked between the cushion and the wall in the very booth where they overheard the crew's plan. It was the key. Along with Dreatte's cousin, a grawback with a much more skewed moral compass than the sweet creature sitting beside him, made the opportunity too good to pass up.

"What's Cin doing with her share anyways?"

"Filing a suit against the company on the basis of sexual harassment. She hired Gretta Goodbeak. She'll likely own the bridge when all's said and done. Cin knows how to get what she wants."

"Apparently it's a family trait." Kell grinned at Dreatte, who cast her eyes downward. She wasn't sure how to feel about the emotion in his eyes when he looked at her. He saw through her wit and attitude straight to her heart, and she loved him more than life.

"What?" she asked, brushing her hands through the blue feathers framing her face in the way she did when feeling self-conscious.

"Nothing. You're just beautiful."

"If you say so."

"It's true, but I'm not wasting time convincing you. I do think it's sweet that you feel bad about all this, but you deserve to be happy, so I'm going to need you to stop it. We pulled their asses out of the sun. They'd be statues if it weren't for us."

"It was the least we could do with them handing us this money. So very much money."

"Drea, you're an amazing creature, and you deserve a good life—the one we're starting together. We didn't hurt anyone, we helped some misguided souls, and we got rich doing it. Take it for what it is. A good thing."

Dreatte smiled and nuzzled her head onto Kell's shoulder, which was at the perfect height for snuggling thanks to the booster cage. For the first time in her life, she enjoyed watching the sun rise, its oranges and reds illuminating the road ahead. If the money weren't enough to convince her that everything was ok, Kell certainly was. The future was bright for them.

Kell cranked the music and kept driving down the empty highway.

3 8

THE END

To Fillig!"

"To Fillig." Granu adjusted her apron as she climbed into the booth across from Kradduk at the end of a long day shift. The sounds of the tavern settling in for the day rumbled gently through the cavern as the last of the louder partiers left for home. A few tables of softly chattering groups remained along with a slew of regulars sitting in ones and twos along the bar. Ginger, the curvy zimble barmaid, the newest member of Goron's, flirted with the stragglers from behind the bar.

"We lost a good troll. May he finally find love in the ever mountains," said Granu, raising a flagon.

"And may her rump be the size of one," said Kradduk. They clanked their flagons together.

"And may he never have to clean another sniggle in the afterlife," added Granu before raising the drink to her lips.

They sat in amicable silence for a long few moments, Granu gazing blankly into space as Kradduk scanned the room. The loss of Fillig was profound for each in entirely different ways. Granu had lost her support system, the troll who'd had her back no matter what, and who hadn't been afraid to tell her when she was too much in her own head. Kradduk had lost a wingman, the troll who'd made him look so good with his awkwardness and made Kradduk secretly look inward at his own worth. Now, they sat together, old friends unable to see the path forward.

Kradduk cleared his throat. "So, how's the cash flow these days?"

"Not as good as Ginger's, I'd wager," Granu replied, nodding toward the zimble, who was leaning suggestively over the bar as she cleared dishes from in front of a sad-sack regular named Colton. Kradduk chuckled. "But better than I imagined, especially if I wear a short skirt. Turns out, there's a subset of underlings who have a fetish for trolls who look like human hybrids. Sick, really, but I'll take what I can get."

"Human hybrids. Ridiculous. Next they'll be saying that platypuses are real."

"I know, right? But there's an entire movement dedicated to the fantasy genre of books, movies, and games, and apparently, I look a lot like one of the characters in their table-top game. *Fields of Corpses* or something like that. You see that group over there," Granu motioned to a quiet table of swogs and molents crowded into a booth made for far fewer, heads down as they whispered to one another while staring in Granu's direction, "They asked me to cosplay the character at an event coming up. They're willing to pay."

"You're not thinking of doing it, are you?"

"Why not? They're offering a good deal for a few short hours of playing dress-up."

"Granu, you wouldn't take a job in the tar pits, but you're seriously entertaining *this* idea? What if they don't only want you to dress-up?"

"Relax, Kradduk. They just want me to wear a costume and mingle. Honestly, it sounds like fun. Though, I do need to read the portions of their manual dealing with Kittera so I can stay in character. I'm not turning it down. It's next week."

"Alright, Kittera, just make sure they keep their paws to themselves."

"Sure thing, Dad. But, you know, some of them have hooves." Granu batted her eyes. Kradduk rolled his.

"So, are you enrolled in school yet?" Kradduk stuffed a handful of fried fairy wings in his mouth, chewing loudly.

"Not yet. Cut-off for fall is in two weeks," said Granu.

"What do you plan to do with a business degree anyways? Manage a daycare center?"

"I don't know. I thought it might open some doors for me. Secretarial work, retail management, something. What is up with your interest in my personal life these days? Losing Fillig seems to have made you a tad overbearing. You don't need to take over his role in our little group, you know."

"Nah, I'm just thinking about the future a lot lately. You know, about what we're both doing with our lives."

"Um, I guess," said Granu.

"We could be statues tomorrow. Life isn't guaranteed. It isn't something to take for granted. I want to do something with my life before it comes to a brutal end. Something more than be a clean-up boy for the worst company in history."

"Work is what you do to pay for life. It's not the end all, Kradduk. Maybe you should look into settling down with a nice girl if you're feeling empty."

"It's not that. It's something else. I'm feeling anxious, or something. Antsy?"

"Kradduk waxing philosophical. Who would have thought?" Granu was staring at her best friend with concern. Something was going on in that big, handsome head of his, and she wasn't sure what he was getting at. His face was drawn, and he didn't even notice the pack of attractive females that walked into the bar, one of whom was wearing a tiara. Normally, they'd be prime targets for a classic Kradduk conquest.

"Kradduk, there's nothing wrong with doing what you must to make ends meet. Most of New Metta would kill for your job, and a secretarial gig is better than nothing for me."

"We lost Fillig. Don't you want that to mean something?"

"How can it? The money is gone, and we're lucky to be alive ourselves."

Kradduk looked unconvinced. "If you won't believe me that you're meant for something bigger, then at least let Fillig's death bring the message home. We came close to greatness, as close as I've ever been. I don't know about you, but I can't go backward."

"Alright. You want this to be some kind of wake-up call? Sure. I'm wide awake, and I'm looking toward the future. I'm making changes. Maybe I'll become an entrepreneur. Start up a business or something."

Kradduk nodded and took a swig of grog. When he set it down, he raised his head to look Granu directly in the face, a suggestive smile pulling at his mouth, his eyes nearly sparkling with some unexpressed thought.

"Or," was all he said. A loaded, open-ended word left hanging in the air.

Granu smiled reflexively, though she wasn't sure why. Kradduk was leading her, and she struggled to see where. Over the past few months, he seemed to change from the shallow, womanizing troll she'd known into someone else altogether. She couldn't put her finger on the change, but it was as if he'd found something in himself. Now, his eyes darkened, taking on a hungry look. Granu shuddered under the intensity.

"Or what?"

"Is this really the life you want? Taking whatever odd jobs come your way, getting a business degree so you can go push paper somewhere? Do you want to waste your life chasing after the mediocre, the making ends meet? Is this what Fillig would want?"

"There is nothing wrong with my life. I'm happy taking control of it, thank you very much, and I'd appreciate a little less judgy-face from you. Who are you to judge me, anyways?" The audacity of Kradduk, the troll who'd spent years slaving away for an immoral corporation just so he could exact petty revenge, acting like she were beneath him. "Support is what I want. That's what Fillig would offer."

Kradduk sighed. "That's true, he would. But is it what he'd want for you Granu? Really? He knew you were meant for more, I know it, and, deep inside, I think you know it too."

"Made for more? I don't even know what that means. If I'm not destined for the mediocre, then for what? If I have some greater purpose, feel free to enlighten me. What is this great life I'm meant for?"

Kradduk's face relaxed and his easy, crooked smile returned. He shrugged. "You tell me, boss."

THE END

ACKNOWLEDGMENTS

My deepest thanks to the person who goes down the craziest conversational paths with me, my sounding board, best friend, and love of my life Alex Sover. To my mom, Colleen Caron, who taught me to love books and embrace the magic in life. To my dad, Paul Caron, who showed me what chasing your dream looks like. And to my brave critique partners and beta readers: Sara Bond, KJ Harrowick, Stéphanie Sauvinet, Max Caron, and Ben Humphrey. This book would not be what it is without every one of you, so it's all your fault!

Thank you to The Parliament House for giving me my first yes and to Falstaff Books for always having my back.

Thank you to Dr. Hew Joiner, who saw something special in me and taught me to embrace the strange workings of my mind. To all the teachers who helped shape the writer and person I am: Dr. Fred Richter, Dr. Bill Irby, Prof. John Parcels, Ms. Emily Beals, Dr. Lisa Tilley, Dr. Doug Wagner, Mr. Rick Friedman, and Mr. W. Clark. You've all made an impact that I'm sure you don't fully realize.

Thanks to Mike Horton for putting far more hours and imagination into our wonderfully ridiculous game #BewareTheGoats than either of us planned. Thanks to Susan Larson, who taught me the falue in rejection—that first letter is still framed in a box in the garage.

Thank you Michelle Hauck, Laura Heffernan, and Diana Pinguicha for the amazing Nightmare on Query Street experience that left me with a shiny query and a ton of new friends.

And thank you to the rest of the writer support group who helped make this book a reality: Angela Super, Glen Delaney, and the Debut '19 authors.

And most of all, thanks to the people off their rockers enough to enjoy this book.

ABOUT THE AUTHOR

Sarah J. Sover is the author of the Fractured Fae Series from Falstaff Books. Her comedic fantasy novel *Double-Crossing the Bridge* became an Amazon Best Seller in humorous fantasy, and her oddball short fiction appears in all three JordanCon Anthologies.

Writer's Digest featured Sarah in the Breaking In column in September 2019 then invited her to write a post for WritersDigest.com. The success of that blog post led to appearances at the 2019 Annual Writer's Digest Conference and at the Writer's Digest University Breaking In conference in 2020. Sarah has articles appearing in both the Nov/Dec 2021 and the March/April 2022 *Writer's Digest* magazines.

Sarah has a degree in Biology, which she utilized to write a piece for Dan Koboldt's *Putting the Fact in Fantasy*, releasing from Writer's Digest books/Penguin Random House in 2022. When she's not writing, Sarah can be found paneling at regional SFF conventions such as JordanCon, Multiverse, and Monsterama, blues dancing, or sipping a good IPA.

ALSO BY SARAH J. SOVER

Fairy Godmurder

FRIENDS OF FALSTAFF

Thank You to All our Falstaff Books Patrons, who get extra digital content each month! To be featured here and see what other great rewards we offer, go to www.patreon.com/falstaffbooks.

PATRONS

Dino Hicks

John Hooks

John Kilgallon

Larissa Lichty

Travis & Casey Schilling

Staci-Leigh Santore

Sheryl R. Hayes

Scott Norris

Samuel Montgomery-Blinn

Junkle

CPSIA information can be obtained
at www.ICGtesting.com
Printed in the USA
LVHW112042151122
733219LV00004B/108